THE PAST
COMES ALIVE

THE PAST
COMES ALIVE

M.R. LOVELACE

Xulon Press

Xulon Press
2301 Lucien Way #415
Maitland, FL 32751
407.339.4217
www.xulonpress.com

This is a work of fiction. All names, characters, places, and incidents either are the product of the author's imagination or used fictitiously, and any resemblance to actual persons, living or dead, businesses, companies, events, or locales is entirely coincidental.

This book has been made possible by the grace of God and the people he has used to bring it to completion. My wife Carolyn whose prayer and support are invaluable. Jon who has provided endless hours of patient technical help to a slow learner. And Carl who has given all he has to the editing of this book. When I look back writing was the smallest part.

Unless otherwise indicated, Scripture quotations taken from the Holy Bible, New International Version (NIV). Copyright © 1973, 1978, 1984, 2011 by Biblica, Inc.™. Used by permission. All rights reserved.

Paperback ISBN-13: 978-1-6628-1752-6
eBook ISBN-13: 978-1-6628-1753-3

THE GOSPEL ACCORDING TO JOHN
CHAPTER ONE

1 In the beginning [before all time] was the Word (Christ), and the Word was with God, and the Word was God Himself.

2 He was [continually existing] in the beginning [co-eternally] with God.

3 All things were made and came into existence through Him; and without Him not even one thing was made that has come into being.

4 In Him was life [and the power to bestow life], and the life was the Light of men.

5 The Light shines on in the darkness, and the darkness did not understand it or overpower it or appropriate it or absorb it [and is unreceptive to it].
(AMP)

Inspired by the Holy Spirit
Dedicated to God

Edited by Carl Hall
Technical support by Jon Lovelace

Prayed over by my wife, family and friends
Written by me. M.R. Lovelace

IOWA CAST OF CHARACTERS

Charlene "Charlie" Ruth Anne Bolton – A seventeen year old, five foot, blue eyed, blond, with a sometimes explosive, no fear personality, like an iceberg, only ten percent is seen.

Pastor William Boyd- Ex Navy SEAL, now the pastor of Life Church in Oak River Iowa, and Charlie's co-guardian until her eighteenth birthday

Jack Donavan- Rebellious son of TJ Donavan, who was murdered at his wife's grave site.

Jennifer "Jen" Donavan- Jack's sister

Chris- Jack's ex-fiancée and Jennifer's best friend

Paula Collins- Defense Attorney and co- guardian of Charlie, Charlie lives with her.

Jerry Watson- Chief of Police for Oak River

Leon Summer- Detective for the Oak River Police department

Bud Markowitz- Co-owner of Markowitz Realty in Oak River

Julie Markowitz- Bud's wife and partner in Markowitz Realty

MONTANA CAST OF CHARACTERS

Dr. Jacob Bullock- Professor of Paleontology at the University of Chicago

Dr. Glenda Pearce- former student of Dr. Bullock now Professor of Paleontology at Montana State University

Steve Bell- PhD student University of Chicago

Linde Phillips- PhD student University of Chicago

Ruth Biskup- PhD student Montana State University

Tim Blocker-PhD student Montana State University

Lester G. Crenshaw- Dealer in rare fossils

Jonathan "Bugs" Wilson- ex Navy SEAL good friend of Pastor Boyd

Henry Staten- Ruth's uncle Alumni Fellow Yale Corporation

TABLE OF CONTENTS

PROLOGUE
EARLY NOVEMBER 1732
IN THE LAND OF THE FIRST PEOPLE

Silver Wolf lay dying in his teepee. A week before he had slipped and fallen while hunting with his two sons. The rock ledge had not been high, only about two feet, but he landed badly on a rock the size of a small melon, twisting and falling with all his weight on his right leg. It had broken below the knee leaving a splintered bone sticking out through his skin. His sons carried him back home. There his wife and younger son had held him down while the older son had pulled on his foot straightening out the leg and letting the bone slip back where it belonged. Next his wife bandaged it with a mixture of moss and herbs she had prepared. Finally, she placed two pieces of a lance she had cut to the length of his leg, one on each side to keep the leg straight, and bound them in place with leather strips.

As the days passed, he seemed to be getting stronger but, on the fourth day he awoke with a fever. They cleaned and retied the leg splint. The leg was now red and swollen and the wound was oozing puss.

A week from the fall he was going in and out of consciousness and he could smell his flesh rotting. He knew death was as near as the winter snow and his family needed to travel back to the winter camp where the rest of their band would be. There they would have the safety and support of the tribe. Now he regretted taking his family off alone, because of an argument he had with his father.

Silver Wolf called his eldest son over and gave him the responsibility as the new head of his family: to see that his body was taken care of, and to ask his father for forgiveness, for his temper and harsh words. Then he began to sing his death song. The following morning, he died just before sunrise.

As the sun reached its zenith, the three grieving souls started out, leaving the flesh but not the spirit of the man known as Silver Wolf. They headed southwest following an old game trail. The day had started out bright and sunny but by midafternoon clouds began to roll in and it started to snow, becoming hard to see. They made camp that night in a coulee out of the wind, which continued to blow all night. At daybreak they looked out and there was no snow the wind had blown it all away. The sun came up to a clear blue sky.

After a cold breakfast their mother had prepared for the trail before they left, they started out again. Soon they came to an ancient riverbed and began following it.

The older son, whose name means "he who runs like a squirrel," was in the lead. Rounding a bend and coming up on a rise, he saw tracks in the stone. They were larger than anything he had ever seen. To him they looked like giant bird prints with human prints following, sometimes overlapping. It was as if the stone had melted at their touch. He could tell the man and bird were both running. Getting down on his knees he felt the prints, smooth and cold to his touch. By now all three of them were staring at the tracks. They followed them about fifty feet until they disappeared under the ground.

"What animal can melt the stone with his foot and what hunter can follow the same way?" he asked his mother.

There was no answer. They continued as if they could still see the tracks. On the other side of the mound they picked up the trail again, about a hundred yards farther they found the climax of the chase. The beast had been caught, surrounded and killed. Its skeleton lay on the ground, melted into stone. Under the beast's great tail, was the skeleton of one of the hunters.

They sat down on some rocks conveniently placed a short distance away just to look at such a marvel. For some time they sat there in silence, then they began discussing the question that had gone unanswered. What kind of man and beast was it that their tracks melted into the stone? And what kind of giant bird was so large and had such a great tail?

Their mother finally said, "It must have taken place when the earth was new and wolves could talk."

They heard an eagle scream overhead and they moved on again.

That spring, after a long and snowy winter, the snow melted quickly as if eager to release the land of the harshness. As the water ran down the ancient river bed it undercut a hill of dirt above where the epic battle had taken place, and covered it again with soil to hide it for another time.

SPRING 1887
JONAH STRIKER RANCH MONTANA TERRITORY

Drought followed by a severe winter had devastated Jonah Striker's herd. Most of his money was gone and he was hunting for his food. All he had managed to save were his horse, his bull and two of his best cows. All five of them had wintered in the dugout where he lived and a lean- to he had built on the side. Now with spring, the grass was greening again and with it, hope.

He saddled up and set out, looking over his ranch, but all he found were the remains of his cattle. Some in draws, bunched together where they had died of starvation and cold. Some alone, where the wolves had claimed their share in the battle to stay alive themselves. After four days of looking, hoping some had survived, he was heading home, wondering how he would get the money to start over. He was following a stone canyon. At a place where the rock had sluffed off during the winter, there, sticking out of the rock, was what looked like a giant bone. He dismounted and looked it over. He had heard of a man by the name of Cope who was looking for bones like this, and it was said, he would pay well for the right ones. Jonah returned home, loaded up his wagon with some tools and supplies and returned to the site.

He spent the next week digging up several fossils, including a skull which appeared to be in perfect condition. He loaded them into his wagon and went in search of Cope. He had heard he was down in the Judith Basin.

CHAPTER ONE
APRIL 9 MONDAY CURRENT YEAR
OFFICE OF LUTHER PETROLEUM
AUSTIN TEXAS

The Luther brothers, Isaiah and Jacob, birthed Luther Petroleum, in 1928. The depression began the following year and for Luther Petroleum it never left. The only oil company to not get rich. Just enough good wells to keep paying for the dry ones. Never enough to make it big. The carrot was always one step ahead.

A grandson, Daniel (Dan) Luther, who just celebrated his fiftieth birthday, now runs the company. Dan is heavy set 5'8" with thick black hair. He wore a new gray Armani suit, white shirt, striped gray tie, and sported Santoni double buckle shoes in lava gray. No more off the shelf clothes, he was going to dress for success. He was also determined to make Luther Petroleum a success... at any cost. He left the office and took a cab downtown to the Speakeasy, a restaurant and bar. Waiting inside was Archie Deerman, a college roommate. The contrast between the two could not have been greater. Archie was 6'1" weighed 158. He had bought his brown suit at Goodwill for $10 on a sale rack including two pair of pants. It hung on him like he was a clothes hanger. He had on a light blue shirt, no tie, and his shoes were black, in need of polishing and came from the same store.

Dan knew Archie would do about anything for enough money and more important, he knew he could keep his mouth shut.

Together they had broken into the chemistry professor's office and stole the answers to the final exam. Archie was caught with the answers and thrown out of school. But he had never ratted out Dan, even with the offer of reinstatement if he revealed who else was involved.

He had not seen Archie since. But a week ago he had run into George Whitcomb, another college buddy and in the conversation, George brought him up to date about several of their classmates, including Archie. He even had Archie's phone number. Archie was just the one he needed to put his plans into effect.

When he saw Dan walk in, Archie grabbed his drink, his second, and followed Dan to a back table.

"It looks like Luther Petroleum is doing very well Dan. I haven't seen you since College."

"I should have kept in touch but, I have an offer that will help make up for it."

After ordering, Archie listened as Dan explained what he wanted done.

"Remember in college when we broke into Professor Harlan's office and stole the answers to the final? I have never forgotten what you did for me. If you want it, I have a very similar job for you, only this one will pay $20,000 up front and a six-figure income as a full-time consultant for Luther Petroleum."

"That's a lot of money. What do I have to do, kill someone?"

"No, I need some papers that are in a lawyer's office in Billings, Montana. They've been there for over seventy years. I doubt anyone even knows they're there. They concern an oil lease for all the Striker ranch, almost 160,000 acres.

I was with my grandfather as he was dying; he rambled on a lot about the old days and his brother. Some of it was interesting and some of it didn't make any sense. But the day before he died, he told me they had bought the oil rights to the Striker ranch. All the papers have been signed. Before he could act on them, my grandmother gave birth to twins. They were born prematurely just ten months after my father. The medical bills went out of site and Jonah Striker loaned my grandfather $3500 from the lease purchase to cover the hospital bill. He had six months to pay it back or lose the lease. Four months later, the twins died one day apart. They couldn't come up with the $3,500 in time and lost the lease. Jonah was free to lease to someone else, but for some reason he never did. I checked. My grandfather said it was the most promising sight they ever tested. They had put all their eggs in that basket and lost. Well I intend to get it all back. I want you to take out the promissory note, which includes the expiration date and bring it to me. I found the Luther Oil copy of the lease, which we will exercise, and begin drilling. The ranch is still in the same family. A Carl Striker owns it now."

Archie left, folded up the address of the lawyer's office and put it in his pocket. When he was in his car, he took out the tape recorder from his shirt pocket, rewound it and turned it on again; it was crystal clear. He drove to his sister's house where he was living, packed a suitcase for his flight tomorrow, and went down to the Easy Pickings bar, grabbed a drink and was buzzed into the back room. He left about 9:30 early for him three hundred to the good. His luck had finally changed. He was in bed by 10:30.

APRIL 10 TUESDAY 5:00 A.M.

Archie was up early to catch his morning flight.

He felt better than he had in years. Soon he could get a place of his own again and pay off all his gambling debts.

Tickets were waiting for him just as Dan said. The flight was scheduled to land in Billings at 11:20 which would give him plenty of time to clean up, rest and have dinner, before going to work on the lawyer's office.

After going through security, he reached his gate just as they were starting to board. His first-class ticket got him right on. He had never been first-class before... anywhere ...anytime. He knew this job was going to be a piece of cake. He had finally gotten the break he was hoping for.

The first leg to Denver went without a hitch. Then everything went wrong. He was supposed to change planes and go straight to Billings, but the plane went down for maintenance. He was rerouted to LAX, then Spokane, Washington, Missoula, Montana, and finally arrived in Billings at 9:30 pm. Archie was tired and irritated. He went over to get his luggage. His never came out the turnstile. Somewhere along the way they lost it. With a promise they would find it and call him, he walked over to Hertz to pick up his rental car.

Stepping out of the air-conditioned terminal it was hot and dry. The smell of oil refineries hit him in the face. "That's the smell of money," he said to himself, "and some of it's going to be mine."

Instead of going to the motel he drove to the offices of Abbot, Bellingham and Craves. It was a three-story brick building in the old part of town. He drove around checking out the area and then drove down the alley behind Craves office. There was a fire escape running up the back of the building all the way to the roof. He parked his car three blocks away in a residential area and walked back down the alley and up the fire escape. "No time like the present," he thought.

The lock was no problem. He slipped his credit card in between the lock and the door jam and just like that, he was inside.

"What a hick town," he said to himself. Going down the hall he found the door labeled "Abbot, Bellingham and Craves", written in faded gold lettering. He opened the door the same way as before and went in, so far so good. Looking around, he found the reception area paneled in oak wainscoting with hunter green paint above. Next was what looked like a client meeting room, followed by a restroom and down the hall was another meeting room. It had a large oak table and six oak chairs with padded leather seats. The next room said "Abbot" on the door. The door was unlocked, he let himself in. The room was empty. The door across the hall read "Billingham", he found it the same. Next, on the same side was "Craves," all the names were in faded gold letters just like the entrance. Craves office was furnished. He turned on the light and looked around. It had the same Oak wainscoting and green paint. It looked like they had not remodeled since the building was built. On the far end was a large oak desk with an oak and leather office chair. In front of the desk sat two oak chairs covered in the same worn leather. Built-in bookshelves filled the wall behind the desk. On the wall next to the door were four oak file cabinets. They were all freshly alphabetized. It was the only thing that looked newer than one hundred years old.

Archie pulled open the drawer labeled So-Tm, and found the file he was looking for. Then all hell broke loose! Sirens were screaming in from two directions. Quickly he looked through the file, found the paper he needed. Jammed it in his pocket, returned the file and slammed the drawer shut. Then flipped out the ceiling light, only to have it replaced with flashing red and blue lights sparkling through the windows and onto the ceiling. He went to the window and looked out. There were two squad cars, the officers were already out and looking up where he was. He heard a third car in the distance, coming to join the party.

He ran through the office, down the hall to the back door, opening it just in time to see the lights of the third police car flashing down the alley. Instead of going down, he climbed up the ladder onto the roof, ran across to the next building, climbed over a short wall, and kept going. At the end of the third building, he was out of breath, out of buildings and out of ideas. He put his hands on his knees and bent over to catch his breath. When he could stand up again, he looked around and saw what looked like a shed built onto the roof. Seeing a door, he went over and turned the handle, it opened. He grabbed the flashlight he had in his back pocket and looked in. It was an elevator shaft. The elevator car appeared to be on the first floor of the three-story building. Just inside the shaft on the left was a ladder, he climbed onto it, shut the door and started down. It was hot and dark, everything he touched was covered in dirt and grease. When he reached the top of the elevator, he stepped onto what looked like a piece of framing, but it gave way and he fell through into the elevator. Just then he heard the door open above him and a light shine down. He froze. Then he heard the policeman call out for him to stay there. Standing up, he discovered he had sprained his left ankle. He pushed the button for the door to open and ran out limping. Running as fast as his ankle would let him, down the hall to the red exit sign, he pushed the panic bar and continued into the ally. There was a space just big enough to go between two buildings. On the other side. He came out just as a city bus was pulling up. A couple got off and he gratefully got on. The bus pulled away just as he heard another siren heading for the building he had just vacated. He sat there catching his breath again, not caring where the bus was going. Twenty minutes later it pulled up in front of a motel with a restaurant next to it.

"Last stop." The driver said.

When Archie stood up and put his weight on his left foot, he almost fell.

"Hey, are you alright?" the bus driver asked.

"Yah, just an old injury from the service. It acts up sometimes if I'm on it too much."

He got off the bus, limped into Bartholomew's restaurant and sat down in a booth. His ankle was throbbing and he knew it was swollen. He ordered a double scotch and water, and asked the waitress if she could find him some Ibuprofen. By the time he finished dinner, six Ibuprofen and three doubles, his pain was gone. He carefully walked over to the motel next door and took a room.

After using the toilet, he looked at himself in the mirror. It wasn't good. His face had dirt and grease on it and his clothes were worse. He took them off and had a quick, hot shower. Leaving a mess in the bathroom, he went to bed.

He woke up some time during the night with his ankle killing him. He took six more pills and went back to sleep.

CHAPTER TWO
APRIL 11 WEDNESDAY
BEFORE DAWN CARL STRIKER
RANCH MONTANA

arl Striker rose before dawn, pulled his pants on over the long johns he had slept in, put on his socks, shoved his feet into his well-worn cowboy boots and went to the window and looked out. The full moon was shining brightly, giving a glow to his ranch. He thought it a waste he had to sleep. On nights like this there was plenty of light to work by. He went to the kitchen, over to his wood cook stove, and struck a match to light the kindling he had placed there the night before. Then he walked over to the side window that faced the corral. Pulling the curtain aside and looking out he saw two horses, their saddles still on. One was getting a drink from the water trough and the other was standing next to a body lying face down on the ground. He let the curtain close and fixed his coffee. Carl was past seventy, five-ten and lean. His face was tan and leathery from a lifetime of working outdoors, he was still strong, agile and driven as ever.

11

The cowhand on the ground was called Pearl, because of his teeth. The one Carl could not see behind the water trough, lying on his back was Buck. They had ridden in at 2:38 AM. Although neither of them could have told you the time even if they had a watch, which they didn't, from rounding up three strays, that were even now laying in Carl's front yard chewing their cud. Pearl and Buck were not dead, as you might suppose from looking at them, just dead drunk. After putting on his pot of coffee Carl walked out his front door, across the yard past the cows, turned and walked over to the water trough with a bucket he had brought. He filled it with water and dumped it on Pearl, who jumped to his feet, took a swing at Carl. Missed, and was hit in the head with the offending water bucket. Which put him back on the ground unconscious and missing one of his pearly white teeth. Filling the bucket again, Carl threw the contents on Buck. Not getting the response he expected he filled it again, this time he poured it all, slowly, right on Buck's face. Buck began to cough, sat up, focused his eyes, and with a voice as sweet as could be, said.

"Hi boss. We got the cows ya sent us after." Then stretched and added. "It's gona be a nice day."

That's when the bucket came crashing down and Buck was out again.

It was mid-morning before the two were up. They both staggered into the bunkhouse where they laid down on their beds and went back to sleep. The next time they woke was to the sound of the dinner bell. When they went to get dinner, they each were handed an envelope waiting for them with their name on it. The word FIRED was written across the front in capital letters. Looking at the cook for an explanation, he gave them one.

"It wasn't coming in drunk or even leaving the cows loose in the yard. It was the fact that you should have been back three days ago. That was the problem."

Pearl said, "He can't fire us. He needs us to brand the cattle. Where is he?"

"He left at daybreak, with two new hands to take your place."

The cook turned and went back to his kitchen to check on his apple pie. It was about time for it to come out of the oven.

Pearl and Buck ate their dinner in silence with glum looks on their faces. When finished, they each took a piece of pie and went back to the bunkhouse, telling the cook they would leave in the morning.

Buck got out the checkerboard, and they began to play, in between bites of their fresh apple pie. When the pie was all gone, Pearl rummaged through everyone's things until he found what he was after, whiskey. He found a pint of Jack Daniel's almost full. He unscrewed the cap and wiped off the top, then took a big swig before handing it to his partner and sitting down again.

"Well," Pearl said. "We're sure in a fix this time. We've never been fired before. What are we going to do?"

"Yes, we have. Four years ago, working for that rancher down in Wyoming. What's his name? Ah…ah Smith, no Schmidt, that's it."

"He didn't fire us. We quit."

"We quit after he said. You're fired!" Buck responded.

"That's not fair. It doesn't count. He just said it first that's all."

"Well, if you would a said it before you took a swing and missed, and then got knocked on your backside, you would a beat him. No, we were fired fair and square." Buck said.

"What are we going to do now?" Pearl asked, wanting to move on to another subject, knowing he had lost that one.

"Well, we got almost a month's pay. Let's move down to Texas. I know a guy who can help us get on where he is. He married my sister's best friend. I'll call her and she can call him and he can put in a good word and we'll be set."

"No! Texas is a long ways away and the last time we were down there we got shot at."

"You got shot at!" Buck corrected him. "I was passed out in the next booth and he missed you and hit me!"

"It was only a flesh wound."

"Yah, the flesh was my posterior! And if he'd a had a real gun instead of that sissy .22, the doc said it would'a, went all the way through and well, you know where it would a come out."

"Well let's forget Texas. I want to stay here. I got a score to settle with Carl. He knocked out my tooth." Pearl said rubbing his jaw.

14

"Then I want our jobs back." Buck said. "You forget about your tooth. Tomorrow we can catch up. Tell him we're sorry and we'll never be late again."

As if to settle the matter the sky lit up with lightning and the thunder crashed putting an end to the conversation.

Buck walked unsteadily over, opened the door, and stepped out onto the porch. "There's sure a big storm rolling in. I'm glad we're here tonight. Maybe the cattle will get spooked and Carl will be glad to have us back." Buck said, mostly to himself.

As Buck and Pearl played checkers and finished their new found bottle, the storm raged, shaking the bunk house they were in, and moving right up the valley. Dumping nearly five inches of rain, the storm caused flash floods. One of them ran down an ancient dried out riverbed, washing off the last of the soil on a stone plateau. The lightning flashed, showing prints that were melted into the stone when wolves could talk. After finishing their bottle and tired of playing checkers the two cowboys went to sleep to the sound of the storm.

APRIL 11 WEDNESDAY
BILLINGS MONTANA 9:30 AM
ARCHIE

When Archie woke again, the sun was streaming in his window. He was sweating, hungry and in pain. He looked at his ankle closely for the first time. It was black and blue with the skin stretched tight from the swelling.

15

He tried to stand, but the pain was too much. He reached over, grabbed the phone, and called the office.

"This is Archie in room…" He looked around for the room number but did not see it anywhere. "This is Archie Deerman. I came in last night. You can look up my room number. I took a fall, and this morning my ankle is swollen and very painful. Could you get me some crutches, and recommend a doctor? Oh, and get me room service. I will need breakfast, and I would like to see the manager right away."

"Yes sir, I'll get you room service and the manager."

He was on the phone ordering breakfast when there was knock on the door.

"This is the manager. May I come in?"

Holding the phone to his chest, he yelled, "Yes." And finished his order.

The manager was short, about five four Archie thought. He was dressed in a tailored black suit, white shirt, and a red tie. His nametag, with the motel logo, said his name was Mr. Smith. If that was his real name, he was the first real Smith he had ever met.

"Good morning Mr. Deerman. My name is Robert Smith. I have already called the doctor. He will be right over. I've taken the liberty of telling him the nature of your injury. Don't worry, we will take care of everything." Lifting the sheet, he asked if it was all right for him to look at his ankle. Seeing was believing for Mr. Smith and he quickly put the sheet down again.

"If you tell me how you injured yourself, I'll file a clam right away for you to sign. Was it the tub?"

Archie realized the manager thought he'd been hurt in his room. Not to look a gift horse in the mouth, he didn't correct his wrong assumption, but instead replied,

"No, it was the bathroom floor. When I stepped out, I slipped and fell, turning my ankle. I thought it would be all right in the morning, but now I find it difficult to get out of bed. And it is very painful."

"I can see how it would be." Mr. Smith replied. "Is there anything else I can do for you before the doctor arrives?"

"Yes, there is. Would you please close the drapes and get me a glass of water?"

"Of course, Mr. Deerman."

He quickly closed the drapes, got the water and at Archie's request, handed him the TV remote.

"Will that be all?"

"You've been very kind. The airlines lost my luggage. If you could have some toiletries sent up, that would help."

Archie had been going over in his mind what to do about the car. He knew he had left it unlocked. He made up his mind.

"Also, my rental car was stolen, if you could call someone, I would like to report it."

Mr. Smith, with genuine concern showing on his face, and in his voice, said.

"Of course! I had no idea. You've had a great deal of misfortune. I will see to it right away. If you will give me your size, I will also get you some clothes."

17

Archie gave him his sizes and Mr. Smith left saying, "I'm so sorry. I will have everything taken care of right away."

After he left, Archie had second thoughts about the car. But he was in no shape to go get it, and with the level of the police response last night, he figured they would be looking for anything that did not fit. He couldn't think of a good reason why his rental should be sitting in front of a house where he didn't know anyone, three blocks away from a break-in. No, that was a good decision, plausible deniability. Isn't that what they call it? Maybe he could even get out of paying for the car. He tried to think of everything that happened last night, looking for loose ends. He had worn gloves, no fingerprints in the lawyer's office and no one had seen his face. No worries. His ankle was hurting too much to concentrate any longer. Where was that doctor? He took six more Ibuprofen, and then saw his suit. With much difficulty, he got up and moved it out of the way, making sure the dirt and grease that he had gotten on it wasn't showing. He had just sat down to go to the bathroom when there was a knock on the door. It was his breakfast. He had him wait until he had finished, and then told him to come in. He was more than ready for his breakfast. The man brought it in and set it down on the table by the window. Archie had him help him over to the chair.

Most of Archie's life was sloppy and undisciplined. Except when it came to food. It was, "to be enjoyed, with gusto and precision". No food should touch any other food. Hot foods should be served on a hot plate and, conversely, cold foods on a cold plate. Coffee should always be hot and served black. Milk should always be served in a chilled glass. With all these requirements, Archie rarely had a good eating experience unless he prepared it himself. Breakfast, for example, was to be two eggs sunny side up, sausage, English muffin, a large glass of milk followed by a cup of coffee, the morning paper, and no interruptions.

Archie was lifting the cover on his breakfast when there was another knock on the door. This time it was someone delivering his crutches. They were not even out of the room when the doctor walked in.

"I'm Doctor Unger. I understand you have a swollen ankle."

"Yes, I slipped on the tile floor when I stepped out of the tub last night."

"Let's have a look."

Archie swung around a little in his chair and stuck out his right leg. For his part Doctor Unger got down on one knee and lifted the leg.

"Move your foot up and down for me. Now from side to side."

Archie did as he was told.

"From one to ten, ten being the worst pain you've ever had, how bad does it hurt?"

"Just sitting in this chair, about a seven. But if I put any weight on it, well, I can't. It hurts more than a ten and it won't hold me. I had to hop over to the bathroom and then back to this chair. They just brought me some crutches."

THE PAST COMES ALIVE

Archie answered, pointing to the bed where the delivery boy had left them.

"I don't think you broke it, but we need to take an x-ray just to be sure. Here is my card. Come over to the clinic this afternoon and we will get you in for that x-ray."

Reaching into the bag he brought with him, he pulled out a bottle of pills. "Take one of these now with your breakfast and another one before bed. They should help with the pain."

Without saying any more, he laid his card on the table, closed his bag, and left.

With anticipation Archie lifted the lid on his breakfast, only to be crest fallen at the sight. The eggs were not sunny-side up. They were fried hard. The pork chop was way over cooked as well. His biscuits, almost burnt and the gravy was a white sauce. He stuck his finger in the gravy. It was cold. He was wondering if it was worth it to get over to the phone and order another meal, when there was another knock on the door. Since it was not completely shut when the doctor left, a man pushed it open, stuck his head in and asked if he was Archie Deerman.

Almost glad to focus on something else he motioned for him to come in.

"Good morning, I'm Detective Marsh. You reported a stolen car."

"Yes. It was a rental. I picked it up at the airport last night."

Looking down at some papers he had on a clipboard he said, "At 9:55 P.M. Hertz car rental. Could you tell me where you went and when you noticed the car was stolen?"

"I'm not sure where I went exactly. I've never been here before. I was frustrated because the flight was very late and the airlines lost my luggage. I drove around and found a bar, went in, and had a drink. Actually, I had several. When I left, I couldn't remember for sure where the car was, I walked around looking for it. Then I remembered where I had parked, but it was gone. A city bus pulled up and I got on. I probably shouldn't have been driving anyway, if you know what I mean."

"Why didn't you report it stolen last night? We only got the call this morning."

"I just forgot. I rode the bus for a while and it stopped in front of the motel, so I got out and took a room. I was very tired."

"It sounds like you had quite a night. Are those your crutches?" The detective asked.

"No." Archie replied. "Those belong to the motel. I hurt my ankle in the bathroom and they were good enough to let me use them. You just missed the doctor. He was just here to look at my ankle. I need to go in for an x-ray after breakfast."

"You're not a very lucky man, are you Mr. Deerman? Are you here on business?"

"No. It was just going to be a few days of vacation. But after all I've been through, I'll be going home as soon as I can. Hopefully today."

Archie was starting to get nervous. He had expected only a patrolman, not a detective. He knew this guy had already checked him out and suspected him.

"We found your car. It was a few blocks from a break in last night. The offices of Abbot, Billingham and Craves. They are a law office on East First street. Would you know anything about that?"

Archie tried to sound surprised. "No. Why would I? I just got to town. I don't know anyone here. I've never heard of them."

"We have the car down at the police station. When you finish at the doctor's office, you can come down to the station, pick it up and fill out a report about the theft."

He handed him his card and left. As he reached the door he turned and said.

"Whoever broke in last night took a big fall. He may have hurt his ankle." He looked at Archie for a minute, and then left.

With his breakfast thoroughly cold and unappetizing, Archie pushed it away and took a sip of his coffee. It was lukewarm, and had sugar in it. He hated cops.

Detective Marsh went down to his car, knowing he had been lied to. But he had no evidence...yet.

He drove over to 334 East First Street and went upstairs. On the door in faded gold lettering it said, Abbot, Billingham and Craves, Attorneys at law. He walked in. There was an attractive woman of about thirty, with light red hair, talking on the phone.

22

As he waited for her to finish her call, he looked around. She had pictures of two kids, both girls. They looked like her. And a man he took to be her husband. He picked up the picture. He was a nice-looking guy, dressed in a flannel shirt and jeans. From the look of him, he was in construction, or maybe a logger. He put the picture down. Besides the two pictures on the desk and a fresh bouquet of flowers, everything else in the room looked as though he had stepped back in time. She hung up.

"You must be Detective Marsh." She stood and offered her hand. "I'm Joann. I handle the phone and everything else around here. Can I get you some coffee?"

"Yes, that would be nice."

She poured him a cup of coffee from a pot on the counter behind her. "Cream or sugar?" She asked.

"I'll take it black."

Handing him the coffee she said, "I'll let Mr. Craves know you're here."

She disappeared down the hall to return in a few minutes, with Mr. Craves. He was younger than expected, only a couple of years older than the secretary. And by the resemblance. He guessed they were brother and sister. They both had the same hair color and mouth. Craves was dressed in a blue three-piece suit, with a blue and white pinstriped shirt, dark blue tie, matching suspenders, and a gold watch chain that disappeared into a pocket on his vest.

Mr. Craves shook his hand, introduced himself, and led him down the hall into the last office on the right, with the name "Justus Craves", written on the door. This room had the same well-cared-for oak furniture. An oil painting of Oliver Wendell Holmes hung on the wall. Behind a large oak desk, the wall was covered in built-in oak bookcases with glass doors. They were all filled with large, hardbound books.

The only thing that looked like it came from this century was a Mac laptop computer, sitting to one side on the desk.

"I know it's a little of a time warp coming in here. My grandfather and his two partners, Abbot and Billingham, started the law practice. The office is all original except for what is obviously not, like my computer. I guess you could say I have one foot in each century."

"Are Abbot and Billingham available?"

"Not unless you want to have a séance."

Marsh looked a little puzzled.

Justus continued, "The original Craves, whom I am named after, was my grandfather. Abbot and Billingham were partners and friends. They did a little of everything; writing wills, contracts, settling disputes among ranchers, even some criminal law. Their sons, William Abbot and James Billingham and my father Thomas Craves, in time, took over the practice. Continuing to do whatever work came in the door. William died young. He had one son who wasn't interested in law. The family sold his third of the practice to James and my father. James had two daughters who were married and lived out of state. They were not at all interested in joining the law firm. When my father passed away, James decided to retire. I got my father's share and bought out Billingham for his half. So now it's just "Craves."

"I grew up down here when all three of them were practicing and my grandfather and Otto Billingham were still coming in from time to time. I've left it all the same except for some technology. I only practice criminal law. I find it more exciting than all that corporate stuff."

"They're all innocent until proven guilty." March said. "Is that right?'

"Yes, that's the system."

"It's a broken system if you ask me. Too many of the guilty get off."

"I see. If they were not guilty, you would not have arrested them, is that right.?

"Let me ask you, how many have you gotten off that you knew were guilty?"

"About as many as were innocent who went to jail." Justus replied.

"I'm sure I know who broke in. But unless I can find more evidence, he will be one of the guilty who got away. I would like to look at the tapes from your security cameras."

"When I checked the tapes this morning there was nothing on them. In fact they had stopped 36 hours before the break-in. I don't know what went wrong. I already called the Security Company. They are sending someone over later today. We have had two other break-ins over the last several years, both connected with criminal cases. Each time they were unable to get any information and both times we had them on tape. They were caught and convicted."

"Do you have any idea what he might have been after?" Marsh asked.

"No. Nothing is missing that we can detect. I don't think they had time to get what they were after. Your men were right on it. As soon as the back door opened, the alarm went off at National Security. They, in turn, called the police and reported the break in. Your men were here in less than ten minutes. I'm sure, if you have the right man, you will be able to get the evidence, eventually. Can you tell me his name and what he looks like, so we can watch out for him? Maybe he's connected to an ongoing case."

"I don't want to give you the name of an innocent man. Like I said, we don't have any proof he was involved."

Detective Marsh stood up and left, convinced he had talked to two liars today.

CHAPTER THREE
APRIL 12 THURSDAY MORNING
CARL STRIKER RANCH MONTANA

By sunrise the sky was clear and the air smelled clean, with the scent of pine and grass. Buck and Pearl packed up after breakfast, saddled their horses and rode out to find Carl. They had gone about a mile when Buck opened an old rough woven bag he had hung around his saddle horn. It contained a new fifth of whiskey and some food he had taken before they left.

Seeing the bottle, Pearl quit talking about how he was going to get even for losing his tooth. "Where did you get that." He asked.

"In the cupboard where I got some supplies for our trip. It was behind some cans of baked beans."

Buck opened it and offered Pearl the first drink. He took a long swig and handed it back. Drinking and talking they didn't notice when they went up the wrong valley. By noon they were drunk and temporally lost.

They fell as much as dismounted and sat down in the shade of a drop-off, to "reconnoiter," Pearl said.

Soon they were both passed out. When Buck woke up, the sun was low in a still cloudless sky. He looked around and saw both horses about twenty yards away, drinking from a pool of water left by the rainstorm.

He was hungry and thirsty. Standing up, his head throbbed. He staggered down to his horse, took off his canteen and nearly emptied it. Next, he took a few steps away from the pool and emptied his bladder, then led the horses back. Debris was piled in places where the water had deposited it, but it was too wet to burn. So he opened a can of baked beans, took two slices of bread, sat down with his back to the wall and ate it cold.

He knew enough to leave Pearl alone until he woke on his own. He always came up swinging if you touched him when he was asleep. It was going to be a nice night, he thought. With his meal done and feeling much better, he walked down past where he had found the horses, then climbed up what were almost like stairs, about three feet to the top of the plateau, to watch the sun set. His foot stumbled in a depression. When he looked down, he was astonished at what he saw. There in the stone were what looked like giant bird tracks.

Buck sat down on the rock, but instead of watching the sun set, he kept looking at the tracks. Running his hand over the smooth stone, he was formulating a plan.

Now that he was sober, he knew where he was. They had been here just a few days ago looking for the strays, he knew the tracks were not exposed then.

"It must have been the recent storm. A lot of water had run down here." he said to himself.

There were pools in the depressions, debris piled up on the bends and around some of the rocks that were large enough to have caught some. He could see where the water had over flowed the stream, running up on the rocks where he was sitting.

Buck would not have had any idea what he had found. Except he had met Dr. Bullock the year before last, about ten miles from here. Some supplies were delivered for him at the ranch by mistake. Carl had asked him to take them up to where they were working, instead of having them come down and get it. He had been excited to see what was going on. They had tents set up, two travel trailers plus another one that was converted into a kitchen. Their camp was a very busy place. Besides Dr. Bullock, there were a number of college students and volunteers and, oh yah, there was also a lady in charge, with red hair. Buck thought it looked like about twenty people. Dr. Bullock had taken him on a tour, explaining what they were doing as he went along. They were working on cleaning off what looked to Buck like a very big leg bone. Dr. Bullock explained it was from a... Buck couldn't remember the name, some kind of "saurus", that had lived here millions of years ago. Buck had asked him if cave men hunted something this big. Dr. Bullock had told him the dinosaurs were extinct long before man arrived. They were separated by millions of years. Buck knew Carl didn't own the land he was now on. He only leased the grazing rights from the government. And he figured this information could be worth money.

"We need to go to Bozeman and find Dr. Bullock!" He said out loud.

When he got back Pearl was crawling on all fours, headed over to where the whiskey bottle was lying on the ground. Buck beat him to it, picked it up and threw. The glass shattered when it hit.

"Hey!" Pearl bellowed. "What'd you do that for? I needed that!"

"I'll show you in the morning. We need to be sober. You want to get back at Carl, don't ya?"

"Yah." Pearl said. "But I feel sick. I needed that bottle."

"I'll get you some food. We've got beans, bread and canned peaches. You start on that and tomorrow I'll show ya how we're going to get even… and make some money at the same time.

It was late morning when Pearl woke up with the sun shining in his eyes. He sat up and then laid right back down. He had a splitting headache. It took him a minute to remember why he was sleeping on the ground. He sat up again, looked around seeing his hat only a short distance away, crawled over, put it on, then stood up. Buck was still asleep in the shade of the low cliff. He walked over and kicked the bottom of his boots.

"It's time to get up." he said, too loud for his own good. It made his head hurt more. The horses were down by a pool of water, nibbling on some green grass. He walked unsteadily over to his horse. The canteen was gone so he walked on down to the pool, got on his hands and knees and put his head in the water, lifted it back out and wiped his face with his bandana, lowered it back down again and took a long drink from the pool. Feeling better, he stood up and checked out his surroundings. It was starting to come back to him. Buck had told him something about being able to get back at Carl... Something about tracking dinosaurs... "It must have been the booze talking," Pearl thought. "There aren't any dinosaurs out here," he said to himself. He walked back over and kicked Buck's boots again.

"Wake up. We gotta go." he said, this time in a softer voice. On the third try Buck woke up.

"Mornin, Pearl," he said while getting to his feet. "This is going to be a great day. We're on our way to fame and fortune."

"What are you talking about?" We don't even have a job, or did you forget we got fired?" Pearl moved his tongue around and stuck it out where his front tooth had been. "And I've got a score to settle with Carl."

"Follow me and I'll show you how we're going to do it. You'll have enough money to fill that hole with a solid gold tooth."

"If you're talking about some dinosaur again, there ain't any out here."

"You just follow me and I'll show you what I mean."

Buck led him over to where he saw the prints.

"You just look down there. You see those prints down there? The ones that look like a big bird print."

"Ya, sort of. I guess."

"Those are dinosaur prints. They're special, but look close. You see those other ones?"

"Of course. It looks like someone walked barefoot through the mud."

"Well, by themselves they might not be so much. But you see this one here and this one here, where the footprint and the bird, I mean dinosaur print, are overlapping. That's very special. And that's what's gonna make us rich. And famous." Buck added.

"Well, how is that going to do us any good? If there is any money Carl will get it."

"That's the get even part. This isn't Carl's land. Oh, he owns miles of it all right, but right now we are on BLM land. Carl just rents the grazing rights."

"How do you know?"

"I just know. Trust me. We're going back to the ranch, leave our horses, and take my truck to Bozeman."

Buck led at a fast pace all the way back. Pearl's head was still hurting and he was having a hard time keeping up.

"Let up, Buck! Those tracks ain't going nowhere."

"No, but we are. This is our big break and I ain't going to waste it."

The horses were all lathered when they reached the ranch. They rode into the corral, unsaddled and Buck headed for his truck.

"Wait a minute Buck. I need a drink. I got a splitting headache."

"You can get a drink from the well right over there. I'm going to Bozeman. We're off the booze for now."

Pearl stopped and looked at the well, then at the bunk house, undecided what he wanted most. He headed toward the bunk house.

"I'll leave ya, Pearl."

"You wouldn't do that. All I need is a little drink. Just to settle my nerves and get rid of my headache."

"I'm goin, Pearl."

Buck continued to his truck, got in and started it. Pearl was almost to the porch when he heard the truck start. He turned around to see Buck pull out and head to the drive. He stopped when he was next to Pearl. Pearl slapped his side and swore. But he turned around and got in.

Buck pushed his old truck as hard as he had his horse. He stopped in Lewistown for gas and something to eat. Then right back on the road. He pulled into the University parking lot at 5:15. The place looked deserted. They got out and headed to the nearest building. When they were almost there, they met two students who were leaving and asked directions to professor Bullock's office.

"I haven't heard of a Professor Bullock. Have you?" he asked his friend.

"No. What does he teach?"

"I don't know what the real name is, but he teaches about dinosaurs."

"That would be Paleontology. But it's late. There might not be anyone there now."

He gave them directions to another building.

As soon as they entered the right building, there was another student standing by the door texting on his phone. Buck got further directions and went down the hall where he found a door labeled "Paleontology Department." They went in. A woman was coming down the hall. She was tall and thin, wearing a black dress and a scowl.

"Can I help you?"

"We're looking for a Dr. Bullock. Does he work here?"

"No, but I know who he is. He works with Professor Pearce during the summers. But I'm afraid she isn't here either."

"Do you know when she'll be back?" Buck asked.

"Not until next week. She's at a conference. Can I help you with something? My name is Kimberly. I work with them.

Buck was all primed to do this now. Not next week.

"We have made a discovery and we want to sell the information."

"How much do you think it is worth?"

Buck had $5,000 in his head all the way here. But he suddenly felt bold and said, "$10,000."

This is a university. We don't normally pay for information. Can you tell me what it is? Maybe I could give you the name of a private collector?"

Buck looked around. There was no one else in the office. He took out his phone and brought up the pictures he had taken and showed them to her. After looking at them she asked.

"What is it you think you have found?"

"I know what I found!" Buck said. "I also know no one else has ever found such a thing before."

He took his phone back and went to the first photo.

"That's a dinosaur footprint. Professor Bullock showed me one before."

He flipped to the next picture.

"That is a human footprint. Just about my size. I took off my boot and stepped in it. I know neither of them is very important, but…"

He flipped to the next one.

"That's a dinosaur print and that right there is a human footprint right on top of it. He was tracking it. It's plain as day. And that is very special. No one has ever found one before. Professor Bullock told me dinosaurs and people didn't live together. They're separated by millions of years, he said. Well, I have proof that's wrong." Growing bolder with every word, Buck continued.

"I think it's worth at least $10,000, maybe more! And if you don't want to buy it, I'll find someone else who will."

"Follow me down to my office and I will make a phone call. I know someone who might be interested. But you know we will have to see it in person to verify it."

She led them down the hall into a small conference room and shut the door.

She spent the next half hour grilling them about what they'd found. Then she made the phone call. She explained everything, then after getting some instructions, she hung up.

"As you heard, he is very interested in what you have found. And is willing to pay what you asked... After I have seen the site myself and verified its authenticity."

After finding out where they parked, she made arrangements to meet them there at six the next morning and she would follow them out to the site.

Pearl could hardly contain himself, and Buck had a huge smile on his face. As soon as they got in the truck, Buck said'

"See! I told yah it was worth money! Now we can go get something to eat and get a room for the night."

"You were right Buck!" I saw her face when she looked at the pictures. I knew right then we had something. When you told her $10,000, I thought you overshot and ruined the deal. But you were right on, Buck. After we get something to eat, I know a nice bar where we can celebrate."

"Not tonight Pearl. We're staying sober. We are not gonna be late in the morning."

The next morning they were there twenty minutes early. At five minutes after six, a dark green Jeep pulled in beside them. Kimberly got out and went over to the truck.

"These two gentlemen are going with me today. They're authorized to pay you." She held up a finger. "After I verify it is authentic. There is one more question. You haven't told anyone else? It's very important this is kept secret."

"Like I told ya yesterday, we ain't told no budy. We're not that stupid." Buck said.

At eleven they were all looking down at the prints. Kimberly was down on her knees checking them closely. Carefully she removed some more earth and revealed another set. When she stood up, she did not have a smile on her face.

"This is very disturbing." she said.

"They're real, ain't they?" Buck said. "Just like I told you."

"Yes. I'm afraid they are authentic. I have some work to do here. Mr. Black will ride back with you to Lewistown and get the money from a bank there. Is that all right?"

"That suits us right down to our boots." Buck said.

"Why don't you let me drive." Mr. Black said, as he pulled out a bottle of Champagne and a fifth of whiskey from the Jeep. Pearl's eyes lit up.

"We can celebrate now can't we Buck?"

"Ya, I ain't never had Champagne before."

The three of them headed out across the open range.

An hour later there was a muffled explosion at the site.

CHAPTER FOUR
AUGUST 5 SUNDAY
PALEONTOLOGICAL SITE
NORTH CENTRAL MONTANA
DOCTORS BULLOCK AND PEARCE

You could see for miles across the open country of north central Montana.

There were only a few high clouds to block the sun. Dr. Bullock stood up from his work, stretched and wiped his forehead with his sleeve, and looked around. There were students and volunteers spread out for fifty yards. Up on a rise a short distance away were two travel trailers and a third one converted into a kitchen. Tents of various sizes and colors were set up all around. There were also two large canopies. One used for a dining hall and the other to prepare their fossil treasures for study and transport back to the university. Seeing Glenda under one of the large canopies Bullock headed her way. Stopping to check on Ruth, one of the graduate students, working under a beach umbrella.

"Yes, Ruth. That is a good vertebra. Clean some more of the rock away." Dr. Bullock said.

The area was almost picked clean. Twelve seasons of work had gone by quickly, he thought. It had been a good place to bring students. They had not found anything exciting, but there had been a steady stream of minor finds. Dr. Bullock, a Paleontologist from the University of Chicago, continued walking over to the shade provided by the canopy they had erected. Under it were several tables. Two of them had chairs so they could sit in the shade, the other three had bits and pieces of fossils. Steve, another graduate student, was working with two volunteers, cleaning, photographing, and cataloging the last of their finds for the year. He walked on past and took a chair next to Glenda Pearce, a Professor from Montana State. The two of them had been working together at this site from the beginning. They had met when she was studying under him, earning her PhD.

"We need a new site for next year." he said. "That storm that went through two nights ago brought a lot of rain. There's an old, dry riverbed about five miles north. Why don't you take a couple of students and check it out? Perhaps the rain washed something out."

Glenda glanced down at her watch. "It will be lunch in twenty minutes. I'll leave after that. I'll take Ruth and Steve. They could use the experience."

"That will be fine. I'll have everyone finish packing up after lunch."

When they finished eating, the four of them filled a backpack with water, some protein bars, and a tool case. Each of them also carried a rock hammer in case they found something interesting. They also carried a topographical map, GPS and walkie- talkie. The ride over in the jeep was rough, but finally they came to the old riverbed. They got out and looked it over. There was ample evidence that a flash flood had been through. Branches and sage brush were piled up in all the tight bends and the water had eroded some of the banks, causing mud slides and exposing new rock.

"I think we should split up. That way we can cover more ground."

Glenda said. "The two of you can go east and I'll go toward the west. If that's all right."

"Ok with me." Ruth said.

"Me too." Steve replied. "It's nice to be out of camp."

"When you find something be sure to make a note on your map, so we can find it next year." Glenda reminded them.

After a radio check they set off, with a plan to meet back at the Jeep by seven.

After having gone three miles, carefully checking both sides, Steve and Ruth climbed up the bank and sat down on the rock.

"This is sure a bust." Steve said, unwrapping an energy bar. "If we go overland and walk fast, we should make it back on time."

Ruth took off her backpack, stretched and laid down, using it as a pillow.

"I can't believe we haven't found something. This is a complete waste of time. I would've gotten the vertebra out I was working on by now. We're all leaving today. I hate leaving something undone. You know what I mean?"

"It will be waiting for you next year when we come back."

"I won't be back. I've been accepted at Yale to continue working for my PhD."

"Why are you changing? Something going on between you and Dr. Pearce?"

"Nothing personal. I have a better offer, and access to better resources, that's all. We better head back."

Ruth stood, took her water bottle out of her pack, took a long drink then reached in to get a protein bar for her walk back to the jeep. She accidently tipped her water over while putting on her pack.

"Oh no! That's the last of my water." she said, quickly reaching down to get it. Too late. It ran along the rock and puddled in a depression.

"Steve. Is that what I think it is?" she asked.

He stepped over and stared down.

"Maybe."

he said tentatively. The flash flood had washed the thin soil off exposing the stone, now her water partially filled a dinosaur footprint. Steve got down on his hands and knees and ran his fingers over the depression.

"It's a print, right?" Ruth said. She looked out over the recently exposed surface.

"Give me your water bottle."

Steve handed it to her and she moved in the direction of the print and then poured some more water on the stone.

"It is a print!" Ruth exclaimed.

The two of them followed the prints along until they had found eight of them.

"Let me have my water back." Steve said.

He took it and poured some on two more depressions next to the ones they had found. Then he stood up and took a step back.

"Ruth, I think you should come back here."

As she did, he poured water on three other prints.

"What do you think those are?" he asked.

Steve bent over and took off his shoes and socks. Then he went over and stepped in one of the prints.

"A perfect size 10." he said.

He then proceeded to follow the tracks step by step.

"It's not what it looks like." Ruth said.

"What does it look like?" he asked.

"You know what it looks like. But that's not what it is."

"But what does it look like?" he persisted.

"It looks like a size 10 human print... next to a print of a dinosaur, size medium." she said, laughing.

Steve got down on his knees again, took his trowel and began removing the thin loose soil toward where the next print should be.

"What are you doing? We need to get back."

"This is easy. Give me ten minutes. I'm just curious to see if they keep going. Why don't you help? We can do it twice as fast." he said, looking up at her. "Please, it's the only thing we found all afternoon."

Reluctantly she took her backpack off and joined him. In a few minutes Steve hit something, he began cleaning it off, revealing more.

"I've found something." he said.

Ruth joined him and began helping.

"It's the end of a tail! See the vertebra!"

Now they both started working frantically, uncovering more and more.

Before they knew it, they heard Glenda call on her walkie talkie.

"Where are you two? It's ten after seven and you're nowhere in sight."

"We found a skeleton! Come and get us. We're about three miles from the jeep."

Glenda was a little put out. She was hot, tired, and hungry. It was the last day. She wanted to leave.

Steve and Ruth continued cleaning off their find.

"Over here." Ruth said.

Steve moved over to where she was and helped her. Soon they were staring at what they were both sure was a human skull. They wiped off the dirt and then Steve took the rest of his water and poured it over the skull.

Glenda drove up and stopped.

"Let's go." she said.

The two of them stood up and waved her over. She turned off the jeep and reluctantly came over.

"This had better be good." she said.

"We were wondering if you could tell us what it is." Ruth said.

"It looks like a human skull."

"And what do you think this is?"

they asked, stepping to the side. The two of them had been standing In-front of some more they had uncovered.

Glenda began looking more closely. She checked it out for a full ten minutes.

"You have discovered your first fraud." she said.

"What about this?" Steve said, moving his back pack.

Glenda looked for some time and then asked. "What would you like to do? she asked, looking at them both.

"We would like Dr. Bullock to look at it."

"At least I would." Ruth said, looking at Steve.

"Yes. I would like him to show me the flaws." I know it's fake, but I can't tell how it was done?"

"Very well." Glenda said.

She called Dr. Bullock on her walkie-talkie.

"We need you right away. There has been a discovery. We need you to check it out."

"Can't you take care of it.?"

"No, it's a great teaching moment. We really need your expertise."

Dr. Bullock stared down at the fossil. It appeared to be a rib bone with a spear point imbedded in it. He didn't believe what he saw.

"It's a fake. Someone is playing with us. Why did you call me over for this, Glenda?" he asked.

"They swear it was virgin earth. That it was not disturbed before they started."

Dr. Bullock was not a medical doctor, but held PhD's in paleontology and geology and was a professor at the University of Chicago. He was sixty-eight years old, six foot two, thin, with a leathery face and long white hair tied in back... and had a reputation for not suffering fools. Standing with him doing the talking was Glenda Pearce, also a professor, from Montana State University, in Bozeman. She was five foot six, short red hair, and a personality to match. How the two tolerated each other baffled most people but they had been working together for twelve years, sharing the site five miles from here.

The other two, standing back a step, were Steven Bell, born in Michigan and studying under Dr. Bullock, and Ruth Biskup, from California, attending Montana State. Both were graduate students working on their PhD's.

"Well, what do you two think?" Bullock asked, looking at the two students. Steve answered first.

"It was undisturbed soil. But it obviously must be a prank of some kind. Maybe someone did it a long time ago and we just happened to come across it. But how do we prove it's a fake?"

"Ruth, what about you?"

"Like Steve said, we want to know how to prove it's a fraud. At first glance I would say it's impossible because of the separation of humans and dinosaurs by millions of years. But if we always close off our minds to the impossible, we will never be open to discovering the improbable. I think it's too soon to decide whether or not it's authentic. We should uncover more of it and do some tests before we come to a conclusion."

"We are closing for the season today," Dr. Bullock reminded them, "There isn't time. Just cover it back up. You can look at it next year, if you want to waste your time".

"It won't take long to see if it is real or not." Pearce responded. "I can spend a couple of days. How about you Ruth?"

"Absolutely!"

"I can stay too, Professor." Steve added.

"Suit yourselves. I'm going back to make sure our dig is properly closed."

Bullock headed back to his four-wheeler.

"I'm going with you." Pearce said. "You two pick up your things and bring the jeep back. It's too late to do anymore today. We can come back tomorrow with more help."

"Don't bring any more students over here!" Bullock said. "The fewer people in the loop the better."

"If we're going to finish exposing it, we'll need more labor." Pearce shot back. It might be the best lesson they will learn this year."

The two of them rode the bumpy five miles back to their original dig, arguing all the way. The only thing they agreed on was to keep the discovery a secret until proven one way or another, if it was genuine.

The whole camp was packed and everything was loaded when they got back. Everyone was sitting around waiting to hear about the discovery they had made.

"I know you are all anxious to find out what Dr. Pearce, Steve and Ruth found. All I will say for now is it looks like a promising site. We will be exploring it in detail next year. I want to thank all of you for your hard work and professionalism, and I look forward to seeing all of you back next summer."

You could tell they were disappointed.

Luke, one of the volunteers asked, "Dr. Pearce, could you elaborate on what Dr. Bullock said?"

"I don't want to spoil the surprise. But next season it will have a lot to teach all of us. I would like to thank everyone also, for your dedication and hard work. We are taking back some very good specimens. Dr. Bullock and I are very proud and grateful to all the volunteers. Many of you, like Luke and his wife, Sharon, have been with us for... how long have you been coming? Is it, six or seven years, Luke?"

"This is our seventh season. And we plan to be back next year as well. We want to see the surprise."

"I would like our four grad students to remain behind and we will go over how we are getting everything back to the University. Thank you again. Keep digging, and remember to follow us on Facebook."

There were hugs, handshakes, and a few tears, but soon they had all left. When the last of them pulled out the remaining six stood in a circle.

"Steve and Ruth have found what we are sure will prove to be an elaborate fraud," Glenda said. "They have challenged us to prove it. Dr. Bullock would like to just leave it until next year. Steve and Ruth would like us to go back tomorrow. We have decided to put it to a vote. If we go back, we will be committing to three days only. After that we will leave, no matter what the findings."

"What do you think you've found?" Tim asked.

"All I will say is, you've never seen anything like it." Glenda replied.

"Besides this being a waste of time, and an obvious fraud," Dr. Bullock said, "it has the potential to harm our programs and reputation, if not handled correctly. So you will need to give us your word to keep silent about it, until Dr. Pearce and myself decide how, or if, to share it with the public."

Contrary to his intention, Dr. Bullock's comments assured a unanimous vote to stay.

They unhooked the trailer holding their hoard of fossils for the year and left it. Then the six of them looked like a convoy driving the bumpy five miles to the new site. The light was beginning to fade as they set up their tents. Steve, Ruth and Dr. Pearce, who had missed supper, made a meal of cheese, crackers and summer sausage. Everyone, except Dr. Bullock, had looked at the fossil quickly before setting up their camp. When they had a campfire going, they sat around discussing the find.

"It looks real to me." Linde, another one of the grad students said.

Tim, the fourth grad student responded, "We know it can't be real. Dinosaurs and humans are separated by millions of years. And it's not complete. I bet it will prove not to be a dinosaur, just some other large mammal. Like a large mammoth."

"Large mammoth, right! How do you explain the rock strata we found it in?" replied Linde.

"The problem is not whether or not it's a dinosaur. We all know it is, right, professor Bullock?" Linde continued. "The issue lies with the assumption that the rest of it is a human."

"Human or not, you can't get away from the fact that one Clovis point is sticking in the rib bone of your dinosaur..."

"I thought you said it was a Mammoth." Linde chided.

"Aaaand, two others laying close by, one with part of the shaft still attached to it." Tim continued.

Dr. Pearce got up without commenting, and went to her tent. Bullock did the same.

The four students continued to argue back and forth until, one by one, they went to bed, leaving Ruth the only one up. When the last light was out, she went to her tent and took out her Iridium 9575 EXTREME sat-phone, a gift from a friend. She walked away from the camp and made a call. Then she went to bed herself.

CHAPTER FIVE
AUGUST 6 MONDAY 8 AM
OAK RIVER IOWA LIFE
CHURCH PARKING LOT

Charlie slammed on the brakes, stopping inches from the delivery truck that pulled out blocking her escape. Quickly putting the car in reverse, she stepped on the gas. The tires spun as the car hurtled backwards. Flipping the wheel, she pulled the emergency brake, causing the car to spin around in a perfect 180. Quickly shifting into first, she punched the gas. The tires squealed again, smoke billowing behind her as the car bolted forward, pushing her back in the seat. A dock worker, more involved with his cell phone instead of watching, walked out in front of her. She turned hard to the left going behind him, then instantly back to the right, just missing a fork truck hauling a large coil of wire. Just then the two motorcycles that had been chasing her, turned the corner and headed straight at her, in a deadly game of chicken. As the gap closed the riders pulled out their machine pistols and began firing. She held her ground as the bullets sailed around her.

Too late they noticed the dip in the drive and with only one hand guiding their speeding bikes, they both lost control. One flew past her window and slammed head on into the fork truck, impaling himself. The other one flipped, tumbling over and over until he slid into the side of the truck that had blocked her path. Safe at last, she headed toward the exit. She was almost there when a black SUV pulled in and stopped in the middle of the street. A woman emerged through the sun roof and took aim with a rocket launcher.

Charlie spun the wheel, did another 180 and headed back. Swerving again this time right and then left, the rocket missed her car by inches, exploding in the side of the truck, spreading flaming wreckage. She drove right through the opening. Seconds later she heard another explosion. Looking in her rear-view mirror she saw a wall of flame covering her escape. She slid into a ninety and came to a stop.

"Pretty good huh." She said, looking at Pastor.

"You're getting better, but you knocked over both cones on your second time through the slalom. And your last 180 was off. You drifted into the other lane. But yes, it's pretty good, for a girl."

Charlie's imagination sometimes got the better of her as she ran the course they had set up earlier. At seventeen years old, five-foot-tall with long blond hair and blue eyes, Charlie did not look like someone who would be mastering evasive maneuvers in a custom Mustang, nor would you expect the six foot four, muscular ex-Navy

SEAL teaching her to be the pastor of Life Church but they were.

"Go ahead and park. We're going to quit early today I have a delivery coming, and I'll need your help with it."

Charlie drove across the church parking lot and parked the car in the garage. As they got out, he said. "Bring those two lawn chairs."

She followed him out of the garage, grabbing the chairs as she went. He stopped just outside and held out his hand. Charlie handed him a chair.

"Let's sit in the shade while we wait, we need to have a little talk."

"What about Boss?" Charlie asked as she sat down.

"I've been letting you use my very nice 66 Mustang convertible to practice in. Someone approached me, concerned for my car and your safety. They offered to sell you an old car for you to practice in. After thinking it over I decided it was a good idea."

He looked at his watch again.

"They're bringing it over in a few minutes. I just hope you won't be disappointed. It's really old."

"That's fine. I'm grateful you're teaching me. To tell you the truth, I pray every time that I won't wreck your car. How much does it cost? I can make payments if they're not too much."

Pastor looked at his watch again and then heard a rumble in the distance.

"Well that's just it. I told them the price was too high and the car was in too bad of shape. If they really wanted you to have it, they would need to fix it up and give it to you. I explained you didn't have any money and really don't make enough to make payments."

The sound grew louder as a car turned the corner.

"I think that's it." he said, pointing down the street.

Charlie looked up just as a car pulled in the drive, drove up, and parked right in front of her. Rob, from City Auto, was driving, Phil was in the passenger seat. It was a bright yellow 1967 Mustang convertible.

Charlie sat there, her eyes starting to tear up.

"That's the car?" she asked.

"I'm afraid so. It was in bad shape, didn't even have a motor when they got it."

Rob pulled the hood latch and they both got out of the car.

Charlie stood up. "You're kidding, right?"

"I don't think so." Pastor said. "Are we kidding, Rob?"

"I hope not. We put a lot of work into this old thing."

"If you don't want it, I can call the previous owner and see if he will take it back?" Phil said, as he lifted the hood.

"No. No! I want it. I, I, I."

"Yes? You wanted to say something." Pastor said.

"Uh who. Uh why, Uh."

"Do you need to sit back down?" Phil asked.

"No." Charlie said, going over to the car and rubbing her hand along the side. It was smooth and silky feeling. The interior had tan leather seats, protected by a roll bar. Continuing her way up to the front, she looked under the hood. The engine filled the entire compartment.

54

Rob gave the introduction. "This is a 1967 Mustang convertible with a total custom rebuild. Nothing on her is stock, from the custom sunrise yellow gold paint, the custom tan leather six-way power seats, to the high performance, 600 hp 429 engine. It also comes with a comprehensive four-year owner's package... including, car insurance, a comprehensive four-year warranty, including oil changes exclusively provided by City Auto Repair, and fuel, provided by Casey's Inc, at least the one in town."

"Is this all mine?" Charlie asked, not really believing what she was hearing.

Rob walked over and handed the keys to Pastor, who put them in his pocket. Rob and Phil went into the garage and came out, each carrying a chair. They all sat down forming a circle.

"You had some questions earlier." Pastor said. Taking his seat again. "I'll see if I can answer them. Your first question was, who. I assume you wanted to know who bought it for you. I'm the only one who knows and I'm not allowed to tell you. I will say, it is not one of us, not anyone in the church, not Jack, or anyone else you will think of.

"The next question you asked was, why. If you meant why did they do it, I asked the same question. They said, God told me to do it."

"When I asked for an explanation," they said, "God told me I loved money too much and needed to give some of it away. He gave me a list of twelve things to do. This is the last one. I kept telling him this one was not only foolish and wasteful, but downright dangerous!"

THE PAST COMES ALIVE

"The three of us have discussed the donor's anxiety in giving this gift. Is it foolish? Only if you treat it foolishly. Is it wasteful? Only if you waste the opportunity you've been given. Is it dangerous? You and I have talked a lot about controlled power, and that car certainly has a lot of power. Power can be very seductive. Like the horsepower in that engine. But there is also power in pride of owner-ship. We three, along with Police Chief Watson, want to help you with your control. There is zero tolerance for any traffic violations. Also, you will be expected to offer your-self and your car, to transport others who have a need. Like Mrs. Lemon, who lost her husband two weeks ago and is working on getting her driver's license for the first time. She needs someone to help her run errands until she passes her driving test. You can also help her prac-tice with their family car. And lastly, we will use your car for the rest of your driving lessons, instead of mine."

Pastor reached in his pocket, took out the keys and held them out to her.

"First, repeat after me; I, Charlie, will abide by all the rules as they have been explained to me. And I under-stand that if I break them, I could lose my driving privi-leges, my lessons, or even the car."

After she repeated the pledge, he handed her the keys.

"The car is in my name." Pastor said. "I will sign it over to you in four years, if you follow the rules."

Charlie thought a moment looking down at the keys. Her eyes became red and tears started to drip down her cheeks.

"I don't understand. Why would God do this? I want the car, but..."

She didn't say anymore. Finally, Rob spoke.

"Phil and I have asked God the same question, all the time we were rebuilding it. Last night I think I got the answer. I was praying about today. It's like God said to me, 'The car is a tool I am using to teach Charlie obedience. When it has done it's work, I will take it away."

She looked at Rob. "Thank you for sharing. Somehow, it's not so overwhelming knowing that. Can we all go for a ride?"

"I know we need a ride back to work." Phil said.

"But we don't need to get there right away." added Rob.

The four of them got in the car. Charlie started it up. It was hard to tell who had the biggest grin when she revved it up.

"Where do you want to go?" Charlie asked.

"I would like to see if you are as good as Pastor says you are." Phil said.

"Yah, let's see how good you are right here." Rob added.

Charlie looked over at Pastor. He nodded his head. She put it into first and drove to the end of the parking lot. The first time through was not her best and Phil and Rob both teased her. Charlie soon discovered her new car handled much better than Pastor's and had a lot more power. She ran through the course several times. Soon she felt in complete control.

"What have you done to this car? It is so much better than Pastor's. Sorry. she said, looking over at him.

"We want you to bring it over Friday about four. We'll go over the whole car with you. We're too busy today." Rob said. "We need to be going back to work. We can't play anymore."

Charlie pulled out of the parking lot and cruised over to City Auto and let them out.

"What now, Boss?" Charlie asked.

"It's your car. What do you want to do? I can play the rest of the morning."

"That's easy. I want to go for a ride."

"I thought you might. Go south out of town on the highway. I'll tell you when to turn."

As soon as they left town, she set the cruise control. The last thing she wanted to do was speed on her first day.

In only three miles Pastor told her to turn left.

"Where are we going?" she asked as she made the turn.

"Where do you think we're going?"

"The only thing out here is the old go-cart track."

"That's where we're going. When you get there, go through the main entrance, but turn to the left instead of going into the parking lot. It will take us back to a set of garages and the entrance to the track. When you see the gate, stop and I'll open it."

In a few minutes with the gate opened, Pastor waved her through and relocked the gate. He came around to the driver's side and asked, "Can we change places for a while?"

"Sure."

Charlie got out and they swapped seats. Pastor pulled on in, stopped and shut off the car.

"Have you ever been out here before?"

"Yah, once, in the sixth grade. I was invited to Keith Bluemont's birthday party. We all got to drive the go-carts. It was a blast! They closed down though, not too long after that."

"That's true. But some friends of mine from the Service bought the track, and the surrounding farm and have been rebuilding it. They're expanding their business, and wanted their own facility."

"Are they going to open the go cart track? Only make it bigger?"

"Not exactly. They teach defensive and offensive driving techniques, among other things, to security per-sonnel. He offered me a job teaching I told him it was a very interesting offer, but I already had a full-time job. He didn't like that answer, so he kept at it and, well in the end, I gave in."

"You're going to quit being Pastor?"

"Don't interrupt I now have a "part-time" job on Mondays when he needs some extra help. In exchange I get the use of the track when it's not in use."

"You mean we get to drive on the track."

"Yes." Pastor started the car. We don't have a lot of time left today. So, for today's lesson we will just check out the track. If you don't mind, I'll take a couple of laps and then you can have a turn."

"That sounds great!" Charlie said. Her voice full of excitement.

"Put on your seatbelt." Pastor said, noticing she didn't have it buckled.

He pulled out onto the track and took an easy lap, explaining why the track was laid out the way it was. As he passed their starting point, he stepped down on the accelerator. The tires broke loose and they were both pushed back in their seats. After he took the first turn sliding sideways, Charlie tightened up her seat belt more. Pastor sped around the track negotiating each turn expertly. As he finished the lap he headed toward the gate and at the last second, did a perfect J-turn and let it coast back to the track.

Charlie, who had been laughing with excitement, said "You're going to teach me how to do all of that? Wow! That was Awesome!"

"Only if you want to learn."

"Of course, I do!"

"Then, it's your turn." He turned off the car, pulled out the keys and handed them to her. When she took them, he held on, and with his serious face, said, "Only on the track, only when I am with you. There is much I can teach you, but the most important lesson is also the most difficult, self-control. Stay in the Word, and don't neglect your time with God. He is where your strength really comes from."

"Your sermon two weeks ago was on prayer. You talked about having a prayer partner. Well I don't have one. I was wondering if you would be my prayer partner. I know you're already busy, but you also know my bad side... I would like it to be you, please."

"Yes, I will. But I expect you to keep in touch. If you don't, I'll come after you."

"Good."

Charlie started the car and headed onto the track.

"Take a slow lap first and then each time around, increase your speed. I'll tell you when you're going fast enough."

Charlie felt her adrenaline kick in as she increased the speed. After a few laps Pastor said,

"This time, when you come out of the last turn, stomp it down, then stop at the entrance."

Coming out of the last turn she punched it. Even though they were already going sixty the tires squealed and it fish-tailed a little as the car responded. Soon she saw the speedometer hit 100. She slowed down and came to a gentle stop at the gate.

"How fast do you think it will go?" Charlie asked excitedly.

"I don't know. Well over the 100 you were going. One day we will find out." Pastor said. "But right now I need to get back to the parsonage, see how Jack is doing, and make lunch." He got out and unlocked the gate.

AUGUST 6 MONDAY MORNING
PALEONTOLOGICAL SITE MONTANA

Ruth woke up, rolled over, and stretched. Her hip hurt from sleeping on the ground. She reached under her sleeping bag and pulled out a rock she hadn't noticed the night before. She unzipped her tent door and threw the rock. Looking at her watch she saw it was just after five. Now that she was awake, her mind began going over the day before. Unable to go back to sleep she put on her clothes and hiking boots and got up. It felt cold as usual in the morning. Rummaging through the duffel bag she kept her clothes in she grabbed a hooded sweat shirt and pulled it out. Noticing her sat phone she stuffed it in the bottom and zipped the bag.

Her next thought was coffee. The night before they had arranged what would be their kitchen. It included a Coleman camp stove with folding legs, two coolers, one with ice to act as their refrigerator, and the other one for dry goods. There was also a large cooler with water bottles and ice, plus an extra case of water, also two construction water coolers holding seven gallons each.

She filled the coffee pot from one of those, measured out the coffee, adding a large extra scoop, turned on the fire and waited. It was just starting to get light in the east when the coffee was ready. She poured herself a cup and sat back in her chair. The next one to poke their head out was Steve. He crawled out of his tent, walked over and got a cup of coffee and sat down next to Ruth.

Neither of them spoke. When his cup was half empty he said, "Thanks."

They were both on their second cup when Tim got up. He put a large skillet on the stove and filled it with bacon, grabbed a Mountain Dew and sat down. They were all up by sunrise and on the job by 6:45. The work went well. Everyone was focused. Throughout the day as needed each of them would stop as and get something to drink or grab a bite to eat, and get right back on the job.

By 8 pm it was all exposed. There on the ground before them was about twenty percent of what was undeniably an Edmontosaurus, including the skull. Lying partly under some of the ribs, was about fifty percent of what appeared to be a human, including the skull and part of the lower jaw, the pelvis, and most of one leg and foot.

They were excited, famished, thirsty, and exhausted. It had been a long day, but very rewarding. They cleaned up as best they could and put steaks on the grill.

Watching the Big Sky sunset, they ate supper. After which they drifted into bed without much discussion.

CHAPTER SIX
AUGUST 7 TUSDAY MORNING
OAK RIVER IOWA
CHARLIE

harlene Ruth Ann Bolton, Charlie, woke up before her alarm, like she did most mornings. The sun was shining in her east window, making the soft yellow walls look like shimmering gold. She looked over at her alarm. It was a quarter to six. Normally she would roll right out of bed, put on her running clothes and go for a run. But today was special. She was alive! Her right shoulder hardly hurt anymore where she had been shot, almost eight weeks ago now. And yesterday, God had given her a car. Officially, she was in Paula's and Pastor Boyd's custody. Most people might not consider it freedom, to be in someone else's custody, but the way Charlie looked at it, it was a plus. No, a blessing!

Charlie glanced around at her large bedroom. It had a walk-in closet and its own bathroom. The mattress was now new. The sheets were soft. And with the window open, she could hear the birds singing a song of praise.

How different this was, compared to the way she grew up. Often sleeping on an old mattress on the floor, or on the couch of one of her relatives, who had reluctantly taken her in after her parents were both killed in an auto accident. Frequently her clothes were kept either in a suitcase or a laundry basket. Finally her grandmother took her in to keep her out of the foster system and things were better. She'd had her own bedroom and a regular bed. True, it had a saggy mattress and the chest of drawers had one drawer missing. To Charlie, the four bedroom, three and a half bath, brick home with a wraparound porch that Paula owned, was a mansion.

She got out of bed, opened the window the rest of the way, and joined the birds in singing her praise to God. After a few bars, she stopped, put on her gym clothes, and headed down the hall, down the steps and out the front door, and started her run. She was almost back to her old self. Looking back at the house she began to pray out loud,

"Father, I want to thank You for everything You have given me. We both know I don't deserve any of it. Without Your blessing I would have woke up in Juvenile hall, locked up until I turned 18, instead of a brick mansion in the best part of town. You have saved me, my grandmother, great grandfather, and most of my aunts and uncles who live in town, even two of my cousins. You are awesome! You remember Jack. He is very stubborn and a lot like me, prone to violence and acting without thinking. You know I love him like a brother. Right now, that brother is confined to a wheelchair, and lives with Pastor Boyd. But his broken bones are healing quickly and soon he will be back on his own. I know he has inherited a lot of money. He used some of it to set up a scholarship for me to go the college. I think he did it because I saved his life and was shot in the process. I think he is trying to buy a clear conscience. The three of us know he is going to hell if he dies. I saw it in his face when I was shot and I feel it in my spirit. Why won't he come to You? How can someone know they are lost and not turn to You?

"He also seems to be avoiding me. Is it because when he sees me, he's reminded of that moment? I don't know what to say. My heart's broken over him. Please show me what to do. I would trade all these blessings You have given me for his salvation."

Charlie finished her run, in silence. When she got home, Paula was in the kitchen finishing her breakfast of yogurt and a muffin. She called to her as she was going past the door.

"How's the shoulder this morning? Must be doing better. Your runs are getting longer."

Charlie went in and sat down.

"It's doing much better. It doesn't really hurt anymore. Just sore and stiff sometimes, but it is getting stronger. I have a doctor's visit day after tomorrow. He said if it looks good, he will release me."

"That's good, right? You're strong, stronger than me. It won't take long to get back to where you were.

67

You look down today. I thought you would be all excited after getting your car."

"I am. It's great. I just don't know what to do about Jack. Do you think if I give the scholarship money back it would be like it was before.?"

"I don't think so. I think it would only make it worse, if you tried to do that. And I'm sure Judge Hartley would not approve of it. Having that in your future is part of the reason you are here, instead of in jail."

"You need to give him some time. A lot has happened to him since his father's funeral. He just needs time to put it all in order."

"I'm worried about his soul." Charlie continued, "He doesn't even argue with Pastor anymore. In fact, he calls him Pastor, instead of Bill. And his sister told me he was going to church this Sunday."

"That sounds like a good thing to me."

"Don't it. But his heart isn't in it. He hasn't surrendered, he just quit fighting."

Paula looked down at her watch. "I've got to go." She got up, leaving her plate on the table along with her empty yogurt cup, and headed out the door. She returned in only a few seconds and grabbed her purse. "Can you get those for me? Got to go." This time she did not come back. Charlie could hear her car leave the drive.

"Hope you don't get stopped for speeding." Charlie said to herself. "Well Charlie, you better get ready, or you will be late as well."

Today was her first day working at Dairy Queen.

AUGUST 7, TUESDAY MORNING
JEN AND CHRIS

"Isn't this just the best Tuesday you have ever seen?" Jen asked Chris, as they parked in front of the Oak River Real Estate office.

"It's a pretty good one all right. Clear sky, sun shining, light breeze, a high today of 87… and I have the day off to go house hunting with a lady who recently inherited enough money to buy any house in Oak River."

"That sounds awful doesn't it?" Jen said.

"What part?"

"The part about all the money. I feel unsure about this whole thing. I don't want to become someone whose only value is that she has a lot of money she didn't earn. Oak River is a small town. I'm sure everyone knows more about my bank balance than I do."

"We've known each other how long, since pre-school right? You've been renting that old house on the edge of town. It practically sits in a corn field, and needs more work than it's worth. No one will blame you for not moving into your father's house, after he was… you know, died. You've always worked hard. It's a good thing, a blessing. Now let's go see what's on the market."

They got out of Jen's car, a seven-year-old Chevy Impala, that she bought used three years ago, with one hundred and thirty thousand miles on it.

The office was on First Street, in a building that started life as a barber shop. Bud and Julie Markowitz bought it and turned it into their real-estate office. Bud was born in Oak River and brought Julie back with him when he finished college. They got married the next week.

Julie greeted them at the door.

"You're right on time. I already have some houses I thought you might be interested in." They followed her into her office. "You said on the phone you would like a three-bedroom, two bath with an attached garage, and a nice yard. I found five that fit that description, in the price range you indicated. I know you wanted a one story; they are hard to find, at that price. Three of these are older two story. I thought you might give them some thought. One, in particular, has a very nice yard and is close to the elementary school."

Julie turned her computer screen around and showed them pictures of each house. After seeing all five on the screen, Jen said she would like to see four of them. As they toured each house, they were both disappointed. They all seemed to look better on screen than in person, and none of them were what she was hoping for at all. It was almost noon when they finished seeing the last one.

"What do you think?" Julie asked.

"I don't know about Chris, but I need a break and some lunch." Jen said. "This is harder than I thought it would be."

"I agree." Chris added. "Could you show us a couple of nicer homes this afternoon? Just so we have something to compare to."

"Yes, I saw two very nice ones this morning when I was putting this list together. I'm sure they are more what you have in mind."

"How much more do they cost?" Jen asked.

"They are more money, but they're also much nicer homes. Remember, it's like buying a car. It's only the asking price. The first one I'll show you, the seller is anxious for it to sell. They live out of town and need it to close so they can settle their mother's estate. There are three siblings, none of them live in Oak River anymore. I'm sure they would consider any reasonable offer. What time would you like to see it? We can just meet at the house if you like."

Jen checked her watch. "How about one?"

"That will be perfect. I'll grab a bite to eat and browse through the listings for anything else I think you would like."

After getting the address they parted ways.

AUGUST 7 TUESDAY MORNING PALEONTOLOGICAL SITE MONTANA

They were all up early and after a quick breakfast were back to work.

A grid was set up, extensive photos taken and measurements made. The skull belonging to the hominid was removed, along with the section with the Clovis point and the Edmontosaurus skull. All were completely packed in plaster. Next, the site was carefully covered with a plastic tarp, reburied, and disguised as best they could.

AUGUST 7 TUESDAY
DAIRY QUEEN OAK RIVER
JEN AND CHRIS

Jen and Chris decided to get a sandwich and some ice cream at Dairy Queen. When they got inside, they saw Charlie wiping off tables.

"Hi Charlie." Chris said. "How do you like your new job?"

"Today is my first day. Tony had me come in this morning to fill out some paper work. Then he had Al show me around and watch what everyone was doing. I'm not so good at just watching, so I asked if I could clean tables. I'm off at noon. I even get a free lunch."

"You're on overtime. It's ten after. You want to eat with us?"

"Sure. I need to punch out first. Be back in a minute."

They waited for Charlie to come back, then they all ordered and got a booth in the corner.

"What are you two doing today?" Charlie asked.

"Jen is going to buy a new house. We're out looking."

"Not a brand new one." Jen said. "We looked all morning. Some of them were not much better than the one I rent. Hopefully I can find a nice one this afternoon. We're going to meet the realtor at one. She's going to show us a house at 106 Springdale. Right Chris?"

"Yes. She said it's a real nice brick ranch, on a cul-de-sac in a nice, quiet, safe neighborhood."

"Do you want to come with us?" Jen asked.

"Yah! That would be great. I don't have anything else to do the rest of the day."

The three of them talked about houses; was Jen going to get a new car to replace her four door Chevy; where did Charlie think she wanted to go to College, now that she had a scholarship; and what did they think Jack was going to do when he got his casts removed?

The results were: Jen, no to the car; She was overwhelmed just looking at houses; Chris and Charlie, absolutely yes to the car. Charlie, College, somewhere in the mountains because they're awesome; Jen and Chris, Iowa State because it's close; the consensus on Jack, no one knew what he would do. They were all praying he would give his heart to Christ before his casts came off and he was on his own again.

Time went by quickly. Charlie ate her lunch, a double cheeseburger, fries, and a malt, also the fries Chris and Jen didn't eat, and the half of a grilled chicken sandwich Jen didn't want.

Afterward they all piled into Jen's car and headed over to Springdale. The closer they got the nicer the houses were.

"I can't afford anything over here." Jen said.

"Just give it a chance. Remember, you will have the money from the sale of your dad's house."

"What will that be, a down payment?"

"Just look at it with an open mind. A house and a new car are not an extravagance. The house will go up in value and I can get you a great deal on a new Ford. My dad owns the dealership you know."

They turned the corner onto Springdale and drove down the block. They were all very nice houses with large lots. One 0 six, was on the right side of the cul-de-sac. The realtor's car was sitting in the drive.

"This is beautiful," Charlie said, "look at how big the yard is and a three-stall garage!

Jen parked behind the realtor's car. They all got out and looked around.

"This is going to be way too expensive." Jen said. "That's why she didn't tell us the price yet." This must be the most expensive part of town."

"Look at the yard! It will be a great place to live and raise a family."

While Jen and Chris continued their conversation, Charlie walked up to the house. The door was open so she went inside.

"Hello. We're here."

Charlie said, as she went further into the house. The large living room blended into the dining room, with the kitchen off to the side. Charlie announced again as she went into the kitchen.

"Anyone here? We're here to see the house."

Not seeing anyone in the kitchen, she said loudly,

"We're here. Is anyone home?" She looked down and next to the kitchen island, she saw a shoe on the floor. She went over to pick it up. "Hello. We're all here."

Charlie reached for the shoe. On the other side of the island she saw the body of a woman lying face down. Charlie hurried over to her. She could see a large amount of blood at the base of her skull and an iron pipe not far away. Charlie knew she was dead. Her head was split open. But she bent down and felt for a pulse. That's when she saw someone run through the back yard. She went out the back door and gave chase. He was carrying something and when he got to the privacy fence, he threw it down and started to climb up. She caught him before he got over. Grabbed his legs and pulled him down. He landed on his stomach and rolled over. She jumped on top of him and was about to punch him in the face when she recognized him.

"John! What are you doing here? Did you kill her?"

"No, No I didn't even go in the house. All I did was see someone lying on the floor and then you came in and we ran!"

There was a scream from inside the house. Jen and Chris had found the body.

"You said, 'we' ran. Where's Willie? You two are always together."

"He's back there hiding in the bushes, I think. We took off in different directions."

"Pick up your metal detector. We're going around front and wait for the police."

Charlie collected Willie on the way. When they reached the front yard, Chris was calling 911 and Jen was repeating, "Nice house. It's just a dead body. Not a problem." She repeated it three times that Charlie heard, then asked,

"What do you think of the house, Charlie?" Then, noticing John and Willie, she said, "You two are in the youth group, right? You didn't kill her? Of course not!" Seeing their metal detector, she said, "You're looking for buried treasure, right? Find any?"

Chris interrupted. "The police are on their way. I called Pastor. He's coming too."

Charlie went over and sat on the steps in the shade. Everyone else followed.

"I think it's a great house," Charlie said. "What I saw of it, big back yard."

"I think so too," Chris added. "I would like to see the rest,...after the realtor is gone, that is."

Everyone burst out laughing, except John and Willie who were trying to think of some way not to get into trouble when they got home, if they got home, and what's it like to get arrested.

A few minutes later two police cars and an ambulance showed up, followed shortly by Pastor Boyd.

AUGUST 7 TUESDAY MORNING
LIFE CHURCH PARSONAGE
JACK

Tuesday, for Jack, started slow, mostly because Monday didn't end until almost three Tuesday morning. He'd turned on the movie channel when he went to bed.

First he watched a western, followed by a thriller, then a Bruce Willis shoot-em-up. During which he finally fell asleep. Anything to keep his mind off his shooting. He h'd had the dream again Sunday night, and that's all he could think about Monday.

Today Don and Gloria were coming over at 11:00 to get him. There was one more thing he wanted to do, to settle his dad's estate. It was almost 10:00 when he woke up. Pastor was gone and he had to call him to help him get out of bed. Jack hated being an invalid and couldn't wait to get his casts off. Pastor had just gone back to work and Jack was sitting at the kitchen table sipping on his third cup of coffee when Don and Gloria pulled in the drive. He waved for them to come on in.

"You look like you just got up." Gloria said.

"Didn't sleep too well, but I'm ready to go. I see you remembered the ladder." Jack said.

"What do we need a ladder for? I thought we were going out to lunch." Don responded.

"We are. But we have a stop first."

It was the first time he had been out without Pastor or Charlie to help. He showed them how to get his wheel-chair on the lift and locked into place in the passenger spot. Gloria drove the van and Don followed in his truck.

"Where are we going Boss?" Gloria asked.

"We're going to the Thirsty Irishman. I think you know the way."

Don and Gloria had worked for his dad, helping to run the bar for pushing twenty years. Now his dad was dead, and the tavern burnt to the ground.

"I don't like going by." Gloria said. "Too many memories, I guess. I miss your dad. The three of us worked well together. It was more like a family than an employee-employer relationship."

"That's part of what I want to talk about today. You and Don are like, aunt and uncle, closer than most of my blood relations."

The rest of the short ride was quiet. Each lost in their own thoughts of the past. Jack had her pull up in front, with enough room for Don to park behind them.

There was not much left standing to the Thirsty Irishman, that had not been consumed in the inferno. What was left had collapsed into the basement. The arsonists had done a good job. Jack hoped not everything had gone up in the flames.

After they had gotten him out of the van, he directed Gloria to push him up to just about the middle of the remains of the building, now mostly just a hole in the ground.

"Get the ladder Don and put it down just to my left and go down. There should be one stone in the wall with a faint outline of a skull and cross bones. I know, dramatic. I was ten when I carved it. You brought the hammer and prybar with you, right?"

"Got them in the back of the truck." Don said.

He lowered the ladder in place and then, carrying the tools, he descended into the basement, took one step to the left and there was the carving, right where Jack said.

"I found it."

"You should be able to pry the stone out. Inside you'll find a suitcase. Bring it up."

Don did as instructed. He had a little trouble getting the stone to move but when it did, it came right out. He reached in, grabbed the suitcase, and pulled it out.

"It looks like the fire didn't hurt it any at all."

Don stuck his hand in and reached around. Finding a small metal box, he took it out also. He climbed up and handed Gloria the suitcase, next he brought up his tools, set them on the sidewalk and went back down after the tin box. When he got to the top of the ladder, he handed it to Gloria.

"Here, give this to Jack. See if he remembers what's in it."

Jack took one look and smiled.

"Those are my baseball cards! Boy, that was a while ago."

Don put the ladder and tools back in his truck.

"What do you want with this old suitcase?" Gloria asked. "That's a strange place to keep your clothes."

"It's not full of clothes. Is it Don?"

"No, it's not clothes. Do you want me to tell her what's in it?"

"No, I don't think so."

Gloria picked it up and tried to open it.

"It's locked. What do you have in it, more toys?

She shook it and felt the things inside move but there was no sound.

"Now, I'm curious. What's in here?"

"Let's go to the Cafe and I'll show you."

They loaded Jack, his suitcase and baseball cards, in the van and headed down the street. The Oak River Cafe was only a few blocks away. While Gloria drove, Jack became reacquainted with his tin box and what once had been his treasures.

Jack had reserved the back room, which was normally for parties and meetings. Once they were seated, he asked the waitress to bring three beers.

"How many more are coming?" she asked.

"Just us." Jack said.

She left and returned with the drinks.

"We are having a meeting first and then we'll have lunch. Please shut the door on your way out." He told the waitress.

When they were alone, Jack took a big drink of his beer.

"Dad's was better." He said. "Gloria and I were talking on the way over to the tavern. You two are more than just friends. You're like family, and I don't have many. Both of you used to help me with my homework. You were often at our house. Don, how many times did I sleep in your spare room when I was in High School and had a falling out with my dad? That's enough of that." Jack said feeling his emotions rise. "I want to ask both of you a question. Just tell me straight out what you think." Jack hesitated a minute and then asked, "Was my father saved when he died? Did he really ask Christ into his heart, and was he really different after?"

They looked at each other, not speaking.

"I need to know. Did he say anything to either of you?"

"Yes." Gloria said. "One Monday night after we closed, we were sitting at a table. Just talking and relaxing, you know. He told both of us what had happened at church, how God had changed him. He said, "forgave him." and how he was able to forgive himself for a lot of things, including his relationship with you after your mother died. And yes. He was different. All the stress in his face was gone. I didn't know it was there until it left. He so wanted to talk to you. To apologize and ask your forgiveness. He asked us if we wanted to ask Jesus into our lives, our heart, he said. I didn't say anything. I was over-whelmed, I guess."

"Don."

"Gloria has it right. I didn't say anything either."

"Is it real?"

"It was for your father." Don said.

Jack pulled the suitcase in front of him, dialed the combination and opened it.

"Don knows what's in here. It belonged to my father. He saved it from the tavern."

Jack turned it around so Gloria could see it. Her eyes got big.

"Is that real?"

"Yes, it's real. I saw him putting some in the safe once. The door to the bedroom wasn't closed all the way and I was peeking in to see what he was doing. He put his finger to his mouth, gave me a wink and said, "Operating funds." That was it. After I got older, he gave me the combination to the safe. In case anything happened to him, he said. The tavern is gone, you both know Jen and I are set. I want the two of you to split it. There's $235,000. Call it a bequest from my father."

Don started to protest.

"Don't even! You will really hurt my feelings if you don't accept it. Now one of you go tell the waitress we're ready to order. This party is to honor my father. Don took the suitcase out to his truck, put it behind the seat and locked the door. Then he told the waitress they were ready to order.

After lunch, with the door to the room left open, they continued talking and drinking. As the afternoon wore on, someone would walk by and Jack would invite them in and the party grew. Word spread. And by five-thirty there were fourteen. They decided to call a few more to come down and have dinner. Once there, they all stayed and reminisced, each telling some story about T.J. The talking and drinking continued until they closed at ten. Then thirty-five people spilled out of the room, out into the summer night.

Jack couldn't drive. Gloria and Don weren't fit to drive. So one of the guys gave Don and Gloria a ride and Frank

Johnson took Jack home and helped him to the door where Pastor met them.

"Hello, Pastor Boyd. We brought Jack home. Do you need any help getting him into bed? He's had a little too much to drink. Sorry."

"No, we're good. You can leave the van right there. Thanks Frank."

Pastor wheeled Jack back to his room, with a quick stop on the way for Jack to relieve himself and throw up.

"I bet I'm the first drunk you ever tucked into bed." Jack said, lying back in bed.

"Not even in the first hundred."

"They said my dad was really saved, that his life was changed. He even witnessed to Don and Gloria... I'm glad he was saved. I guess that only leaves me."

Jack closed his eyes and was gone.

AUGUST 7 TUESDAY 1:52 PM
BACK AT THE MURDER SCENE

Police Chief Jerry Watson and two officers got out of their cars. He looked around, saw Charlie, and motioned for her to come over.

"What's going on? It looks like a lawn party. We were told there was a probable murder here."

"It's not probable. The body is in the kitchen. She was a realtor, going to show us the house. When we got here her car was already in the drive and the front door was open."

83

"Who found the body?"

"I did."

"Figures."

Chief Watson had told his officers and the paramedics to hold back. Now he motioned for them to go on in. As they walked past, he said,

"It's a murder scene. Tape it off. And keep Jennifer and Chris on the porch. I'll be over to talk to them in a few minutes."

Pastor Boyd drove up. Seeing Chris and Jennifer, he started to walk up to them, but Chris motioned for him to go over to where Charlie and the Chief were talking.

"Tell me the whole story." the Chief said.

She gave him the whole thing; pulling up to the house, finding the body, where the probable murder weapon was, seeing John running in the back yard, chasing him down, John and Willie and their treasure hunt.

"What did the boys see?"

"They haven't told me yet. They're very scared. I think Wille saw something. If you want, I can talk to him later. Maybe tomorrow."

"You seem to have it all figured out. Who did it?"

"I don't know yet."

The Chief smiled at the word, 'yet'.

"But the boys might. And if the killer knows they saw him, they might be next.

I want you to talk to them now! The best way to keep them safe is to catch the killer. I'm going to take statements from Jennifer and Chris. I'll let you and Pastor talk to the boys first, then I will. It'll be easier, and we'll get more if they tell you first.

Chief Watson went to meet his forensic team who'd just pulled up, while Charlie and Pastor gathered the boys. There was a gazebo in the side yard, out of the way. As they each took a seat, Charlie got Pastor's attention and put her finger up to her mouth and shook her head 'no'. They all sat there in silence, the boys with their heads down, not wanting to make eye contact. After a few minutes Willie blurted out.

"I saw them! They came out the door in the back of the garage, ran across the back yard and went between the fence and the bushes."

Charlie waited a minute then asked, "How many were there?"

"Two."

"Did you see their faces? Do you know who they are?"

"No."

"Was there anything weird about them?"

"Yes. They were both dressed like boys but they ran like girls."

"John, tell me everything you saw, and don't leave anything out."

"We didn't kill her."

"I know, but you have to tell us everything so we can catch who did. You understand?"

"Where do you want me to start?" John asked.

"Why did you come here?"

"We came here to see if we could find the treasure. I overheard my mom talking to Willie's mom on the phone. She was telling her what she'd heard at the beauty shop."

John paused.

"What did she say?"

"That the lady that lived here was rich, and that she buried her money in the back yard, so no one could find it. But she got sick. You know, where you can't remember things. Then her family came and took her away somewhere. And now they're going to sell the house. We wanted to find the money so we could give it back to her before someone moved in and found it and kept it. Honest Pastor!" John's eyes were turning red and he was having trouble holding back the tears. "We weren't going to keep it." He wiped his eyes with the back of his hand.

"I believe you John. But we need to know what you saw."

"We just got here and put our bikes over beside the house. Willie and me walked around back. We thought no one lived here. We were walking past the back patio door and my eye caught some movement. You know, you don't really see what it is. You just know something moved. So I stopped and looked. It was Charlie walking into the kitchen. Then I saw someone laying on the floor. Charlie went over and knelt beside her and touched her neck. Then she turned and saw me, and I yelled at Willie to hide. He was behind me. Then I took off running, but Charlie was faster and caught me climbing the fence. I thought she was going to hit me, but she didn't."

"Did you see anyone come out of the garage?" Pastor asked."

"No. I was just trying to get away from Charlie. Sometimes she hits people. I know she's saved now, but I didn't want to take any chances. I'm sorry Charlie, I shouldn't a ran."

"That's ok. I understand fight or flight."

"Willie do you remember anything else about the two people you saw?" Pastor asked. "Like what they were wearing?"

"They had on pants and T shirts... and baseball hats. Blue, I think Yah, blue. No black! All their clothes were black."

"Did you hear either of them say anything?"

"No. Yes! Well, I think so."

They waited for him to continue.

"What did they say?" Charlie asked.

"They stopped with the door open and looked around before they ran. One of them saw me and said, "There's a kid hiding in the bushes. I think she was going to grab me or something but the other one said. 'Now. Let's go!' And they took off running. It was a girl. I don't know who she was, she had sunglasses on. I don't think I ever saw her before. She's going to kill me isn't she Charlie?"

"We won't let that happen, Willie." Charlie assured him.

"How old do you think she is?" Pastor asked.

"About the same as Charlie. Only she's much bigger." Willie answered.

"How do you know the other one is a girl?" Pastor continued.

"They both ran like girls. You know, they don't run the same as boys. Except Charlie, she runs like a boy and hits like one too. I asked my mom once. She said Charlie was just a tom-boy. She would grow out of it when she's ready. I told her that was good because Charlie sure is pretty. She doesn't look like a boy."

"Thank you, Willie," Charlie said. "Did the girl you saw look like a boy too?"

"She had her hair cut short and it was black and she had black lipstick and black above her eyes. No, not like a boy, but one of the scary girls. I see some of them at the High School sometimes that look that way. They all hang out together. They look scary. I try to stay away from them."

"Do either of you remember anything else?"

They both scrunched their face and thought hard.

"Not me." John said.

"Me neither." Willie echoed.

"Pastor, is Chief Watson going to lock us up?"

"No, I don't think he will do that. Which one of you owns the metal detector?" Charlie asked.

"Uh, we sort of borrowed it from my cousin." John said. "We were going to take it back before he gets home. He's at baseball camp. Could you please talk to our moms? We're supposed to go to Church Camp next week and well, we don't want to miss it because we're grounded."

"Yah, we'll probably be grounded the rest of the summer for this." Willie added.

Chief Watson walked up.

"Did you boys tell everything to Pastor Boyd and Charlie?" he asked, looking very serious.

"Yes sir, we did." John said.

"You too Willie?"

Willie nodded his head yes.

"OK. If you remember anything else tell your mom or dad to call me right away."

They both nodded in the affirmative.

"OK. You two go over and stay with Chris and Jennifer."

After they were out of hearing range, he asked Pastor and Charlie what the boys knew. They gave him the complete rundown. When they told him how the girls got out, he got on his radio and had two of his officers check out where they went through the fence and find out if anyone on the other side remembers seeing them.

"What are you going to do to protect them?" Charlie asked.

"And their families. They could all be in danger if they recognized Willie." Pastor added.

"The same thing I did for Jennifer and Jack. I can have their houses checked on but, you know I don't have the manpower to give them bodyguards. I'm going to call their folks and let them know what's happened, and see if they can pick them up."

Then he looked over at Charlie. "Aren't you supposed to have your arm in a sling? By the way, you and Boyd stay out of this one. I don't want you shot again. I need to check on my men."

The Chief heard another car drive up, and turned to see who it was. "You and the girls can go tell everything to my detective. His name is Leon." Jerry motioned for him to come over to the gazebo.

Then he left.

A few minutes later Jen and Chris came over and joined them. Leon took written statements from the four of them, going over each detail more than once. When he finished, he thanked them, and gave them his card.

"If you think of anything else, give me a call."

They watched him walk away.

"Is it true?" Jen asked. "Was Willie face to face with one of the killers?"

"That's what he said. He gave a good description, all things considered." Pastor answered.

"So now the killers will be after Willie, because he's a witness."

"Maybe." Pastor responded.

"Can they leave town or something? Maybe go on vacation?"

"We need to do something to help." Chris said.

"Jerry told us to stay out of it. There's a good chance the girl Willie saw goes to High School here. I'm sure they will have Willie look at school photos, and pick her out yet today. This time we need to let them do their job." Pastor said. "You know they really are good at it." Pastor looked at his watch, five after four. "Sandy has left the office for the day. Let's go home."

"When do you think we can look at the house again? I really like it." Jen said.

"Well, you can call another realtor and ask. Should be cheaper now." Chris said. "I wonder if all the furniture goes with it?"

"I like the house too." Charlie said, "But what are we going to do about Willie and John? The best way to protect them is to find the killer. The way I see it, they either had a personal grudge, knew she would be here and waited to kill her. Or, they were here looking for something worth killing for. That's the one I'm going with. What we need is a metal detector, and start looking."

"I know we're supposed to stay out of it, uninvolved," Jen said. "But my dad had a metal detector. It's in the garage at home. We can go get it, grab another burger or something and come back with plenty of time to look before it's dark."

Chris and Charlie both looked at her in amazement.

"What has gotten in to you?" Chris said.

"I've been afraid of everything my whole life. I couldn't go to bed unless the light was on. Afraid to go out after dark. I don't know, I was terrified when Chris and I were kidnapped, I was sure we would be molested. No, raped and killed and no one would ever find our bodies. When I got loose in that motel and hit Jimmy with the lamp, something just snapped. I'm not afraid anymore."

"Well, I'm ready. Let's go get it." Charlie said.

"Chris are you in?" Jen asked.

"It's stupid. If Jerry catches us, we'll all be in trouble."

"For what? Trying to find my earring." Charlie said.

"Really?" Chris said, sarcastically.

"Honest. I must have lost it when I pulled John down off the fence."

"Then you can count me in." Chris said. "We must find that earring."

Jen turned at the next corner and headed to her dad's house. Once there, they found the detector hanging right where it belonged. Jen got it down, turned it on and ran it over the garage floor.

"Hear that beep? There's a re-rod right there."

She moved it around the floor and it would beep every time she passed over one.

"Dad said they are on twenty-four-inch squares."

She shut it off, and they headed out to find an early dinner.

"Where do you want to go? We need some place to plan it out." Jen said.

"McDonalds." Charlie said.

"That's the worst place in town. I never go there." said Chris.

Jen responded the same. "Me either." That's the last place you would find me."

"That's my point." Charlie said.

"Mickey D's it is." said Jen.

The place was almost empty. When they pulled into the lot there were only two other cars, one from out of state and one from another county.

"Looks like you were right, Charlie. This'll be a great place to hatch a plan." Jen said.

Jen and Chris both ordered a salad, Jen got a Bacon Ranch Grilled Chicken, Chris a Southwest Grilled Chicken. Charlie ordered a Deluxe Quarter Pounder with Cheese, fries and Coke, Biggy sized.

While they were waiting for their order, Chris asked Charlie.

"Where do you put it all? You always eat like that, and do you even weigh a hundred pound?"

"You're close, 103 pounds on the dot."

Jen just shrugged her shoulders, "I can't eat like that. And if I did, I'd weigh 200 pounds on the dot."

They all laughed.

Once they had their orders, they took a booth in the back corner, and began discussing what they would do.

"Do you really think she buried money in the back yard?" Chris asked. "The house is still furnished. Maybe she just put it in a drawer or something. If there even is a treasure."

"They didn't break in for nothing. It might not be money or jewelry. It could be something valuable only to the family."

"Like a will. It sounds like she has Alzheimer's, and they're expecting her to die." Jen said.

Charlie looked up. "Check out who just walked in. That girl fits the description, right? Short black hair, black lipstick, nose piercing, all black clothes."

Charlie took her phone and snapped a couple of pictures.

"I don't think Willie said anything about a nose piercing." And I know who they are I think that's her dad, Sawyer, or something like that, I can find out later. They bought a new car about three months ago. I think they go to the Baptist Church. She was with him when he picked up the car. She looks weird, but she's really nice. She said she works in the church nursery and wants to be an elementary teacher." Chris said.

"You can't judge someone just by the way they look. No one would think you've done half the things you have, Charlie." added Jen.

"Thanks." Charlie said. "We need to find the motive. Then I bet it will be easy to find the killer."

"How do we do that?" Jen asked.

"It's just like you see on tv. First, we need to find out who lived there. What did they do, are there any enemies, you know, did he run a company, and cheat people out of money? Then we can branch out to the rest of the family. Are there any family feuds? Maybe one of them wants to find the will and destroy it."

"How are we going to do all that?" Jen asked.

"Internet." Charlie and Chris said in unison. "You can find out almost anything." Chris continued.

"Well, let's get started. Hopefully the police are gone." Charlie said.

On their way out, Charlie took several pictures of the car the Goth girl came in. It was a new Ford Explorer, copper colored Limited Edition, license CGY-379, from Johnson County, with a sticker on the back from the local Ford dealership.

When they got close to Springdale, Jen slowed down and drove past the turn. It was a good thing. When they looked up the street there were still two police cars parked at the end of the cul-de-sac. She drove on by.

"What should we do now?" Jen asked.

"Let's drive around the block and see where the killers came out. They just might be neighbors." Chris said.

They circled the block a couple of times. On the third time a guy who was sitting outside his open garage door waved.

"I think that's enough. Go past Springdale again and see if the police are gone." Chris said.

"We need to stop and talk to him. Maybe he saw something." Charlie said.

"The last thing we need is for someone to call the police and report us for snooping around. If Jerry finds out we're trying to find the killers he'll give us a ticket or something."

"It's not against the law to go around the block." Charlie said.

When they turned the corner to check on Springdale, they saw another police car turn, and go up to the house.

"They're going to be there all day. We might as well go home."

said Jen.

"We can come back tonight." Charlie suggested. "After dark."

"What if the killers come back tonight also." Chris said.

"Then we call the police and the case is solved."

"What do you think Jen?" Chris asked.

"I'm with Charlie. Let's come back just before sunset. I can drop the two of you off with the metal detector then park the car on the next street and walk back. We can stop on the way home, pick up some flashlights, and then see what we can find on the computer about who lived here."

"That's a good idea." Chris said. "Maybe we can figure out what they were after."

Jen stopped at the hardware store. Charlie and Chris each bought a flashlight and Jen bought one that straps on your head like a coal miner, so her hands would be free. Then they picked up Jen's laptop and went to Chris's.

Chris lived on a farm her grandfather bought, to save a friend from having it foreclosed on during the farm crisis, then rented it back to him. After the friend retired and moved to town her grandfather built a new house on the property and moved in. Then he tore down the old one. There was a small barn off to the side. Chris asked if she could fix it up and live in it. He said yes. She started working on it but, in the end, her grandfather did most of the work. He finished last year and Chris moved in with Colonel Wilhelm Schmidt, her 7-year-old German Shepherd. It was small for a barn, just 26x40, but with an open floor plan it was a very spacious house. There was a loft over half of it, with a wide stairway leading up to the bedrooms and bath. The floor was stained concrete. The kitchen sported hickory cabinets and a granite top with an under-mount sink. Most of the furniture was white wicker with some antique tables and a sideboard, handed down through the family. One corner served as an office with an old oak desk, a year-old Mac desktop sat in the center.

This was the first time Charlie had been there. When they entered, Schmidt greeted Chris, then came over and smelled Charlie's outstretched hand, and gave it a kiss.

"Wow! He is beautiful." Charlie said, bending down to scratch his head behind his ears. Schmidt responded by wagging his tail in approval and gave her a couple more kisses.

"Well, I guess you're in the family. You have the Schmidt seal of approval."

"What happens if he doesn't approve?" Charlie asked

"Well, a deep growl, while baring his teeth, then he will back you to the door, unless I come and rescue you."

There was a laptop computer sitting on the corner of the desk. Chris went over and handed it to Charlie, then followed her over to the dining room table where Jen was already sitting. She signed on the computer for Charlie, then went to her desk, and started looking for information on who had lived at 106 Springdale. In a few minutes she had the lady's name.

"Her name is Clara Kingsley. We can all start there."

Charlie started looking through the local paper for what she could find. Chris started with the Ford dealer archives. And Jen googled her name. When it was time to go on their treasure hunt, they had quite a bit of information. Clara was born in 1932, her husband's name was Edward, died 1998, was an electrician. Clara worked as a secretary for Dr. Green, retired in 1997. They had three children: Edward Jr. 68, a retired dentist, living in Seattle; Timothy 66, a retired truck driver, living in Lincoln, Nebraska; and Robin 54, living in Iowa City. Clara had a good credit score; the house was paid for, along with the three-year-old car in the garage. She is now living with round-the-clock care from Helping Hands care givers.

Robin never married and is a Nurse Practitioner, working for a Dr. Ortigas.

Ed is married to Cora, no children.

Tim is on his third wife; her name is Angel. They have two girls, Lisa and Tisa.

When it was time, they all left to go back to the house. Jen drove past Springdale just before sunset.

"I think the police are still there." Chris said.

"What do you want me to do?"

"Pull over and let me out." Charlie said. "I'll walk up and see if it's really the police."

They dropped Charlie off at the corner. She walked up the street to see if they were still there, while Jen drove around the block, On the third time around, Charlie was waiting for them.

"Two policemen are standing out in the yard. I over-heard them talking. Some more are coming over to spend the night, hoping the killer will come back for the treasure.

"We might as well all go home." Jen said.

AUGUST 7 TUESDAY EVENING
CHARLIE

Charlie spent the rest of the evening at home in the library, sitting in her favorite chair by the window, reading in her Bible and praying. The day had started so free and liberating. Now there was a murder, and she had found the body. Everything had moved so fast; she hadn't had time to really process the magnitude of it all. Someone had killed another human being. She had felt the body. It was still warm but there was no life left. Now she was in heaven or hell. Charlie wondered if she was a Christian or not, whether she had invited Christ into her heart, to be her Lord, her Boss. Charlie also wondered who would be grieving for her. Was she married? Did she have any children? She wasn't that old. Surely her parents were still alive.

She continued reading and praying. She prayed for her family, whoever they were, her coworkers. Prayed that the police would catch whoever had killed her before, anyone else was hurt...or killed. She prayed for Chris and Jen, especially Jen. Charlie wasn't sure she was as tough as she had proclaimed today. She prayed for who-ever had been involved, that they would turn themselves in, that they would find forgiveness and be able to forgive themselves. Then she prayed for herself. She prayed in English and she prayed in the Spirit. Then she went to bed.

AUGUST 7 TUESDAY EVENING
PALONTOLOGICAL SITE MONTANA

Everyone pulled out at seven that evening. Bullock and Pearce left in the four-wheeler with the fossils. The girls followed in the university pickup pulling the trailer, and the guys brought up the rear in the jeep. When they reached the Striker ranch the four-wheeler and jeep were parked in the shed they used. The fossils were transferred to the trunk of Bullock's Cadillac convertible, and then they all left. Ruth drove Dr. Pearce's car, with Linde. The guys followed in the pick-up. Leading the way was Bullock and Pearce in the Cadillac. They were all heading for Jordon and something to eat.

Before they were out of the drive Bullock and Pearce were arguing over the fossils.

"The fossils are going with me." Bullock said. "You can ride back to Bozeman with the kids."

"That's not how it's going to happen. I am not going to let them out of my sight any more than you are. Bozeman is a lot closer than Chicago. It makes sense to go there. We have a state-of-the-art facility and I can control the project until we're ready to release it to the public. No one will find out about it. And don't forget, the museum is right there."

"It'll be public within days, if it isn't already. Those students probably have it on social media, pictures and all."

"They will keep quiet. You made it quite clear what would happen to their careers if it gets out and then is proved a fraud."

"Which it is." Jacob reiterated. "All our careers are on the line here. It should've been covered up, as I said, and forgotten. Everyone will expect us to be in Bozeman for just the reasons you named. That is why we can't go there."

"Chicago is no better. There are all kinds of people crawling around your labs."

"You're right, not Chicago either."

"Then where?" Pearce asked.

"Oak River Iowa."

"What's in Oak River?"

"Lester G. Crenshaw is in Oak River, actually on a farm outside of town."

"I've never heard of Oak River or this Les guy. How is he going to help?"

"Don't call him Les. He hates it. He is the only one I know who knows more than I do about paleontology. But don't tell him I said that."

"I've never heard of a Lester G Crenshaw. If he's as good as you say, I would have heard of him, or at least read about his work. What university does he teach at?"

"None. That's the best part about Lester, he is totally off the radar. If you have any more questions you can ask him when we get there."

It was almost eight before they pulled into Jordan and made a right onto Highway 200. Just at the edge of town was the Elk's Run Bar and Café and across the parking lot was the Elk's Rest Motel. There was only one car in front of the motel and three at the café. When they walked in, the juke box was playing a country song and two guys were playing pool in the corner.

A waitress stopped wiping off tables and came over.

"If you're looking for food you just made it. We close the restaurant in fifteen minutes, but the bar is open until two."

"Yes. We would like something to eat." Dr. Pearce said apologetically.

She showed them to a table for six, and handed out the menus.

"Do you know what you want to drink?" she asked. "We have Pepsi products, or I can get you something from the bar. We have a special on the chicken dinner, two dollars off, if you're interested. But there are only four left." There wasn't really a special but the chicken was sitting back in the kitchen under a heat lamp.

All four students ordered beer. Pearce and Bullock had coffee. When the waitress came back the orders were simple. All the students ordered the chicken dinners, Dr. Bullock a grilled chicken sandwich and Glenda had a cheeseburger. She took the order to the kitchen smiling all the way. They wouldn't need to throw out the chicken after all.

When the waitress left, Ruth asked, "What's going to happen now? I don't want to go home. I want to stay and work on what we brought back."

Steve spoke up next. "I agree with Ruth. This find will make us all famous!"

"Or infamous!" Bullock shot back.

"All the same, we all want to continue working on what we've found." Linde added.

"All of us." Tim interjected. "You are taking them to Bozeman, right."

"No one will be left out. Glenda and I will secure our find until school starts. We will need to work out a secure lab to work on it until we're ready to go public. We've made some phone calls and will probably rent a small warehouse in Bozeman to set up a lab. Glenda and I will need to work out our teaching schedules. There's a lot to do between now and the time school starts. I need all four of you to continue with your plans, as if nothing has changed. We will see all of you the first day of class.

Do you know how the California Gold Rush started?" Dr. Bullock continued. "One man discovered gold. And like a fool, couldn't keep his mouth shut. The next thing you know, people are coming from all over the country and it was all out of control. He was killed, and others took over what should have been his. This is potentially far more valuable than finding gold. I am very serious about keeping this all to ourselves. He only told one person. Do you know who it was? A trusted friend."

The waitress brought over their food, and set it down. "Is there anything else I can get you?"

"I would like another beer." Steve said.

"Me too." added Linde.

"I'll bring over four more, is that ok?" Receiving no objections, she left, and in a few minutes returned with their drinks.

The conversation turned to what they were all going to do with the rest of their summer.

When the professors having finished eating, Glenda announced,

"Dr. Bullock and I are going to take his car. Ruth, would you mind driving mine back to the school and leaving it in my parking spot? You can put the keys in my mail box."

"Sure, but aren't you coming back with us?"

"We have some things to do first. If you would please park, the truck and trailer in the garage. All of you can head out for your well-earned time off." They said their good byes and left. Once in Dr. Bullocks car, Glenda asked, "If we are not spending the night here, then where?"

"On the road. We're going to see Lester."

After Bullock and Pearce left, the talk quickly changed topic, back to their discovery.

"What's with that? You know they're going to cut us out, don't you? I'll bet they're not even going to take them to Bozeman." Tim said.

"They sure left here in a hurry. Do you think they're going to Chicago?" Linde asked.

"No!" Steve replied. "You don't know Bullock like I do. He would never share this with anyone. And they are not going to rent a warehouse in Bozeman either. We've seen the last of those fossils. And the last of the dig. They took all the hard proof with them. Next season, we'll probably be moved clear off the Striker ranch, maybe even to a different state like Wyoming or Utah."

"He can't do that. Dr. Pearce will not let it happen. He can't cut her out. She has the connections to the ranch, and they left together." Linde said.

"It doesn't matter." Ruth cut in. "It's a fraud."

"It's not a fraud. The fossils are real, undisturbed, and in the right strata for the Edmontosaurus. We all looked at it very carefully. That is a Clovis point sticking in the rib, even if it is broken off. You need to come to grips with the facts, Ruth. This find will rewrite all we know about humans and dinosaurs." Tim responded. He was now a firm believer.

"Someone planted it there, carved it out and moved the skull from somewhere else. It is clearly impossible. We will discover how they did it in the lab." Ruth responded.

"I'm telling you, we will never see them again. We need to go back tomorrow and work on it until we get the rest out and in plaster. Then we'll have something to bargain with."

"If we don't get caught removing it. Where are we going to hide it? And how long before all of us are arrested?" Tim asked.

"Arrested for what? Grand Theft dinosaur". Everyone burst out laughing." We're just working on a University project." Steve said. "And they wouldn't want the publicity from arresting us."

They ordered more beer.

They didn't leave until the place closed at two A.M. Then they staggered over to the rooms they had booked earlier. Ten minutes later one of the doors opened and a shadowy figure got in the back seat of a waiting car. A few minutes later a man emerged from behind the motel and got in the front seat. The car pulled out and headed east.

CHAPTER SEVEN
AUGUST 8 WEDNESDAY
OAK RIVER

Charlie woke up wet with sweat. Her shoulder was hurting, probably from pulling John off the fence. She looked at the clock, almost 2:30 am. But that was not what woke her. It was the dream. The same dream she had before. She was a spectator watching from the side. She watched the motorcycle pull into the parking lot and head right for them. She tried to warn them but they couldn't hear her. The rider raised his gun and fired. Elijah fell to the ground and the gun he had stuck in his belt dropped out toward her, her other self. She ran for the gun as the motorcycle made a big circle and headed back, this time straight at her and Jack. She picked up the revolver, stood in front of Jack, aimed and slowly pulled the trigger. She knew she had hit him. He went over backwards off the bike, his gun firing as he went, striking the van and then her. She fell back onto Jack's lap and their eyes met. Next, she saw Pastor walk over to the shooter and take off his helmet. When she looked down to see who it was…it was her. She got out of bed and sat in a chair by the window and looked out. The yard was flooded with moonlight, bathing everything with peace. As Charlie watched, a rabbit hopped out of the shadows and began to eat some grass. She softly prayed, with tears running down her face. She began to praise God and softly sing 'Amazing Grace' to Him. Then a peace came over her and it seemed like she was sitting in His lap and nothing could harm her. She went back to bed and slept soundly.

AUGUST 8 WEDNESDAY 3:30 AM
ELKS REST MOTEL MONTANA

At three thirty, the Elks Rest Motel exploded, leaving only a large hole in the ground.

AUGUST 8, WEDNESDAY EARLY
PARSONAGE

About the same time in the parsonage, Jack woke up and desperately pushed the call button on his hospital bed. In seconds Pastor was there. He didn't need to ask what Jack needed. He grabbed the waste basket and held it up under his chin. For the second time he threw up. When he finished, there was nothing left.

Pastor took it out and disposed of it and put in a clean bag, and returned to see how Jack was doing. Jack was clearly embarrassed.

"I'm very sorry. I really don't drink much, mostly protein drinks and spring water. More of a health nut really, I've been drinking here because I wanted to irritate you. I am sorry. It won't happen again."

Pastor pulled up a chair and sat next to the bed.

"I wasn't born a pastor you know. I grew up on a farm and joined the Navy right out of High School. I've been where you are more than once, before I committed my life to Christ."

"You said you were a SEAL. That's not an easy club to get into. How long were you in?"

"Twenty years. Most of the last one I spent in the hospital riding around in a wheelchair just like you. Well not just like you. I looked a lot better and I didn't get there by falling down the stairs backwards like a sissy."

Jack laughed. "It was pretty stupid. I've always had a problem controlling my temper. Wanted to be a Ranger, but I was kicked out of the program after hitting my commanding officer. He could've had me court-martialed. And I would have been, except no one else saw it. You know what he did? He got up, wiped the blood off his mouth, looked me straight in the eye and said, 'I'm disappointed Jack. You have everything it takes to make a good Ranger, except self-control.' Then he turned and walked away. On my eval., he wrote at the bottom 'Excellent skills, No self-control.' He never told anyone what happened."

"Charlie is dealing with the same problem. You might be surprised how many gifted people have a lack of self-control. It's listed in the fruit of the Spirit. You'd think it would be the first on the list, instead it's last. In Galatians chapter five Paul begins by reminding us how Christ has set us free, but we are not to use our freedom to satisfy our own selfish desires. Instead Paul directed us to 'be controlled by the Spirit.' He explains that as we yield ourselves to Christ, the Holy Spirit begins producing good fruit: Love, Joy, Peace, Patience, Kindness, Goodness, Faithfulness, Gentleness, and Self-Control. I think it's listed last because it's the most difficult for us to learn. You've seen the change in Charlie's life. He can do the same for you."

"I'm glad, grateful, impressed, maybe envious. I hope she makes it. But I can only hold it together so long... long as I don't have a reason to lose it. But when a real test comes, I fail."

"Charlie isn't controlling her temper all on her own. The Holy Spirit is working with her. It doesn't mean she will never have a control issue again. But it does mean God, the Holy Spirit, is helping her. And each time she succeeds, she's getting stronger."

"And if she fails, what then? Is she kicked out like I was kicked out of the Rangers?"

"No. If God threw us out because we made a mistake, 'sinned again', no one would make it to heaven. If we truly ask for forgiveness and desire not to continue in our rebellion. He will forgive us and we can start over, hopefully wiser and a little more determined."

"How many times do we get a do-over? Some days I would need more than one."

"The Apostle Peter asked Christ a similar question, how many times am I supposed to forgive someone who wrongs me, seven times? I think Peter thought he was being generous. But Jesus told him, 'not seven times, but 70 x 7.' In other words, unlimited."

Jack lay back and closed his eyes, ending the conversation. He heard Pastor get up and softly close the door. Jack opened his eyes again and lay there unable to go back to sleep. He finally dosed off about daylight.

AUGUST 8 WEDNESDAY EARLY MORNING MURDER SITE

Burt Hansen and Stan Rengold spent the night at 106 Springdale. Stan had his wife bring over their dog, Rogue, a six-year-old mixed breed, German Shepherd and Poodle, a Shepadoodle. His coat had the markings of a black and tan Shepherd, but with the texture of a Poodle. Rogue was well trained and rarely barked. Instead he would give a low deep growl until he had Stan's attention.

They both tried to stay awake all night. At first they talked quietly, and would walk through the house periodically but, by 3 am they were both asleep. Stan on the couch and Burt in a recliner. They had walked in from four blocks away in civilian clothes just after dark. The only one who slept well was Rogue. The night was uneventful. At six am, Toby and Jim relieved them.

"How long are we going to keep up this surveillance?" Burt asked as soon as they were inside.

"Until further notice, is what I was told. See you two at six tonight." Jim answered.

"Remember. Stay out of the windows." Stan said. "No one is supposed to be here."

"Oh," Jim continued, "The Chief said Boyd is coming over to check out the 'treasure room' this morning."

"Whatever." Burt said. "This is a waste of time. They're not coming back. I wouldn't. I would figure the cops already found the treasure, if there really is one, which I doubt."

"Except we didn't, did we." Toby responded. "I know it said 'treasure room' on the door, but there was no treasure just a creepy room."

"Have you thought it's something else? Those boys were here with a metal detector. What if she did bury something outside?" Jim said. "People do weird things all the time."

"Well, me and my dog are going home. Maybe I can get some real sleep." Stan said.

"See you tonight." said Burt, closing the door.

AUGUST 8 WEDNESDAY 7:AM
JEN'S HOUSE

Wednesday for Jen was not her best day. As she said to the mirror "You have looked worse, but not for a while."

She had found it hard to sleep. She kept hearing noises in the house. Twice she got up and checked all the doors and windows looking outside. But all she saw was a beautiful night, with no one about. One reason she had rented this house was because it was at the end of the street and had fields on two sides, which were now full of corn taller than she was. The second time she got up she fixed herself a hot chocolate, and sat at her kitchen table reading her Bible. When she opened it, it was Psalm 68. She read the whole Psalm twice. Then she prayed, "Lord I need You to give me power and strength. I know I sounded brave today, but You know down inside, not so much. I can't believe what happened yesterday. I need You to scatter my enemies. Blow them away like smoke. Melt them like wax in a fire. And I will sing praises to Your name. Father, I don't like living alone. I want a Godly husband, and children... Please... soon." She closed her Bible and went to bed. Surprised she'd put into words her desire for a husband. Something she had never done before, not even to God.

She slept well the rest of the night, was up by six-thirty and at work by eight.

AUGUST 8 WEDNESDAY AM
FORD DEALERSHIP OAK RIVER

Chris entered the office at seven-thirty. She didn't start work until nine, but she had a lot to do before then. She went out to the shop, got a cup of coffee and a donut, then went to her desk. She wanted to add to what they had found out the night before. Oak River was a small town and a lot of people had a media presence. By nine o'clock she had the entire Kingsley family tree on both sides, back to Clara's great grandfather and up to and including her children and grandchildren. There were a few kinks here and there, but nothing to suggest her family had anything to do with the break-in. She was living on Social Security and a comfortable pension. There was no evidence she had any large sum of money, or jewels, or anything else of great value to steal. Just her clothes and the furniture. She would have to work on Bud and Julie Markowitz later.

AUGUST 8 WEDNESDAY MORNING 6:30 AM
LIFE CHURCH PARSONAGE

Nate Strong's started his day with a phone call from Pastor Boyd, while he was still in bed.

"Hello, someone better be dead!"

"Nate this is Pastor Boyd. No one's dead and I know it's early, but you said you would like to help Jack. Well, he will need your help this morning. Usually I'm here when he gets up and I take care of him before I go to the office. This morning I have an early appointment, and Jack is sleeping in."

He explained about the night before and what Jack would need.

"If you could come right over it would be a big help."

"I'll be right there." Nate said.

Nate pulled in at ten after seven and Pastor left a few minutes later for a breakfast meeting with Charlie.

At seven thirty-three Charlie opened the door to Pastor's Mustang convertible and got in.

"Where we going Boss? I'm sure ready for breakfast. I usually eat at seven. After my run."

"How's your shoulder today? You know there's a lot of prayer going up for your recovery."

"Yes, I am very grateful. It's really doing fine. Just a little sore, that's all. I think I hurt it a little pulling John off the fence yesterday. Tomorrow is my last visit with Dr. Clifton. I should be released. What else are we doing after breakfast?"

"Who said there is anything else? Can't I just take you out to breakfast if I want?"

"Sure, anytime. But this is the first time. It must have something to do with yesterday, right?"

"Yes, it does."

He parked in front of the Oak River Cafe and shut off the car.

"I have a couple of reasons. The most important is, I am concerned for you. How was last night?"

Charlie was going to just tell him it was fine. Then she looked at his face.

"You know, don't you?"

"I know how something like yesterday would bother me, if I were in your shoes."

"I had the same dream again. The one I told you about. I got up and prayed and read His Word. And then sang Him a song. I was all right after that and slept well."

"Are you up for going back over there today and help me unpack some of the treasure?"

"Is there really treasure there?"

"To her, it is the most valuable thing in the world."

"What is it? There can't be so much it takes two of us to unpack. Besides, the police would do that. It must be something else."

"You'll see when we get there. Now let's go get some breakfast."

"If I guess it, will you tell me?" she asked."

"If you guess it correctly, I'll tell you."

All through breakfast she tried to reason it out, but every guess was wrong. As

Pastor pulled up in front of the house and parked he asked, "Do you have any more guesses."

"No, what is it?"

"Let's go in and I'll show you."

The yard was all taped off and there were barricades across the drive. They ducked under the tape, walked to the front door, and rang the doorbell.

"There's no one home is there?" Charlie asked.

"There better be."

The door was opened by officer Jim Cummings.

"Come on in, Pastor. Jerry said you would be over this morning. Hi Charlie I heard you were the one who found the body. How are you doing this morning?"

"I'm fine, thanks for asking. Are you here to guard the treasure?"

"No one here has found any treasure that I'm aware of."

Toby walked into the room from the hallway.

"Good morning you two. You're here to see the treasure, right?"

116

"Jim just said there wasn't any." Charlie responded.

"That's not what it says on the door. Follow me and I'll show you all the riches."

Toby led the way back down the hall. There on the right was a door with gold letters that spelled out, 'Treasure Room'. He stood back and let Charlie open the door. She stepped in and immediately felt the Presence of God. Pastor felt the same as he entered. Jim and Toby left them to it without going in. The room was meant to be a bedroom, but the only furniture was a small table with a straight-backed chair, and a small cushion laying on the floor. There was a well-worn Bible and a notebook laying on the table. On the walls were pictures, mostly of individuals, but some were of couples or families. Most of them not in frames but all of them had the name of the person printed on them with a black marker.

"Jerry said none of his officers wanted to come in, they said it felt, 'creepy'. That's why he asked me to come over and see what I thought."

"It's the Presence of God. It's not creepy. This is wonderful! What did she do in this room?"

"She prayed."

Pastor went over, picked up the Bible, looked at it, then handed it to Charlie.

Next, he picked up the note book, opened it and turned to the last entry. The date was two weeks ago. It was a prayer.

"Listen to this, it's the last entry. 'Lord Jesus, thank you for meeting me here again, I have prayed for everyone

You have given me. I don't understand why You haven't healed me. My prayer journals are full of Your answered prayers. You have touched so many others I have prayed for, and You have answered prayers for my family and husband. I know I can't continue to live here alone. The only time my mind is clear is when I'm in here with You. My daughter is coming over this morning to take me to a home. I know You will go before me, and with me, but this is the hardest thing I have ever done. Will You meet me there in prayer just like here? That is all I ask.

Thank You. I will take You at Your word. It has always proved true.'"

"What was wrong with her.?"

"Jerry said she has Alzheimer's"

"What does he want us to do?"

"He wants us to go through a year's worth of prayer journals. See if we can find out what why someone would break in, and be willing to kill."

"He thinks the answer might be here in these Journals?" Charlie asked.

Pastor walked over to the closet and slid the door open. Inside were book shelves almost filled with note-books, each one with a beginning and ending date on it. "Jerry said they found almost thirty years worth in the basement. stacked neatly on shelves just like these."

"Wow! That's a lot of prayer."

"I called her pastor. He said he is really going to miss her. Said she was probably the most important person in his congregation. The best prayer warrior he has ever met. Said she hasn't been able to come to church in over a year. Ladies from the church were coming over every day and checking on her. Until it became too much, then they hired round-the-clock nursing care. Finally, they agreed with her daughter, it was time for her to go to a facility. That was two weeks ago."

"Aren't we breaking some rule? I mean these are private. It will be like reading her diary."

"I look at it more like it's God's diary, a record of what He has done through her. Her pastor has a signed letter giving him all the journals, and permission to use them as he sees fit. When I talked to him, he said he has been out of town at a conference for almost a week, and hasn't gotten around to pick them up yet. We have permission to use them. He will get them as soon as the police release them."

Pastor started with the one at the desk. Charlie took the next one in order and sat on the cushion. The handwriting was clear and very easy to read. She had written only on every other line, leaving room to come back later and make notations about results, which were all written in red and dated. The result was a history of her prayers and God's answers. Not everything was answered the way she expected and some were still waiting for answers. They both became engrossed in what they were reading. Finally, Charlie said, "It's time for lunch, and I've got to use the rest room." She got up and left. Pastor looked at his watch-twelve 0 five. He finished what he was reading then got up and stretched. Charlie called to him from the bathroom. He found her standing in the door way holding a painting. It was only about ten by fourteen inches and looked like an oil painting of an angel hovering over Christ's tomb.

AUGUST 8 WEDNESDAY
OAK RIVER CAFE

They say a man's car says a lot about him. If that is true, then Dr. Bullock's showroom quality, 1959 bright red Cadillac Eldorado screamed, 'Here I am!' He parked it in front of the Oak River Cafe, at a quarter to ten the next morning. Jacob had driven the whole way himself, with the top down, stopping only for gas. No one else was permitted to drive his car, ever.

He got out and stretched, walked up to the restaurant door, and held it open waiting for Glenda to fix her hair. She had spent most of the night sleeping in the back seat, switching to the front right after sunrise during a gas stop. When she finished, they went in. There were four others ahead of them, Glenda watched the hostess grab a handful of menus and lead them back to a large table. She was about her age she thought, thin with a quick easy smile. When she returned, she picked up two more menus and escorted them to a booth halfway back.

"You're not from here." she said, setting the menus down. "I think I know just about everyone in town. You must be visiting. Welcome to Oak River." Her voice was as genuine as her smile.

"You're right. Never been here before". Jacob lied.

"Seeing family? That's about the only reason people come to Oak River."

"Just passing through. Do you know if a Billy Boyd still lives here?"

"If you mean Pastor Boyd, he sure does. You can find him at Life Church. Do you know him?"

"We've met."

The bell on the door rang as more people came in. She left to take care of them.

"Who's Pastor Boyd? I thought we were here to see Les."

"Don't call him Les, it's Lester. He hates Les and he can be sensitive. We don't want to start out on his bad side."

"Ok, Lester. Who's Boyd?"

"He's my nephew. I haven't seen him since his father's funeral. Someone told me he was here in Oak River. I thought he might come in handy."

"For what, his take on creation vs evolution?"

"No, protection. He was a Navy SEAL before he got religion."

"Why would we need protection?"

"I received a phone call while we were stopped for gas early this morning. You were in the restroom and getting something to eat. I let it go to voice mail. Yours rang right after. When I finished filling the tank, I checked the messages. They were both the same, from the sheriff of Garfield county."

Jacob paused.

"Just say it. What was it about?"

"They're dead."

"Who's dead? she asked.

"Everyone who was in the Elks Rest Motel last night, including our students."

"That can't be!"

She knew from the look on his face that it was. She began frantically looking for her phone, tears filling her eyes, but she couldn't find it.

"Where's my phone? What have you done with it?"

"We can't call back right now."

"Why not? We need to call, and go back right away."

"They were murdered, and we are probably next on the list, if they can find us."

"That's crazy. It must have been an accident of some kind."

Just then the waitress came over.

"Hi. I'm June. Have you decided what you want to drink?"

Looking at the tears on Glenda's face, she started to say she would give them more time. But Jacob spoke first.

"We'll both have the special and coffee."

Feeling awkward, she left to get their order.

"I need to call right now." she said, standing up. "I want my phone. We must go back. Now!" She stood there looking at him.

"Why didn't you say something when you got the call?" she said accusingly. "We need to go back right away! How could you? Why would you keep this to yourself?"

122

The waitress brought their coffee and set it down, hurrying away.

"Sit down and drink your coffee. We can't go back unless you want to be murdered also."

"They weren't murdered! It was an accident. And why would anyone want them killed in the first place? Not over the fossils."

Her eyes started to fill with tears again. She sat down and took a sip of her coffee.

"How do you know it was murder?" she said, forcing calm into her voice. "Did you call someone?"

"No! But we have both stayed in that motel numerous times over the years. The only thing in those rooms that use propane is the furnace. It was 98 degrees the day we left. The owner has the propane shut off all summer. The only way there was a gas explosion is for someone to turn it back on, at the tank."

"We still need to go back. We are responsible for the students. We need to call their parents. The University needs to know where we are."

"Twenty-four more hours. Then we can go back. If we're still alive."

"No! Now! We need to go back. I'm going to call Bozeman."

Glenda reached for her purse to get her phone, forgetting it wasn't there.

That's when Jacob set a small electronic device down on the table. It, was smashed.

"What's that?" she asked.

"I'm not a professional, but I would say it was a GPS tracker."

"Where did you get it?"

"I found it under the rear bumper of the car."

"But how?"

"I was looking for it. That's when I put both of our cell phones on a semi, hauling lumber to Minneapolis."

"You what?"

"You heard me. Someone committed mass murder. The only possible motive I can think of, is our find, which is only 72 hours old. Someone had to tip them off. It wasn't me. That only leaves five other people."

"You wanted to see how I would react in public didn't you? That's why you sprung it on me here. Well, did I pass the test?"

"I had to be sure. Now the question is, which one of the students left the motel before it exploded? Or I suppose they might have killed the informant along with everyone else."

"I want my phone. You owe me $2,000. I want it now! Write a check. You can afford it."

"Your phone didn't cost that much."

"The rest is for anguish. After all these years working together, putting up with you. You didn't trust me. That's what hurts, Jacob. You didn't trust me. Now write the check."

He started to protest.

"I'm not kidding. Write the check Jacob."

He took out his checkbook, wrote out the check, signed it, and handing it to her, he said again in defense, "I had to be sure. I'm sorry."

The last two words were hard for him to say, and she knew it. They were worth more than the check, but she still took his money.

"So, what do we do now?"

"Eat. Then we go see Lester."

Just then the waitress showed up with their meals. Relieved to see the crying was over, she asked, "Can I get you anything else?"

"What is it?" Glenda asked.

"Clam chowder."

"Can I have a cheese burger and fries to go with it, please."

"Sure."

Glenda slid her bowl over to Jacob.

"You ordered it; you can eat it."

Having already started on his, Jacob said, I"t's really good, you should try it."

"I don't eat anything that makes its living eating off the sea floor."

"Suit yourself."

When they were almost finished, the waitress brought over the check.

"Would you like dessert? she asked.

"No thanks." Glenda responded. Then she stood up. "I'm going to the restroom to fix my makeup before we see

Lester. I don't want to upset his sensibilities. You can pay for the late breakfast."

To say Lester lived out of town didn't quite give you the whole picture. First Jacob headed north out of town about five miles, just past the county line he turned right on a gravel road, followed it for another four miles, then turned left on another gravel road that had a sign, 'dead end'. He followed it until it ran out, then turned down what was little more than a dirt path. It wound its way through corn and bean fields before entering a wooded area. Another quarter of a mile, sitting on the right side, was an old white farm house in severe need of painting. There was an old Ford truck sitting next to the house. A large black dog of mixed breed announced their arrival, who, to Glenda's delight, went around to Jacob's side and put his paws on top of the door and just stared, showing his teeth, with drool running down his jaw onto Jacob's seat.

A short time later a man in bib overalls and carrying a shotgun came out of the house. Seeing him, Glenda, trying to hold back her laughter, said,

"Somehow this is not what I imagined. A paleontologist of his renown looking like an angry Elmer Fudd."

Lester more than filled out his overalls on the sides. He was maybe five foot six, Glenda figured, bald, with a brown and gray beard that was long enough to hide his double chin. His grumpy, 'I would rather shoot you than talk to you' face, changed over to an, 'I can't believe it's you' smile.

"Is that you Jake? Well, I'll be. Get down Red. You remember Jake. It's been what? All of ten years. Always did drive a fancy rig. Get down Red." he repeated, this time grabbing him by the collar and dragging him back. "Come on, you can get out now. Red won't bite you. Who's the pretty lady? You get married?"

"My name is Glenda. No, he hasn't proposed yet. But maybe tonight."

she said, getting out of the car.

"I'd like to drive around to the barn," Jacob said, "I've something to show you."

"It must be very unusual, to bring it here. Sure, go right ahead. You know the way. Your little lady and I will just follow along behind."

Jake drove off around back of the house, disappearing from view, while Lester and Glenda followed on foot. Not surprising, Lester was not a fast walker. Red, for his part, had taken off, keeping pace with Jacob.

"What do you have in your trunk? Lester asked. "Must be real important, for Jake to bring it here."

"I think you will find it interesting. How do you know Dr. Bullock?"

"He didn't tell you about me, did he? I'm not surprised. We've always had, how should I put it, a shadowy relationship. I met Jake on a dig in Wyoming. He was seventeen I was twelve. He was with a High School science teacher and about five other boys hunting for fossils. We had a high old time, we did. You should ask him about it sometime."

127

Rounding the house, Glenda saw a barn. There were hints of red paint, but only hints. The roof had holes in it, and part of it was gone completely. There was a large sliding door, but it was off its track, hanging by one roller, waiting for the next gust of wind to knock it off.

"That's your barn?" Glenda asked, not believing she had ridden over 900 miles for this.

Lester didn't answer. He just kept walking, past an old tractor with weeds growing up through it, and several other pieces of farm machinery. The only thing they had in common was, they all looked like they had sat there for longer than she had been alive. When the thinly graveled drive faded out, they followed the path made by Jacobs car through the grass, then through a stand of pine trees, which blocked her view. Walking around the last one she stopped and just stared. The building she was looking at was not new. The paint had faded, and she could see dents and rust on the overhead door. But it was massive. She would learn later it was 60x180 feet with 20-foot-high side walls.

"What is that?" Glenda asked, almost too stunned to speak.

"That's the barn."

"What's in it?" she asked, hurrying to catch up.

"You'll see."

They found Jacob standing behind his car with the trunk open, and Red beside him.

Lester looked in the trunk at the plaster casts.

"Let's get those inside." he said. The door had an electronic lock, and needed Lester's handprint to open. After unlocking the large sliding door, he slid it silently aside with a gentle push. Then Lester disappeared inside.

They each took an end of the long cast containing the rib and were carrying it in when a spotlight suddenly went on. Glenda almost dropped her end. She found herself looking in the wide-open mouth of a Tyrannosaurus Rex only a couple of feet above her head.

"Over here."

She looked in the direction of Lester's voice, and saw him standing beside another door. This one, she discovered, led into a well-equipped lab.

"You can set it down on that table over there." he said.

Lester followed them out to retrieve the other fossils, then shut the trunk of the car, closed and locked the sliding door again, then joined them in the lab.

"What do you think? Not bad for a fat old farmer in bibs is it?"

Glenda was torn as to what to look at first. The lab was well lit and spotless, containing every piece of equipment she could think of. But she turned and went back out and looked up at the T- Rex, standing there like the star of the show, which he was.

Lester began turning on more lights until the whole warehouse was bright as day.

The T-Rex was not alone. There were others, many others, including a Triceratops, two Velociraptors and a Troodon, all complete. It looked like a museum. There

129

were also displays of partially complete skeletons, and lots of tables containing only a few bones or maybe a partial skull.

"Where did you get all..." Glenda spread her arms out and turned around... "this?"

She had been excitedly walking around. Lester and Jacob caught up to her.

"Here and there." Lester said.

"The better question is how much do they cost, and were they stolen?"

"I have never stolen anything!" Lester said empathically.

"Maybe not personally, but most of the specimens come from suspicious origin."

"Jake here is just still miffed because I have the T-Rex, and he doesn't. You must need my help or you wouldn't be here. So, what's important enough for you to bring me some of your fossils? Why aren't they sitting in Chicago or Bozeman? You didn't acquire them on the black market, did you?" Lester said as he headed back to the lab.

Glenda held Jacob's arm, stopping him until Lester was far enough away not to hear. Then she looked him in the face questioningly. "I'll explain later." Glenda cocked her head and gave him a look. "He buys and sells fossils. I've known him since we were kids. He knows paleontology. He has an instinct. He has the equipment we need and, he will keep his mouth shut."

Lester had stopped by the lab door.

"Come on you two. We have work to do. I'm dying to see what you brought me."

They carefully removed the casts from the fossils. After carefully examining them, Lester asked, "Where did you find these? In Montana where you've been working? They were together?"

"Yes, and yes." Glenda said.

"How many of your students know about them?"

"Maybe one." Jacob answered.

"How many others?" Lester asked, looking up from studying them. "I assume you have done basic tests. Where are the pictures? You did take pictures."

Ignoring the jab, Jacob opened his laptop and opened the file. After looking at them closely, and carefully examining the fossils again, Lester said.

"Tell me the whole story. Where are all the students?"

"Presumed dead." Jacob said.

There was a pause.

"And?"

"I believe they were killed when the Elks Rest Motel blew-up."

"On purpose. They were murdered?" Lester asked.

"I believe so, yes."

Just then several red lights started to flash on and off in the lab.

"What's that.?" Glenda asked.

"Security. We have visitors."

AUGUST 8 WEDNESDAY,
CRIME SCENE 106 SPRINGDALE

"Do you know what this is?" Charlie asked, holding up the painting, and grinning ear to ear.

"A nice print of an angel."

"No. It's an original oil painting by Isaac Carl."

Pastor stood there with a blank look on his face.

"He's a famous Caribbean artist."

Still nothing.

"He's dead. His paintings go for over $100,000 each. If you can find one for sale. He was a Christian artist, painted religious scenes like this."

"Oh, that Isaac Carl." Pastor said. "How do you know how much it's worth?"

"Antiques Road Show." Charlie answered, with a big grin returning to her face. "They had one of his paintings on a show I watched. It's been about a year ago. Grams likes to watch the program. Grams says she must be worth a fortune, because everything she has is old. Anyway, his paintings stand out. They are different from what you're used to seeing. You can see his name on the front. On the back, he signed, dated, and named it. See." She turned the painting around and showed him. "Also, there's the tag from the art dealer where it was sold."

Charlie was quite pleased with herself.

"What do you think? We need to look around. Maybe there are more. You know, on the show, some people buy paintings at a garage sale for only a few bucks, that turn out to be worth thousands. Sometimes they're even found in the trash."

She had forgotten about lunch, and was now on the hunt.

"Are you sure this painting is the real deal?"

"I'm not an art dealer, right, but I'm sure enough that we need to check the rest of the house, and have this secured. It might be what the murderer was looking for."

"Let's go tell our friends in blue." Pastor said.

They found the officers in the kitchen eating their sack lunch.

"We, Charlie that is, may have found something worth killing for."

He showed them the painting.

"What's that?" Jim said, taking another bite of his Sub-Sandwich.

"We think it is an original Isaac Carl painting, worth at least $100,000."

"Oh!" said Toby, who was just about ready to take a big bite of his sandwich. "In that case, we need to call the Chief. He said to call him right away if you two found anything." Then he took the bite that was waiting right in front of his mouth. "You call." He said with his mouth full.

Pastor called Jerry and filled him in on what they'd found. He said he would be right over.

"Bring an extra-large pizza and two cokes when you come. We're both hungry. Yes, everything on it."

Charlie gave him a fist bump.

While they were waiting for Jerry, and their lunch, the two of them took a tour of the house, coming up with two more paintings, both from her bedroom. Charlie googled the artists name. If authentic, the total value for all three was between two and three hundred thousand dollars.

"That looks like a motive for murder to me." the Chief said, looking at the paintings, while helping himself to another slice of pizza. "When we finish eating, I want to go over the whole house and garage again and make sure you haven't missed anything. I wonder how they could afford that kind of art."

"The ones we found in the bedroom have been there a long time. The paint around the pictures is all faded. You can easily see where they were hanging." Charlie said.

"Have you found anything in the diaries yet?"

"Yes," Pastor said. "A look into Oak River I never saw before, an understanding of the power of prayer I didn't have before and didn't fully realize was possible."

"But nothing to show any insight into our murder?"

"No. But we've only started. It will take several days to go through a year's worth of her prayer journals."

"You can stop looking at them. I think we found what we're after." They finished lunch, and then the three of them went through each room, then down to the base-ment where Jerry opened an old trunk. It was filled with pictures, old cards, a few stuffed toys, and other memorabilia.

"Charlie, come over here," Jerry said. "Check this out. See if there is anything in here worth killing over. Well that about does it, Pastor. Let's go upstairs and I'll call Clara's daughter. Let her know what we found, and ask her to have them appraised, to verify what they're worth. Now that we know why, we just have to find the who."

Charlie heard them go upstairs. She wanted to continue reading the prayer Journals, but did what she was told. She soon figured out the newer things were on top and the deeper she went the farther back into their lives it went. Charlie emptied out the whole trunk and organized it. Then she began going through everything in order and putting it back in the trunk when she finished looking at it. Starting with the oldest things first, she had just started when she found an old birthday card. It was from Clara's husband. When she opened it a receipt fell out. She was about to just put it back in when she read what her husband had written in the card. "I bought these paintings from a guy I met, when I was in Florida at the convention. I have never seen anything like them. I just saw Gods hand in each one. I know it's a lot of money, but I know you will love them too. Happy Birthday to the love of my life." The receipt was for three oil paintings–$100 dollars each. Charlie grabbed the envelope and took it all up stairs.

"I found it!" she exclaimed as she ran up the stairs. They were all in the kitchen.

"Found what?" Pastor asked.

"Everything! Who bought the paintings, when, why, for whom, and how much they cost. Here."

She held it all out. Pastor took it, looked at it, then passed it on to Jerry who, when he finished, set it on the table, Toby and Jim quickly picked it up and read it.

"That ties up all the loose ends." Jerry said. "You two can go on home." he said to Toby and Jim. "And you two," looking at Charlie and Pastor, "are finished too. I'll take the paintings and the card back to the office." He put the card and receipt back in the envelope, told Jim and Toby to lock up and left, taking the pictures and card with him.

Jim and Toby had picked up their mess from lunch, and were waiting for Pastor and Charlie to leave so they could go home.

"I left a mess in the basement." Charlie said. "We can lock up when we go."

"Be sure you do." Jim said. And the two officers left, closing the door behind them.

"What else do you have in mind?" Pastor asked. "Besides cleaning up your mess in the basement?"

AUGUST 8 WEDNESDAY
LESTER'S BARN

Seeing a short, old, fat man, run the forty feet to the other end of the lab was quite a sight.

"Follow me." he yelled as he ran toward a room at the end of the lab. Once all of them were inside, Lester closed and locked the heavy steel door.

"Unless they brought a lot of explosives, we're safe in here." Lester quickly sat down at a table. There were twelve video screens, each with a different view of the outside. He quickly scanned them, changing cameras on some until he found what he was looking for.

"There they are." he said, pointing to a screen. There was a black SUV parked by the house. Red was up on his hind legs barking, and growling. Lester turned on a mic in front of him. chose a switch labeled HF and spoke. "Red sit." They saw Red back up a step and sit, but not taking his eyes off the driver's door.

"Who are you and what do you want?" Lester said, in his 'I would rather shoot you than talk to you'. voice.

The driver's window came down and a man stuck his head out, keeping an eye on Red. We are looking for Drs. Bullock and Pearce. Have you seen them?"

"Who are you? You're not from around here."

"My name's Tom."

"Tom who?"

"Tom Smith. Have you seen the professors?" he asked again.

"I sure have. Haven't seen Jake in twenty odd years. Then he shows up out of the blue earlier today, said he needed my car. Drives around back, empties out his trunk and puts some plaster covered things in my car, says 'thanks Lester', and leaves as fast as he came." What am I going to do with his big old boat? Thank God I still have my truck, drive it most of the time anyway."

The man stuck his head out a little farther, which was greeted by a deep-throated growl from Red. He pulled it back where it was.

"What kind of car did they take?"

"I have a white Ford. You're asking a lot of questions. I live back here so I won't be bothered. Now you guys get, before I turn Red loose and come out there with my shotgun."

He tried to ask if he knew where they were going. But before he got it all out. Lester shouted out one word.

"Red!"

He needed no more prompting. Red jumped at the window. Tom saw him coming and got his head back just in time. Red nearly jumped in the car window. There was a cry of pain then the car pulled backwards, throwing Red to the ground. The window went up as the car spun around with Red back at it, jumping on the driver's door, barking louder than ever.

Lester called Red off, and they watched the car spew gravel down the drive.

"Who did you tell you were coming here?" Lester asked, visibly upset.

"No one! That's one reason I'm here, so no one would find us." Jacob replied. "I don't know how they knew we were here. I removed the GPS they stuck under my bumper."

"Well, there must be another one somewhere."

Lester switched one of the screens and they could watch the car continue to drive away.

"How many cameras do you have out there?" Glenda asked.

"Enough to make sure they go all the way back to the blacktop."

There were some blind spots but finally they saw the car turn on to the highway and head back toward Oak River.

When they were on the highway, Lester went to a cabinet and took out an electronic device.

"We're going to check out your car, and remove anything else they may have added." Lester went over it very carefully, removing two more GPS trackers, one under the hood in a hard-to-see-area and another one under the carpet. He also found and removed a microphone from under the dash.

"Not only could they follow you, but they could hear everything you said. These devices are not what you buy at Walmart. This is professional stuff. These guys will be back tonight Jake. I want you to take your car and move it to the back of the house and put the top up. When they come back tonight, they'll find your car just as I told them. Make sure it's unlocked. If they find it locked, they'll just break in. Glenda, here are the keys to my car. I want you to drive back the way you came in and turn left at the first gravel road, it's one mile. In two more miles you will come to a blacktop road. Turn left. Pull in at the first farmhouse you come to. It will have the name 'Miller' on the mail box. There will be someone there to meet you and show you where to park the car. Then they'll drive you through the farm and show you a path to take through the woods. You will come out right outside the lab."

139

"I got it." Glenda said. "Back down the road take the first left. Go to the blacktop. Turn left. Pull into Miller's drive, and they'll take it from there."

"Right."

While Jacob and Glenda were dealing with the cars, Lester went back toward the house. There was an open shed with a tractor, with a wagon hooked on the back. He unhooked the wagon and drove the tractor down to the barn and back covering up Jacob's car tracks. Returning, he hooked the wagon back on and parked it in the way leading to the barn.

Jacob was waiting when he returned to the barn. He let them both in, then went straight to the security room. On one of the security screens, he saw Glenda approaching the lab. He opened the door and let her in. He sat back down in front of the security system, making some adjustments. When he was satisfied, he led them back to the lab. There was a table and six chairs, Lester sat at one end and motioned for them to take a seat.

Lester opened his laptop. There was a message waiting for him.

"The car was rented in Bozeman, Montana, three days ago, to a Tom Jenkins I guess he forgot his last name when I asked. You two are in a lot of trouble. If they'll blow up an entire motel, I don't think they will stop at anything. How do you two want to handle it?"

"Handle it! I want the police to handle it, I'm a paleontologist, not one of Charlie's angels. We need to call the police, or sheriff, or whoever it is you call out here in the middle of a corn field. The FBI, that's it. They crossed the state line that makes it a federal offence, right?" Glenda said. "Then we need to go public. Take what we have to Bozeman or Chicago and call in the press. Once it's out, there'll be no reason to kill us anymore." Glenda said.

Jacob sat there thinking, while Glenda was growing impatient, waiting for him to say something.

"There are two ways to look at it." Jacob said. "We've been assuming they don't want the find to be made public. But maybe that's not the case. They might be trying to take over the discovery for themselves. Either way, we need to do two things right away. We need to decide if it's genuine or not, and are we willing to stake our careers on it,,, or not. We also need to secure the site in Montana before someone destroys it, or removes it. If it's not too late already."

"I just might be able to help you with both of those things." Lester said. "For a price. How much is it worth to you, a million?"

Glenda gasped. "We don't have that kind of money."

"He doesn't want money." Jacob answered. He has all the money he needs. What he wants is his name on the discovery."

"Is that true Lester?" Glenda asked.

"Yes, equal credit with the two of you. You can have the full use of my lab and I can have four men on the site in less than two hours, all armed. Just give me the GPS coordinates."

Jacob didn't speak.

"Well, Jacob. What do you want to do?"

"What are we going to do when they come back here tonight? They will come back. Right Lester?" Glenda asked.

"I would, maybe even before dark. If you killed everyone in a motel, an old man with a dog way back in the boonies, is not going to stand in your way. But to answer your question, we can call the sheriff and see if he will send out some men to shoot them. Or we can wait for them. And when they break into the house, we can shoot them ourselves."

"Is there something we can do that doesn't involve shooting them?" Glenda asked.

"Yes." Lester responded, "We can let them shoot us."

"We can all leave, then no one will get shot." Glenda said.

"In that scenario they will, in all likely hood, prowl around, find the barn, see the security lock, find a way to break in, and who knows what they will do out of their frustration at not finding us or the fossils. Probably steal and destroy, and then hunt us down and shoot us."

In the end they agreed to give Lester equal recognition for the find. He called the team he already had in Montana and gave them the coordinates.

"Well what do you want for lunch? Lester asked.

"What are the options?" Glenda asked.

"Let's go upstairs and see."

After a lunch of leftover roast beef sandwiches, which Glanda made some chips and coffee, they returned to the lab and began working on the fossils.

AUGUST 8 WEDNESDAY
PARSONAGE

Wednesday for Jack, as you recall, started about 2:30 am. Part two began at 1:28 in the afternoon. He woke with a splitting headache and a desperate need to use the bathroom. He reached over and hit his call button. Nate tapped on the bedroom door and went in.

"I have to go to the bathroom now!" Jack said as he heard the door open.

Nate grabbed Jack's wheelchair and brought it over to the bed.

"My name is Nate."

Jack didn't care who it was at the moment. He just needed to go, now! Before he knew it, he was in the wheelchair and heading to the bathroom. When he was all set Nate left the room leaving the door ajar.

"Just yell when you're finished." he said.

Yell, that's exactly what he wanted to do, but his head hurt too much.

Jack sat there and stewed. Who was this guy? Where was Pastor? It was bad enough letting him help, I was used to him Jack thought.

Now there was some stranger here. He needed drugs, and a shower, and clean clothes and food. He just realized how hungry he was, and he wanted Pastor, not some stranger to get it all for him.

Nate went to the kitchen and waited. He was just getting ready to make some lunch, when he heard Jack call. Going to the bathroom he opened the door.

Jack looked at him for a minute hesitating, before he spoke.

"Could you get me four Ibuprofen? I was in a bad way in there. Who are you again?"

This time Nate stuck out his hand.

"Nate Strong, I'm a retired Physical Therapist."

Jack shook his hand the best he could with the brace on his wrist.

"I attend Pastor Boyd's church. He called me early this morning and asked if I could come over and take care of you until he gets back."

"When do you think that will be?"

"I don't know for sure. He didn't say. It looks like you had a rough night. If you like, I can help you with a shower and then fix you something to eat."

"What time is it.?" Jack asked while trying to decide what to do."

Nate looked at his watch.

"It's almost two."

Jack decided he was too miserable to be picky.

"I do stink. It was a rough night and I,m really hungry."

Nate smiled.

When Jack was ready for his day they went out to the kitchen.

"Interested in some coffee?" Nate asked, as he pushed Jack up to the table.

144

"You read my mind."

"What would you like to eat?"

"Breakfast would be good. Eggs and bacon or whatever's in there."

Nate turned on the coffee maker he had set up earlier, went to the refrigerator and got out what he needed. Then he turned the stove on and put the bacon on to cook.

When it was on the table, he got himself a cup of coffee and sat down across from Jack.

Jack bowed his head for a minute and then started to eat.

"What do you do now that you are retired?" Jack asked, between bites.

"My wife and I have always been active. We bike a lot. Did RAGBRAI once. We used to camp out in tents with our kids and kayaked. The kids are all grown and gone. We just bought a travel trailer, and are planning on using it this fall and winter. We haven't really traveled much out of state. We would like to check out some of this country we live in."

It didn't take Jack long to finish his breakfast. He was getting much better at eating with his wrist brace on.

"Would you like another cup of coffee?"

"Thanks. That would be great."

"I am sorry about the loss of your father. We were out of town and didn't hear about it until we came back."

"Thanks. Last night was the first time it really hit me that my father was not coming back. That I would never see him again. I guess I didn't handle it so well."

"Your father was saved. His body died, but not his spirit. He is still very much alive, with Christ in Heaven."

"That's what I've been told. If it's true, I won't see him. I'm not a believer. There are too many things in the Bible that science has proven to be untrue. I guess the way I see it, it's all true or none of it is true."

AUGUST 8 WEDNESDAY
106 SPRINGDALE

Charlie was quiet for a moment then said, "It just doesn't fit. No one knew those paintings were worth any money. They've hung there literally for decades. Julie was hit from behind, in a large open space. I don't think those two goths snuck up behind her and hit her in the back of the head and killed her. And if they had seen or heard anyone they would've just left, and come back later. I think someone else was here. Also, I don't think she just happened to be here at the wrong time. I think she was the intended victim."

"That's not how the police see it. What evidence is there? Not to mention, how were they able to slip in and out without anyone seeing them? If the pictures are not the motive, what do you think it is?"

"I don't know yet. But those two girls might have seen the whole thing. We need to find them before the real killer does. I'll bet they can tell us a whole lot."

"How do you propose we do that?"

"We need to get some High School yearbooks for the last two or three years, and take them over and see if Willie can pick her out. I also have a picture on my cell phone, someone we saw come in while I was having lunch with Jen and Chris.

"Also, it would be a good idea to track down the source of the rumor that there was a treasure here. See if they were talking about the 'Treasure Room' or some monetarily valuable treasure, like the paintings."

Their first stop was at one of Charlie's friends. She went in and, after a brief time, came out with the last three year books. Then they headed over to John's home. Mrs. Windsor answered the door.

"I'm glad you have come over Pastor, I was going to call you. Yesterday was quite a shock to John and I. Not every day the police call and ask if you can pick up your son, and tell you he's involved in a murder. I understand you were there."

"Yes. I arrived right after the police. Do you know Charlie?"

"Certainly. Everyone knows Charlie. I understand you were there also. The police told me you were the one who discovered the body. That must have been terrible.

"My husband and I are concerned that the girls who did this may try to harm John and Willie. What do you think we should do? My husband thinks we should take our vacation early. We've been planning to go see my sister. She and her husband live on a ranch in South Dakota. We were planning to go next month after John Jr. gets back from Church camp. Do you think we should leave right away? My husband only has two weeks. If we use it up and they haven't caught them, what would we do?"

Marla was beside herself and was holding back tears as she finished.

"You and your husband need to decide what's best for your family. Church camp starts Monday for John's age group. You might consider going up early. I know the director, and he can always use some help. You might talk to Willie's mom and the four of you go up early. You would be out of town and surrounded by people. That way you can keep your original vacation time."

"That might be a good idea. I'll talk to John when he gets home. He will probably have more questions. Is it all right if he gives you a call?"

"Sure. I'll give you my card. It has my cell number on it." As he got his card out, he continued, "John said he overheard you talking about there being a treasure over at that house."

"Yes. That's how this terrible thing got started… John listening in on our conversation, and then going off with Willie to dig up buried treasure. I swear those two have enough imagination to fill a book. Don't think he didn't have a talking to last night. We were so thankful they weren't hurt, but also furious for lying about where they were. John sent him to his room until we can figure out what else to do about it."

"If you want, I can have the camp director put Willie and John on kitchen duty. Cleaning up after 200 campers plus staff, might give them time to think about what they've done. They generate a lot of dirty dishes."

The thought of that brought a smile to her face.

"He hates doing dishes. That would be worse than being grounded. I'll be sure to tell John about that."

"So, if it wasn't buried treasure you were talking about, what was it?"

"You've been there. You must have seen her Treasure Room. It's printed in gold letters on the door. Edith, she's a friend I see at the beauty shop. We have our hair done the same time every month. She is also a friend of the Kingsley family and has been over there and seen it. We were talking about her prayer closet. It's just like in the movie."

"Thank you very much." Pastor said. "Can we pray for you and John?"

"Yes, we could sure use your prayer. This has been very stressful."

The three of them held hands and Pastor and Charlie both prayed for all of them.

Back out in the car he called Willie's house and asked if they could stop over. Mrs. Tomsky was excited to hear from him and thanked him for calling.

"That was sure easy." Pastor said. "I think both of Willie's parents are home."

Before starting the car, he asked Charlie to pray for their meeting.

The atmosphere at Willie's house was in panic mode. They could hear them arguing before they got out of the

THE PAST COMES ALIVE

car. Charlie's look was flight-not-fight as they opened the car doors.

"Don't worry. You prayed, right?"

"Paul prayed a lot and he was beaten everywhere he went."

"It's a good thing he prayed then, isn't it. Might have been worse."

"Like when they stoned him and left him for dead."

"He got back up and went right back into the city."

They were both laughing as Pastor rang the doorbell.

Willard Tomsky wasn't laughing when he opened the door. His face was turned, and he was yelling at his wife. "We are not leaving and going to your mothers!" He turned to face Pastor. "Who are you?"

"Hi. I'm Pastor Boyd and this is Charlie. Your son comes to our youth group."

Willard's face changed completely, and his volume lowered by half. Stammering he said,

"Uh,...A this is a bad time... Uh, Charlie, are you the one who found the body yesterday?"

"She is." Pastor Boyd answered. "I know you have a lot to decide. If we could come in, perhaps we can be of some help."

His wife pulled the door open all the way.

"Pastor Boyd. This is my husband, Willard. I don't believe you two have met. Please come in. We're both very disturbed by what happened yesterday. The police were over, even Chief Watson was here. Things like this don't happen in real life. Frankly, we're scared. I didn't sleep a wink last night. And now what are we going to do? Marla said they are going to take their vacation. We just can't afford a vacation right now. Willard says nothing is going to happen. The police will take care of it. On top of all that, we don't know what to do about Willie's behavior."

"It's not just bad behavior." Willard said. "He lied! You know how I hate lying. And they took that metal detector without permission. That's stealing!"

"I know how upsetting all this must be." Pastor said. "We just came from seeing Mrs. Windsor. She has the same concerns you two have. The church camp is hosting the younger kids right now and they can always use some help in the kitchen. It would be a way of getting Willie away for a while. And cleaning up dishes for over 200 people will give him time to think about his actions."

"We can't afford to send him to extra camp. It was all we could do to pay for next week." Willard said.

"Under the circumstances," Pastor said. "he will be working and it won't cost anything. In fact, he can work next week as well, and we could return the fee. There is also a senior camp following. If necessary, we would love to have him stay for that, at no charge, of course."

It was obvious getting his money back was a big incentive for Willard.

"Work is just the thing." Willard said. "They will make him work, right? Not just goof off."

"I'll give them instructions myself if you like." Pastor said.

"I think that is a good solution. It will help give Willie a good work ethic. And," looking over at his wife, "keep him safe at the same time."

"Is that what Marla is going to do with John?" Katie asked.

"They haven't decided yet, but there is more than enough work to keep them both busy. Karen is in charge of the kitchen. I wouldn't say she's a slave driver, but she is a real stickler. There's no goofing off on her watch. She makes sure everything is done just right, for health reasons."

"I don't know how well Willie would do, being away from home for so long." Katie said.

"It would be fine if one or both of you wanted to go along to make sure he's ok. You wouldn't have to work. The camp has guest cabins you could stay in." Pastor said.

"Well Willard, it does seem to solve all our problems. I could go along with him. That is if you don't mind. You would have to take care of yourself for a couple of weeks."

Willard was thinking of the two weeks he would be able to do anything he liked. He could have the guys over to his house for a change, to watch the game, and maybe even play cards.

"That is the least I can do for our son's safety. It's settled then. I think it would be best if he could go today. For safety's sake. What do you think Pastor aaa?"

"Boyd. Yes that can be arranged. Camp is not too far. They could be there in time for supper. Is it ok if Charlie and I talk to him before you go?"

"Yes. He's in his room, upstairs and to the right." Willard said, trying to hide his obvious delight at being home alone.

As they ascended the stairs, Charlie and Pastor could hear Willard.

"You go and pack what you need and when they come down, I'll help Willie get his things ready."

Pastor knocked and he and Charlie went in. Willie was sitting at his small desk in the corner, thumbing through a fishing magazine.

"Wow! It is great to see you two! Dad said I couldn't have any company until I was 18, or something like that."

"You will be going to camp as soon as we leave." Pastor said.

Willie interrupted. "Camp? I get to go to camp? Wow! I was just praying about that and telling God how bad I wanted to go. And if He would let me go, I would never lie or steal ever again. What about John? Is he going to go too?"

"His mom and dad are thinking about it. There's a good chance he will be able to go also."

"But camp doesn't start till next week. How can we go today?"

"Your mom will explain that. Could you look through these pictures and see if you can recognize the girl you saw yesterday?" Charlie asked.

"Sure. But she had sunglasses on so I don't know if I can. But I will try really hard."

He looked at all the pictures and twice he stopped, pointing at one, but in the end he said he didn't recognize anyone. Charlie took the books back and handed them to Pastor.

Remembering the one she had in her phone, Charlie pulled it out. "Here. Check this picture out." she said, handing the phone to Willie.

He looked at it really close, then a big smile lit up his face. "That's her! That's her!" he said excitedly.

"Are you sure?" Pastor said. "We need you to be positive."

"I'm positive those are the earrings she was wearing. Fish. See the earrings. They're all black. But that fish is a rainbow trout. It's the wrong color. It should be pretty with rainbow stripes on the sides."

"You're sure?" Charlie asked.

"I know fish. That is what she was wearing."

"Thank you very much, Willie. Enjoy camp."

His dad must have been waiting outside the door because he burst in as soon as they were finished.

"Very good son." Willard said. "We need to pack now so you can be off to camp. You don't want to miss supper."

Pastor and Charlie showed themselves out. As soon as the front door closed, Charlie asked, "Is Karen really a slave driver?"

"I didn't say she was a slave driver, just that she wants everything done right. I do know however, that all the kids who work in the kitchen ask if they can do it again the next year."

154

"He's going to have a good time then, isn't he?"

"As you might say, he will have a blast."

When they were in the car Charlie asked. "Where to now Boss?"

AUGUST 8 WEDNESDAY PM
FORD DEALERSHIP OAK RIVER

At 3:25 pm Chris gave Jen a call.

"Good afternoon Dr. Springer's office. What can I do for you?"

"This is Chris. Is Jen available?"

"Let me check. I think she's just finishing up her last cleaning."

She pushed a button on the phone. "Jen, you have a phone call, line one. Being in that same house with poor Julie, just lying there murdered. That must have been awful." the secretary said. "Here's Jen."

"Can we meet somewhere. I found some more information." Chris said

"I can meet you in about fifteen minutes. Where do you want to go?"

"Mickey D's. It's easy and I could use a cup of coffee."

"Mickey D's it is."

When Jen arrived, Chris was already in line waiting for her order.

"I got us both large coffees. I also ordered a chicken sandwich and fries. We were so busy most of the day I didn't have time for lunch. Do you want anything?"

"No, I'm good. What did you find out?"

Chris's order came up they took it to the corner booth.

"I have all the family background. But, I don't think it's going to do us much good."

She handed Jen the sheet she had compiled that morning and waited for her to look it over.

"See. They're all upstanding citizens. I can't find a motive anywhere."

She handed her another sheet. "Remember when Charlie took that picture of the Goth girl? I remembered they bought a car about three months ago. Well, his name is Dr. Jonas Sault. He lives in Iowa City and has a very good credit report. He paid ten thousand dollars down, no trade in for his car. It was on a Saturday. I talked to the salesman who sold it. He said Jonas was in the Saturday before, test-drove three different cars, and said he would be back the next week to decide which one he wanted. Even made an appointment for 10:00 am. He showed up a few minutes early. This time the girl was with him. He thinks he introduced her as his daughter. He doesn't remember her name. But said she was very nice and respectful, and actually asked a few good questions about the car."

"So, she lives in Iowa city." Jen said.

"Unless he's divorced and he gets her every other weekend."

"Why would you buy a car here if you live in Iowa City? Plus, the murder was on Tuesday. What were they doing here together in the middle of the week?" Jen asked.

"We have lots of buyers from out of town. Most of the time our price is lower and our service is always better. Let's call Charlie and see if she's found out anything." Chris said.

"Good idea."

Just then Chris's phone rang. She looked at it. "It's Charlie."

"I was going to call you." she said. "Jen and I are at McDonald's. What are you doing?"

"I'm with Pastor. We know who Willie saw. It's the girl we saw at McDonalds. We decided to go down to the police station and let Jerry know."

"Jen and I will come down also. I have some information on the man who was with her."

Fifteen minutes later, all four of them entered a conference room with Chief Watson. All the women began talking at once. He put up his hand.

"Pastor. You go first. What information have you got?"

"Charlie is the one who found it out. I think she should go first."

"So, you think you know who our killer is?" he said, looking at Charlie.

"I'm sure I have a picture of the girl Willie saw at the house, but I don't think either one of the girls is guilty of murder."

Jerry held out his hand. Charlie took out her phone, found the pictures and handed it to him. He looked it over.

"Scroll on down. That's the car they were driving. The last picture shows the license plate."

"First, how do you know that's the girl Willie saw? Second, where and when did you take the pictures? And third, what's her name?"

"Willie was able to identify her because of the earrings she's wearing. The fish are black. That's the wrong color. Those are rainbow trout. Willie knows fish. I took the pictures here in town in the McDonald's restaurant, the day of the murder. Chris, Jen, and I saw them come in. She looked like she could be one of the girls so I took the pictures."

"If it's ok to talk now," Jen said, "I know who bought the car."

"Just a minute. Take your phone down to my secretary and tell her to print off the pictures. Two copies. Ok, what do you have?"

Jen handed him the paper and he read it over.

"Why don't I just fire my detective and hire you four? Is this address still good?" he asked. "Never mind, we'll check it out. Do you have anything else?"

Charlie came back in.

"Your secretary said she would have the pictures right away."

"What about you Sherlock, have anything else?"

"Yes. I don't think Julie just walked in on something, I think she was the intended victim. The girls might have seen something but neither one of them killed her."

"Why don't you tell me who it is, and save all of us the trouble of figuring it out."

"I don't know. Yet."

158

"You four get out. I've got work to do."

As the four of them left they could hear Chief Watson yelling for Leon, his detective.

Leon held the door open for Jerry's secretary and then followed her in. She handed Jerry the photos she'd printed.

"Thank you, Debby."

As she left, she wagged her finger at Leon and gave him a big smile.

"What was that all about?" he asked.

"Never mind her. How are you coming on the case? Have you found out the identity of either of the girls yet?"

"Not yet. But I've been to the High School and talked to the principal. He said he would put together a list of girls who dress like that and would have it for me tomorrow."

"How about the fingerprints from the garage? Any luck matching them?

"No. I've run them through all the data bases, no hits."

"Do you have any new leads at all?"

"Ah.., no, not really."

Jerry handed him the photos and the paper he got from Chris.

"That is probably one of the girls. The man could be her father or other family member. Speak nice to him, he's a doctor. See if you can bring them in for questioning."

"Where did you get this information?" Leon asked.

"From the ladies who are going to take your place. Let me know when you're on your way back with our suspects. You will have them today."

Leon wondered why he'd ever become a detective. It was a lot easier writing tickets for speeding, or patrolling neighborhoods where little Johnny riding his bike through the neighbor's flower bed was the most serious offence, or arresting the town drunk for crashing his car into an oak tree. Murder never happened in Oak River. Now this was the second one this summer. "Oh, yah," he remembered, "more money. That's why I took the promotion." He went to his office and called Dr. Sault.

"Hello."

"Dr. Sault, this is Detective Summer, Oak River Police Department. Could I have a few minutes of your time?"

"I'm about to leave the office. What can I do for you, Detective?"

"You were seen in McDonald's yesterday afternoon. Was the young lady with you your daughter?"

"She's my niece. Why?"

"I would like to talk to her about something she may have seen. Could you tell me her name and where she lives?

"Her name is Kelly Sault. She lives at 802 10th. Avenue there in Oak River. Is she in trouble? She's had a tough time of it lately. Our whole family has. Her father, my brother, died of cancer a few months ago. What's this all about? You're being very vague Detective."

"A woman was murdered at 106 Springdale yesterday. I have reason to believe she was at the scene and may have seen something."

"That's ridiculous. She would have told me. Do we need to get a lawyer?"

"She is entitled to a lawyer, Dr. Sault, but we only want to ask her a few questions, find out what she saw, if anything. Her mother and you are both welcome to come down. In fact, it would be easier on her if all of you came down together."

"When would you like us to come?"

"As soon as possible. You're in Iowa City. Why don't you pick her and her mother up and be here... say, in an hour?"

"And if we don't come?"

"Don't make this harder than it needs to be Dr. Sault. I will look for you," Leon checked his watch, "at say six?"

"I think we can make it."

"Thank you, Dr. Sault. See you at six."

Leon went back and told the Chief. He was not overly happy.

"You should've gone over and just picked her up. What if they run, or concoct some story. And she will probably alert her friend."

"If she runs, we'll catch her. If she lies, you will know. I just wanted to give her the benefit of the doubt. She just lost her father, and like you said, he's a Doctor. Where can he go? This way we save them some embarrassment by not picking her up in a squad car."

"I'm going to call my wife and tell her I won't be home for dinner. You go to the Café and pick up something to eat. I'll take their pulled pork sandwich with fries and a coke."

161

Leon started to leave. "Oh, get me an order of cole-slaw also."

"Right Chief."

Chief Watson ate at his desk, while working on the new schedule for his men. With a knock on the door his duty officer came in.

"The Sault family is here. And they brought some others with them."

"How many?"

"Three, looks like a dad and mom with their daughter. Both girls are dressed in black, lipstick and all."

"Take them back to the conference room. I'll be right there.

He put his work aside, ate the last three fries and drank the rest of his coke. Then he headed down the hall, stopping at Leon's office on the way. Opening the door he said, "They're here." and continued down the hall. Jerry opened the door to the conference room and walked in, Leon right behind.

All six of them were sitting on the far side of the table. Dr. Sault had a concerned look, but was ready to fight. The parents looked bewildered and scared. The girls had their faces down. When they looked up there was fear mixed with guilt on both faces. They'd been crying.

"Hi. I'm Chief Watson. This is Detective Summer. I'm glad you could come down. Why don't we start with introductions."

"I'm Dr. Jonas Sault. This is my sister-in law Helen Sault, and her daughter Kelly."

"I'm Ben Kiger. This is my wife Audrie and our daughter Sherrie."

"A woman was murdered at 106 Springdale yesterday" Jerry said. "We have been talking to everyone who was there. One of them identified Kelly as being at the scene. There was another girl there also. Was that you Sherrie?"

She raised her head. "Yes sir."

"Would one of you tell me and Detective Summer what you were doing there, and what you saw?"

Jerry waited for one of them to speak.

"It's ok Kelly. Tell him what happened." Dr. Sault said.

"Sher and I, we were going to find the treasure. You know, the one that the lady buried in the flower garden."

"What kind of treasure do you think is there?" Jerry asked.

"I don't know, jewels I think."

"Where did you hear about it."

"From my mom."

Audrie wanted to interrupt. But Jerry put up his hand.

"You will have time to talk later, Mrs. Kiger. Go on Kelly."

"I heard my mom talking to our neighbor. I think she heard it at the beauty shop."

"Tell me how you got there and everything you saw and heard. From the beginning, and don't leave anything out."

She looked like she was going to start crying, Jonas put his arm on her shoulder and she calmed down.

"We walked over to the house and went in through the fence in back, and headed over to the flower bed. Then we looked at each other and said 'shovel'."

"Shovel?"

"Yah, we forgot to bring anything to dig with. That's when we heard them arguing and yelling. We went up to the garage door. The window was already broken out. We tried the handle and it opened. We could hear them better in the garage."

"Do you know what they were arguing about?"

"He was saying something about being cheated, and that it wouldn't happen again. She said something like, 'you were never cheated', or something like that. Then he yelled, 'don't walk away from me'. Then we heard a thump. It sounded like someone fell. Then something metal landed on the floor. We got really scared and were going to leave. That's when I kicked something. It was a baseball. It rolled across the floor and hit a can. Sher and I froze. Then we heard someone say, 'Is anyone home?' I think they said it over again. We went back to the door and looked out. That's when I saw that boy, and he saw me. Then we took off running for the fence and left."

"You didn't break the window or go all the way into the house?"

"No."

"Were you wearing gloves?"

"No. We forgot them too. We didn't bring anything to dig in the garden with. Stupid huh."

"Did you see anyone leave the house?"

"No. I just saw that boy. We both jumped and then Sher and I ran."

"Sherrie, tell me what you remember."

164

"It's just like Kelly said. We didn't see anything, just heard them arguing. I didn't even see the boy. Only Kelly saw him."

"What exactly did they say? Were they arguing over money or something?"

"I think it was money. Somehow, she cheated him out of some money on some deal, I think. I don't really know for sure."

"Do you know when you got there, and how long before you left?"

They both shook their heads no.

"This could be very important. Think hard."

Kelly said, "We weren't there very long, maybe five minutes at the most."

"Kelly, do you know who the boy was? Did you see him come or go?"

"We just moved here after school was out. The only one I know here is Sher. We met at a band competition last year. She just lives down the street from us, so we hang out."

"Mrs. Kiger, tell me about the treasure you were talking about."

"I should be the one to tell you." Audrie said. "It all started at the beauty shop. I was waiting my turn and I overheard Betty, and another lady I don't know, talking about Mrs. Kingsley having to go to the rest home. And they were wondering about her treasures and who would take care of them now that she was gone."

"So, what do you think the treasure is?"

165

"I don't really know, I thought they were talking about her flower garden."

"Do any of you know Clara Kingsley? Or heard of her at all?"

Jerry looked from one to the other starting with Dr. Sault.

Everyone answered 'no'.

"Do any of you know the victim Julie Markowitz, her husband Bud, or have you done any business with Markowitz Reality?"

Again, everyone said 'no'.

"Helen, who did you buy your house through?"

"We saw it online and bought it through Jim at Oak River Reality."

"Thank you. You've been very helpful. You can all go. But don't go far. Are any of you expecting to go out of town?"

They all shook their heads no.

"Show them out, Leon, then come into my office."

When he came back Jerry said. "Shut the door and sit down. Well that was a bust. All this over some beauty shop gossip they didn't even hear correctly."

"I think it's progress. We removed two people from our suspects list."

"So, who does that leave?"

"No one. The husband has a rock-solid alibi' He was showing houses out of town all afternoon to the new owner of Oak River Hardware. He's moving here with his family from Ohio. He was with both husband and wife and

166

their four kids. Not his best afternoon, he said. Told me he took four ibuprofens, when he got back to the office. Then we called and told him his wife was murdered."

"I want a list of everyone who has been in that house since it was put up for sale. Maybe one of them recognized the paintings, came back for them, and ran into Julie. Also, check the past on both husband and wife all the way back through High School. How long they've been in town, where they came from, everything. Check their parents, brothers, sisters, the whole family."

"That'll take days."

"Then you'd better get started."

AUGUST 8 WEDNESDAY
LESTERS LAB

They worked hard all day. At eight o'clock Glenda stopped.

"You two can work all night if you want to, but I'm going back upstairs and get something to eat. Then I'm going to take a shower and get some rest before our friends come back."

"We all need to stop." Lester said. "We can go up to the house, the accommodations are better."

"We are not leaving the fossils here. If we go to the house, they're coming with us." Jacob said.

"I have a walk-in safe right here." Lester said, pointing to the other end of the lab. We can put them in there. They'll be fine, trust me."

167

"I am. That's why we're here. But the fossils are going with me."

"Ok, Jake. There's a four-wheeler in back. I'll get it and we can take them up to the house in it." Lester said.

Once there the three of them carried them into the house and upstairs to the spare bedrooms. Just like the rest of the farm, the inside of the house was much different than the outside. The outside looked like a rundown farm house on its last leg. The inside was completely remodeled, with period antique furniture. Once in the house Lester took Glenda and Jacob upstairs to the spare bedrooms, each with its own bath. Jacob had the fossils put under the bed in his room. Then he cleaned up and laid down on the bed fully dressed, and went to sleep.

AUGUST 8 WEDNESDAY EVENING, POLICE STATION

Jerry sat back in his chair and pondered the whole case. It shouldn't be this hard. There were people all over the place. How did someone get in, kill her, and leave, without being seen? It's impossible, at least almost impossible. Maybe they didn't leave the house. Maybe they just hid until we were gone. Not likely, I had officers and a dog in there overnight.

He picked up his phone and called Pastor Boyd.

"Hi, Jerry what do you need?"

"I need you to get Charlie and meet me at 106 Springdale."

"When?"

"Now if you can."

"Charlie is here along with Nate Strong who's been taking care of Jack today. He stayed for supper and we're just finishing up. Charlie and I can meet you in about twenty minutes."

"Perfect. See you there."

The Chief was already there when they arrived, the door to the house was open.

"This is just like it was when we got here the other day. Wow. That was only yesterday. Seems like it should be longer than that." Charlie said as she opened the car door. "You don't think the Chief is lying dead in there do you?"

"No. But let's go in and check."

They went in the front door.

"We're here. Chief." Charlie said.

There was no answer. She started to walk back to the kitchen.

"Don't play any games. This is spooky enough." she said, while continuing.

Then she saw the shoe and ran around the counter. He was lying face down, just like Julie, only there was no blood on the back of his head. Charlie knelt, and felt the side of his neck for a pulse. It was strong. Just then he clicked his stop watch and rolled over. To his surprise, she didn't scream. Instead she jumped on his chest and slapped him on the cheek.

"Don't ever do that again!" she said.

Pastor, who was watching, couldn't control himself. He doubled over laughing. Charlie was still sitting on him and smacking him on his cheek. He managed to roll back over and get up. When he was standing, Charlie was on his back holding on to his neck.

When Pastor could finally speak, he said,

"I told you not to do that. She doesn't react like you would think."

Jerry was still trying to get her off his back.

"Take her off! I don't want to hurt her."

"Charlie, get down and quit playing with him."

"She's not playing."

Charlie jumped down.

"Yes, I was. But it's not nice to scare me like that. I love you don't you know."

"She was playing, Jerry. Clearly you've never seen her when she is serious." Pastor said.

"You were timing how long it took me to reach the body weren't you?" Charlie said.

Jerry took a minute to straighten his shirt. He turned around to tuck it in. Mostly he was trying to deal with what Charlie said. The list of people he thought cared for him was short. Turning back around he said,

"Yes. It was 24 seconds. I don't know if you could've choreographed this whole thing better. Did he come over with her? Did he hide in the house and leave later? If he didn't ride with her, how did he get here? There was no other car anyone noticed."

Jerry scratched his head. "I'm stumped. It's impossible that no one saw him."

"You're right about the timing. Here's what I think happened." Charlie said, "I've been thinking about it a lot. He hits her over the head." Charlie began acting it out. "Shocked at what he or she has done, it could be a woman. They dropped the pipe. Then they hear the girls in the garage and a few seconds later he hears us pull into the drive. He must act fast. I think he heads down the hall before I get to the door." Charlie quickly walked over to the hallway. "Without hesitating, he goes down the hall into the master bedroom." Pastor and the Chief quickly follow her. "Goes over to the patio door, opens it, turns the lock, like so. Steps out onto the patio and takes a quick look around, goes around this one section of privacy fence into the neighbor's yard and quickly walks along the hedge into the next yard, then out to the street where his car is waiting. Gets in and quietly drives away."

"So, Sherlock-does he, or she, already know the back door is there, or is it just a lucky break?" Jerry asked.

"I think they knew."

"So, they are familiar with the house."

"Yes."

"So, did he come in the same way?"

"I don't know. But if you look down," Charlie said, staring down by her feet. "There is a partial footprint, right here." Charlie pointed down at the dirt between the bushes and looking closer. Said "And here are some bent branches."

Charlie stepped back and let Jerry and Pastor look.

"What do you think?" she asked.

"It has possibilities." Jerry said.

Charlie followed as they both stepped through the hedge and carefully walked to the end of the yard to where the hedge turned a corner. The grass was too thick to see anything, but about five feet from the corner they found what they were looking for- another small opening in the hedge and an almost complete footprint heading in. "Don't step on that footprint I'll have my men come over and take a cast."

The hedge opened at the back of a flower garden but there were no more prints. Jerry stepped through and was immediately challenged by a woman holding a hand hoe, in a threating manner.

"Now, I caught you. I'm calling the police."

Jerry stepped carefully on through the flower bed, followed by Pastor and Charlie. The woman stepped back flabbergasted.

"There's three of you! You stay still. Don't come any farther."

She got her cell phone out and was trying to watch them. While holding onto her garden hoe, and call the police at the same time.

Jerry got out his badge and showed it to her.

"I am Police Chief Jerry Watson. This is Pastor Boyd, and Charlie.

"Oh! Oh my! I don't care who you are. You can arrest these two... And yourself! I don't believe it. No self-respecting Pastor would climb through a hedge and tromp all over my flower garden!"

"You said, finally caught us. Did someone else go through here before?" Charlie asked.

"They sure did! Yesterday! The same day that nice lady was murdered. Are you really the Chief of Police?"

"Yes ma'am."

"And you're really a pastor, and..."

"Yes. I'm a real girl. Did you see who went through here yesterday?"

"No. If I had, I would've called the police then!"

"Would you tell us about the footprints you found?"

"I'll bet you're trying to catch him too. That's why you came through. You could've just come up to the door you know, I would have answered all your questions. We could've had some tea. Would you all like some tea?"

"Maybe some other time." Jerry said. "You were telling us about the prints."

"Yes, I was. There were two sets, one going in and one coming out."

"Was there anything special about them?"

"They were a men's wingtip, size ten. They were neat and careful going in, but not coming out. He stepped right on my geranium."

"How do you know the kind of shoe and the shoe size?" Jerry asked.

"My husband and I owned a shoe store in Clinton, until he died. Then I sold out. Retired here to be closer to my son."

173

"Are you sure about the shoes?"

"Of course I'm sure! Forty-nine years in the shoe business. I know shoes. And yours need polishing. They should look smart and shiny, like Pastor's here. And you, little lady, are wearing yours too tight. You need room for your toes to breath. Also, there was one clear heal print. It showed the name Florsheim. I'll tell you another thing- he walks on the outside of his right shoe. It was all worn down. I can fix him up so he wouldn't do that. If you catch him, that is."

"We'll catch him. Thank you for your help."

Jerry turned to walk back the way he came.

"Oh no, you don't! You go right on through the yard and around the block on the sidewalk."

Charlie looked back when she reached the sidewalk. The lady was down on her hands and knees erasing their foot prints.

"We're making progress. We know it was a man by himself. How he got in and out. Also, he probably had a key and was already familiar with the house." Jerry said, smiling as they walked around the block. "Who would fit in that category."

"Family, friends who were helping to take care of her before she moved." Pastor said.

"Plus, all the realtors." Charlie added. "What we need is a motive."

"$250,000 in art is a good motive." Jerry answered.

"True, but the paintings were on the far end of the house. There was no need to go all the way in." Charlie said.

174

"Maybe they panicked." Jerry said.

"No, I don't think so. All they had to do was go back outside and wait until everyone left." Pastor said.

"You're right." Charlie said. "One, the motive has to be personal. Two, they had to know she was going to be here."

When they reached the house, Pastor said. "I think Charlie and I will head back home, unless you need us for something else?"

"No. Thanks for coming. It was a big help. I just needed the perspective of a former criminal."

"Thanks a lot." Charlie said.

When Pastor backed out onto the street, she said, "At least he said 'former' criminal."

"Yah, that's an improvement."

"What's next, Pastor?"

"I'm going to take you home, then I'm going home."

"I'm thinking we need to go house hunting tomorrow." Charlie said. "I'll drive. I need to help people run errands remember. I can pick you up at say, 9 o'clock. Then we can pick a realtor's office and ask to see some houses. Then when we're out looking, we can ask to see 106 Springdale, and see how they react. What do you think?"

"I think you have a doctor's appointment at 10:00 tomorrow. I'm taking you home and then I'm going home. You can come over after you get through at the doctors. I'll think about the realtors."

CHAPTER EIGHT
AUGUST 9 THURSDAY 1:50 AM
LESTERS HOUSE

Jacob woke with a start and looked at his watch. It was ten to two am.

He looked under the bed. The fossils were still there. He got up and went to the bathroom, then looked out in the hall. It was too quiet. He stepped out and looked in Glenda's room. She wasn't there. He went downstairs and looked around. He found them both in a security room, very much like the one in the barn.

"We can see everything from here." Glenda said. "Even your bedroom. She tapped a button on the computer and Jacob's room was on screen eight. They're all connected to motion and sound detectors too. When you woke up it alerted us and brought your room on the screen. You can see and hear everything in the house, the barn, and everything in between. Every camera is also backed-up on a two-week loop. Lester also told me how he was able to get the T-Rex. He said it's 100 percent complete and in perfect shape. It's the only thing in the barn that is not for sale. He turned down an offer of ten million from a private collector." Glenda said, raising her eyebrows as she looked right at Jacob.

"Yes, I've seen it before. It is a great specimen. But only 95 percent complete. I checked it very carefully once. I assume he told you how he cheated us out of it? He knew how close I was to finding it?"

"Yes. Only he described it as a close call, from his point of view, that is."

Looking around the security room Lester had in his home, Glenda thought he must either be paranoid, or he must be involved in a lot more than Jacob seemed to think. The security alarm went off at 2:20 a.m. They were all watching as Lester gave a blow-by-blow account of the intruder's progress, from the moment they turned off the highway, right up to when they stopped part way up the drive, got out and walked in. Lester had all the cameras equipped with night vision, but when they reached the front yard it wasn't needed. He had two powerful outdoor lights, one in front, another in back. It was lit up like daylight. They went around to Jacob's car first and, without checking to see if the doors were locked, jammed a crowbar under the trunk lid and pried it open. As soon as Jacob saw what they were going to do he screamed, "No! Shoot them!"

Next, they walked over to the back of the house and pried open the back door the same way and carefully walked in. Once in the house the three of them could hear everything, including their quiet footsteps.

Lester let them walk in as far as the living room before stepping out from behind them, cocking his short barreled semi-automatic 12 gauge. That was the sign for Jacob to flip a switch turning on the lights. At the same time Red came out from the other way, with a deep growl and his teeth showing.

"I imagine you remember Red. He remembers you. One thing you have to keep in mind, Red's bites worse than his bark and right now he's telling you to put the crow bar down and lay flat on the floor...slowly."

The end was rather anticlimactic. They simply did as they were told. Jacob and Glenda zip tied their hands and feet, and put black bags over their heads. Then Lester had Glenda empty everything out of their pockets. While she was at it, she searched them thoroughly and put everything on the dining room table. Besides what you would normally expect to find, there were two semi-automatic pistols in shoulder holsters, one with a silencer. A small five-shot revolver she found strapped to an ankle, and two switchblade knives. Meanwhile, Jacob went out and searched through their car. When Glenda finished, Lester handed the shotgun to her and grabbed their wallets.

"You stay here and make sure Red doesn't tear them up. I'll be a while." Lester said, heading back to his security room.

When Jacob came back in, he asked, "Where's Lester?"

"He's back in the office." she said, pointing in the direction of the security room.

After waiting a while Jacob went over and tried the door. It was locked.

"What do you think he's doing in there?" Jacob asked.

"I don't know for sure, but if I were to guess, he's finding out who these two are."

"They're hoodlums, with no respect for other people's cars."

He walked over next to the one who'd pried open his trunk and kicked him in the side. "You didn't even check! I left the door open and the keys in it so you wouldn't need to destroy my classic Cadillac." He gave him another kick, this time a little harder. The victim responded with a groan. "Do you know how much it cost me to buy that car and have it restored? Not to mention keeping it in perfect condition. What did you come here for, besides killing Lester? What were you going to do to the fossils if you found them? Destroy them too?"

Jacob kicked him again even harder than the last one. Just then Lester came back out, he put their wallets back on the table.

"Looks like we've caught ourselves two professional hit men. The question is, what do we do with them now?"

"I don't know. Call the sheriff and turn them in for breaking and entering?" Glenda said.

"I think we should shoot'em!" Jacob said. "Did you see what they did to my car? Besides, if we turn them into the sheriff they'll just get out, and come back after us. They're probably the ones who blew up the motel, killing my students." This time he really kicked him as hard as

180

he could. The resulting groan was much more severe and he struggled to get his breath back. "Plus, I want to know which one of them is the turncoat. Which one of the students started this whole thing? We need to make them talk before we shoot them."

"You can't be serious." Glenda said. "That's murder."

"You're right." Lester said. "It would be murder. But it would be the most prudent thing to do. And it would be most helpful to have the answers."

"Too bad. I already called the Sheriff's office. They should be here any time now."

"Who's going to pay for fixing my car?" Jacob asked.

"Don't worry about that, I'll take care of it in the morning. I don't think either one of these two will be coming back this way soon. They're wanted in Texas for murdering two Texas Rangers, one of whom was the nephew of the governor."

Soon two Sheriff cars pulled into the drive. Lester went to the door and let them in.

'Hi Jim. Who you got with you tonight?"

"Ed and Ellen." Turning to them he said, "You two shackle them and take them out to the car. Make sure they don't get away. Lester here says Texas is mighty interested in these two, after we're done with them. Apparently they like to kill Rangers.

Ed and Ellen cut their feet loose, put shackles on them and escorted them out, without removing the head coverings.

"Their personal effects are over here on the table." Lester said.

Jim looked down at the arsenal. "Maybe we can tag them for some more killings after ballistics is done with these."

"The car down the drive is theirs too. They have some very interesting things in the trunk." Jacob added.

"I'll need you three to come to the office tomorrow, let's say one o'clock.

That work for everyone?"

They all answered yes. Jim left, taking the intruders personal effects with him. He turned at the door. "I'll have the car picked up first thing in the morning." he said, and shut the door.

AUGUST 9 THURSDAY AM
PAULA'S HOUSE

Thursday morning Charlie called Chris, getting her out of bed.

"Who is this again?" And what time is it?"

"Chris. Wake up. This is Charlie. I have a great idea."

"Can't it wait until today? I mean later today."

"Open your blinds and look out the window."

Chris pushed off her covers and went to the window and opened her blinds.

"Ok, I'm looking out. What am I supposed to see?"

"Isn't it beautiful."

"There'd better be more to it than this! What time is it anyway?"

"You sound like you're awake now. I had an idea. You could go into work early. Find all the realtors in town. Then see how many of them bought cars from your dad and we would have all kinds of information. We think the killer might be a realtor. What do you think?"

"I'm going back to bed now." Chris hung up and turned off her phone. Then went over and looked at her alarm. 5:33. The sun isn't even up; it's only thinking about getting up. She crawled back into bed and tried to go back to sleep. Ten minutes later she gave in, got up, and took a shower. The more she thought about it the better she liked the idea. It could be another realtor. They would have access to the house. In Oak River, they would all know each other. Maybe she could find something. She was at work by 6:50, grabbed a donut and a cup of coffee from the service manager, then went to her office. "This is becoming a habit." She said to herself.

AUGUST 9 THURSDAY AM
PARSONAGE

Pastor's morning started a little after Charlie's and Chris's. He was up at six, did his devotional out on his bedroom patio, then cleaned up. At 7:30 he looked in on Jack who was wide awake, a strange look on his face.

"Are you alright?"

"No, I keep having a nightmare. It's always been on Sunday nights. But last night was Wednesday."

"Do you want to talk about it?"

"No. Yes. I don't know. I need to talk to someone. You're a pastor right. I mean you will keep it between us, right."

"Yes."

Jack was silent for a minute thinking, then reaching a decision he said,

"Every Sunday night since Charlie got shot, I have the same dream. You know I'm not a believer."

Pastor was going to say something but changed his mind. "Yes."

"You know I really like Charlie, right. Even before the incident, right."

"I would say so."

"And I put the money up for her scholarship."

"Yes, that was very…" he was going to say nice, but changed his mind and said. "kind."

"So why do I keep having this dream? This nightmare?"

"Why do you think you keep having it?"

"I don't know. That's why I'm asking you."

"You can do better than that."

"When Charlie was shot, our eyes met. It was just that instant, I could see her in heaven if she died and I saw myself in hell if I died. That was just the emotion of the moment. Sorry, nothing personal, but they're not real, heaven, hell, or God, at least not the one you talk about. Not a personal God that you can know."

184

"You told me yesterday that your Dad was saved and that only left you."

"I was drunk that doesn't count."

"Yes, you were. But you knew what you were saying. Your sister and Chris have prayed daily for you ever since they were saved. I know Charlie is very concerned about you also, and prays for you. A lot of the Church is praying for you as well. The personal God that we know hears those prayers, and acts on them. You have been through quite a bit lately, with your father's passing, his conversion, what happened in Montana. This all adds up. Then falling down the stairs, living here with me. I think God is fighting for your soul in answer to our prayers. Let me ask you this. You once said your father's death was a waste, that all being saved got him was killed. Would you be here right now if he hadn't died?

Jack sat there thinking, "No, I wouldn't. Are you saying my father died to bring me here?"

"I'm saying God doesn't waste anything. He didn't cause your father's death but He will use it, not let it go to waste, for His purpose.

"We say salvation is free. I don't like it put that way. It is free in the sense that we can't do anything to earn it. But in fact, I think it's the most expensive thing in the Universe. God the Father and God the Son, Jesus, along with God the Holy Spirit, before the world was created, knew Adam and Eve would sin. And that sin would separate them. God already knew what would have to be done to open the door to bring us back into fellowship. Let me put it this way. You were in the military. What would happen to a soldier who betrayed his country?"

"He would be tried for treason and shot."

"Exactly. God not only created everything...."

Jack interrupted, "That's just it. Did He really create everything? Did He create anything. I hear all about God creating but that's not what really happened. Science tells a very different story. If Genesis is not true, what does that say about the rest of the book?"

"If God created everything that would make Him the rightful Ruler of everything. Wouldn't it?"

"That's a big if."

"Hang with me now. That would make him King."

"I suppose."

"Jesus declares himself to be the "King of all kings, and Lord of all lords." It is not just something we sing. It is fact. When Adam and Eve sinned, they committed treason against their rightful King, and were under a death sentence. How many rulers would let their son take the place of someone convicted of treason?"

"None. I wouldn't. That's for sure."

"Well, that's exactly what God did. His love is so great that even when we were guilty of treason, He sent His Son, Jesus to take our place.

"But He is so careful with our right of free will, that even though His Son died in our place, we must choose to accept His pardon, or not. It cost God His Son. It is not free for us either. When we accept His pardon we, in effect, are also swearing allegiance to Him as our rightful ruler.

Scripture says we were bought with a price. Wouldn't you expect to obey a King who died in your place?"

"Yes, of course. But it's not that simple."

"Sure, it is. Didn't you take an oath when you went into the military?"

"You were in. Everyone has to take the oath."

"Did you mean it."

"Yes."

"Did you ever violate it. Disobey."

"Yes, more than once. You know I even hit a commanding officer."

"I'm glad you brought that up. He gave you grace and had mercy on you, right."

"Yes, you could say that."

"That is exactly what God does for us. Once we accept Jesus' pardon, and invite Him in, He gives us a willing heart to follow Him, to obey him. But we don't always succeed. He doesn't throw us out when we fail. When we ask forgiveness for our failures, He grants it. And we start again with a clean slate. Were you kicked out of the military?"

"No, I quit."

"What would've happened if your Sergeant had turned you in?"

"If I was found guilty, I would have gone to prison and been given a dishonorable discharge."

"Unlike the military, God will never throw you out. No matter how many times you mess up. The only way you can get out, is to quit on your own. Tell Him by action and word you no longer want to be covered by His pardon." Romans 10:13 For "Everyone who calls on the name of the Lord will be saved."

Jack had had enough.

"I'll think on it. I've really got to go to the bathroom. I can't think on a full bladder."

When Jack had his needs met, they both went to the kitchen. Coffee and breakfast was next on the schedule.

AUGUST 9 THURSDAY
OAK RIVER CLINIC

It was after eleven when Charlie left the doctor's office and called Pastor. He answered on the third ring.

"I'm finally out. They were behind schedule. Are we on to look at houses?"

"Yes. I invited Jack. He's not into looking at houses. Said he's not living in Oak River, and is not interested in dealing with it in his wheelchair. I did leave him with a book to read. "I Don't Have Enough Faith to be an Atheist."

Jack read to page 45 where the student confronted the pastor. "Sir I believe you are going to Hell. Then he shut the book and put it in the drawer beside his bed.

"He seemed to be interested. But on the up side, Sandy, my secretary volunteered to come, as long as she gets paid, that is. This detective work is beginning to cost. But it lets me postpone doing the reports another day. She's been trying to trap me all week."

"What reports? Are you taking classes?"

"No. At least that would be interesting. These are reports that need to go to the Church District. She does most of the work. We just go over them together before they're sent in. It's not that hard, it's just that I don't like doing them. I don't think you can quantify what God is doing with numbers on a page. I told her we would do them next Tuesday for sure."

"I'm curious, does procrastination fall under lack of self-discipline?"

"You got me. I need to grow up some more. I think she made a twelve-thirty appointment at Oak River Reality. I'll call the office and tell her you're on your way."

For her part, Sandy would've gone just to get to ride in Charlie's 1967 custom yellow convertible. But she didn't tell him that. She held out for lunch and the afternoon off with pay.

AUGUST 9 THURSDAY NOON
FORD DEALERSHIP

Chris was usually too busy to take an actual lunch break, but today was slow, so when Sue Ellen, her secretary, and Jamie, a sales woman, invited her to go across the street to Kim's Chinese Buffet, she accepted. The restaurant was almost full when they arrived. The hostess led them to a table in the middle of the dining room. They sat down and prayed, then they all went up to the large buffet to choose their favorite dish. Soon they were all seated at the table.

"What do you think of Julie being murdered in that house?" Jamie asked. "I heard you were right there when it happened." she said looking at Chris.

Without giving Chris time to answer, Sue Ellen chimed in.

"What was it like, seeing a dead body? I would have ran right out of the house screaming."

"It was very startling. I'm glad I wasn't alone. Charlie Bolton was the one who found her first, and Jen was with us. Actually, we were looking at the house for her. Did either of you know Julie? I must've seen her around town but I can't say I knew her."

"Well, I don't want to speak ill of the dead," Jamie said, "but I have a friend who bought a house through her. She didn't tell them the basement leaked when it rained a lot. They bought it late summer, like August, I think. Well, the next spring we had a lot of rain. They had a foot of water in their basement. Ruined most everything down there. It cost them almost ten thousand dollars to get it fixed. They got hold of a lawyer, who looked at their sales agreement and told them there was nothing they could do. It was an estate sale; the owner had died. Apparently, it was up to them to have the house inspected if they thought there was anything wrong."

"I heard she was having an affair with someone and was going to leave her husband." Sue Ellen added.

"Do you know who with?" Chris asked.

"No, just that it was with another realtor, from out of town." But they said she was sleeping around with a lot of guys. I guess that's how she closed more than one big sale."

"Did her husband know about this?"

Sue Ellen bent forward and lowered her voice.

"If you want to know the whole story, my friend said they had what's called an open marriage. They both did whatever with whoever. But this was different. She was going to leave him. She said she recently made a lot of money on a farm sale, and was going to leave her husband high and dry."

"What does that mean?"

"I don't know. That's just what she said."

"Who told you all this?"

"I shouldn't say. It's supposed to be confidential."

"She's been murdered. The police need to know who it was so they can investigate."

"I don't want to get involved with the police."

"Just tell me who it is, and I won't tell them how I found out."

"You won't connect them to me, right? I never thought it was important like that. Do you think he could have killed her? Maybe she was going to run out on both of them?"

Chris looked her in the face. "Who told you?"

"Alright it was Jen. Not your Jen. Jenny from Jenny's Beauty Salon."

This put a damper on the rest of their lunch. When they finished, Sue Ellen and Jamie went to the restroom to freshen up, while Chris paid the bill.

"Wow. She really is up tight about all this." Sue Ellen said.

"It's murder, Sue. This is not just some gossip, like when we were in high school. And she is paying for our lunch remember."

"Yah, I guess you're right."

When Chris got back to work, she called the police station and asked to speak to Jerry.

"I'm sorry. He's out of the office. Can someone else help?"

"No. Just ask him to call me when he can. I have some information on the Markowitz murder."

"Do you want me to put you through to Leon? He's handling the case."

"No thanks. I'll wait for the Chief."

AUGUST 9 THURSDAY
LIFE CHURCH PARKING LOT

When Charlie pulled up, Pastor and Sandy were standing out front waiting.

Pastor got in the back, saying,

"I told her she could sit up front."

Sandy took her seat up front, buckled her seat belt, and then said. "Put the pedal to the metal!"

Charlie turned to Pastor.

"I also told her you would show her a couple of turns in the parking lot."

"Controlled Power?" Charlie asked.

"Yes, she wants to do a J-turn."

Charlie needed no more encouragement. She wound up the tach and popped the clutch. The rear tires fought for traction then sped down the parking lot. Just before reaching the end, she did a 180 and headed back where she came from. Coming to a gentle stop at the church exit.

"I always wanted to do that!" Sandy said. "That was exhilarating. Now let's go do lunch."

Charlie could hardly hold it together. This was not what she pictured when she thought of Sandy. Short, brown hair with some gray starting to show, very conservatively dressed, quiet, reserved, and every inch what you would expect a church secretary to be.

While they were waiting for their order at the Café, Charlie and Sandy were still talking about their ride in the parking lot.

"You ladies know it would not be good if the whole town knew we were doing J-turns in the church parking lot, right."

"Ok, we'll change the subject." Sandy said. "Like the whole town doesn't already know. How about parasailing?"

"You've done that?" Charlie said.

"Yes, and I've gone down a zip line and skydived, twice." Sandy continued.

"Where, when, did you do all these things?"

"My husband died three years ago."

"I'm so sorry." Charlie said.

"Me too. I miss him a lot. But we never did anything exciting, adventurous. Well we raised three kids, there were moments. But I mean nothing like skydiving. Clifford fished. So we all fished, and went camping. The farthest we ever went was to Minnesota, fishing. Don't get me wrong. We had great family times. The kids really enjoyed it. We did a lot of things together. Some of their friends grew up not doing anything with their parents. The parents worked and their kids were in organized sports. Which is nice but they didn't actually do many things together. Everyone just kind of did their own thing, I guess. Now they realize how valuable it is to be a family. Clifford was just not into more adventure, that's all. Now that he is gone, I figured, if I'm going to do it, now's the time."

"Can you do that around here?"

"You can skydive. There's a place by Brooklyn. I went there once. They were really nice. It was a beautiful fall day and the leaves were at their peak. It was the first adventurous thing I ever did. I was hooked! The rest I've done while on cruises. Clifford left me comfortably off. He knew I always wanted to do things like that, and when he got cancer, he encouraged me to go ahead."

"So, what's next?"

"Believe it or not the car ride today was the last on my list of those kinds of things. Pastor over there doesn't know it yet, but next May and June I am going on a vacation, oops! It's called a sabbatical, not a vacation."

"Where are you going?"

Magen brought over their lunch.

"Hi Charlie, I bet it's exciting doing those turn things with your new car. It sure looks awesome. We all went out and looked at your car. Pastor Boyd, some of us were wondering if you could teach us how to do it? Those turn things."

Pastor turned his head and looked over toward the kitchen. There were three standing by the door, another waitress and two of the cooks.

"They're called 'J-turns'. You can call Sandy at the church she handles all the scheduling."

"Wow! Great! we will definitely call. Thanks a lot, Pastor Boyd."

"See what you started." Pastor said.

"They already knew before we got here. Megan lives across the street from church. And I've already had two calls wanting lessons, four calls asking who is racing around the parking lot, and does Pastor know what's going on."

Pastor changed the subject.

"What did you order Sandy? Normally you have a chicken salad and a glass of water."

"Today is special and you're paying. So. I'm getting the special, stuffed flounder with rice and grilled vegetables." Charlie's was the tenderloin and fries and Pastor had a Taco salad.

"Since you are leaving on a sabbatical Sandy, you can start your prayer life by praying for our lunch." Pastor said.

"You can count this as my notice for next year."

When she finished praying, Sandy said, "You were wanting a way to reach the young people in town. You may have found it. But you will need to find another place to teach them. One of the calls complaining was Jerry. You know him, the Chief of Police. I told him today would be the last time."

Then she picked up her conversation where she'd left off.

"I want to go to Europe. Big Ben, the Eiffel Tower, the Colosseum in Rome. I want to see all the things you see in movies and read about in books. Some of their buildings and houses are way older than our country."

"Since this is a working lunch, you can tell us what you have set up with the realtors." Pastor mentioned.

Thinking about what she said, while opening her purse she thought, I wonder what insurance would cost to teach the youth J-turns. She took out four sheets of paper and handed them to him.

"What is all that?" Pastor asked."

"What you asked for, plus a little. It's a list of all the real estate offices in Oak river. There's eight, believe it or not. Plus, a list of all the agents who work in those offices, a total of twenty-four agents." She handed him two more.

"These other two are the rest of the offices in our county, and their agents. Eight more offices with eighteen more agents. A number of them are husband and wife offices, just like Julie and her husband."

Pastor started to speak.

"Don't interrupt." Sandy continued, "Some of them are retired. One of those is eighty-six years old and is in a nursing home. You will see a double asterisk by the ones who are inactive." She held up her hand before he could ask a question. "One asterisk means they still have a desk in an office, but don't really look for clients, only taking the ones that fall in their lap. As you can see, all of them come with addresses and phone numbers. Now do you have any questions?"

"Just how are we to sort through 42 names even if one is in a nursing home?" Pastor asked.

"I thought of that. If you approve, there's a realtor and his son who have been in business here for over thirty years and his father before him. I can arrange a meeting with the two of them. Maybe they could help."

"Who are they?"

"The owners of Smith and Son reality."

"When can we see them?" Pastor asked. "We have an appointment with someone at Oak River Reality right after lunch."

"I took the liberty of cancelling that, in exchange for Smith and Son. I thought it would be a better use of our time." Sandy said. "When would you like to see the Smiths?"

"Right after lunch, if we could."

"How about right now, this is a working lunch."

"That would be fine are they close by?"

Sandy put her hand up and waved. A minute later two men were introducing themselves,

"Hi, I'm Red Smith Senior and this is my son, Red Smith Junior.

"Oh, I told them you were buying their lunch also."

"I think I've been set up." Pastor said.

"I think she's scary, but awesome!" Charlie added.

They could have been twins except for the twenty-two years difference in age. Both had curly red hair, blue eyes, and a mouth that turned up at the corners, causing them to look like they were always smiling. They were medium height and build. And both were wearing dark blue suits and white shirts. Senior had on a blue and red tie; Junior sported a red bow tie.

Pastor looked for the waitress to come over and take their order.

"We already ordered at the counter," Red Senior said. "She'll bring our food over when it's ready."

"Sandy asked if we might be able to give you some help on who might have a motive for killing Julie Markowitz. At least as it might relate to the real estate business." Red Junior said.

"It's only a possibility that whoever did this might be a realtor. We need to keep this between ourselves. I don't want to start rumors."

"We understand. Julie and her husband opened their office about four years ago. That may sound like a long time, but not in Oak River. My dad took over the office from his dad, and I'll take over for him. There's only one other office that someone started that came from outside the community and that is Ted Wise. He mostly sells insurance, but also has a realtor's license and if something comes his way, he takes it. But most of his money comes from selling insurance. We're a small community. Everyone knows everyone else. There are no... how should I put this?... No one steps on other people's toes, no cutting in to take someone else's client. If you know what I mean. Bud and Julie came to town convinced they could put all of us hicks out of business. They used cut throat tactics and acted like they were in some big city. It didn't go over well, not only with the other realtors like us, but also with the buyers. They misrepresented some properties and were sued twice. They almost went under."

"I thought Bud was from here." Pastor said. "He is, sort of." Junior said, "He was born here, but his parents were divorced when he was five and his mother left, taking him with her. His father farmed east of town, and Bud came back for summers until he turned 18. Then no one saw him again until he moved back with his wife six years later. During that time his dad had sold the farm and moved to, I think, Kentucky."

"Tennessee." His dad corrected.

"I don't think Bud really runs the show. His wife was the driver. At work and at home."

"Remember what Pastor said, no rumors." his dad interjected.

"Well, I don't know about home but she sure ran the office."

Red Senior shook his head yes.

"I know of one deal about six, or eight months ago. It was a farm sale. She sold the old Hoffman farm, over two thousand acres. Hoffman died and the only heir was a granddaughter who lived back east. Julie told the new buyer, Stanley Granger, that it was certified as an organic farm, but that the certificate hadn't been renewed because the owner was sick, or something like that. They took her word for it. After he took possession and applied for certification, it failed. The ground was full of chemicals. He will need to transition for three years before he can sell anything labeled organic. But there was nothing in writing guaranteeing it was organic. I met the new buyer. He was very upset. He will lose a lot of money until he gets it certified. But he didn't seem like he would kill over it. Also, there was some funny business with the sale. The property was properly appraised but never listed for sale. It was bought by a corporation for sixteen million dollars."

"Isn't that a lot of money?" Pastor asked.

"Yes, but good farm ground is expensive. It's not unusual for corporations to buy farms. But it was resold two weeks later to Stanley, for twenty million dollars, as an organic farm. Which, like I said, it wasn't. I don't know this as fact, but I think she was selling her house and the real-estate business also. She's had run-ins with every realtor in town and probably the whole county. Including my dad and me."

"I'm sure glad Jen didn't buy the house from her." Charlie said. I think she is still interested in looking at it, can she call you?"

Red Senior pulled out his card. "You can call us any time. I will make sure the police are finished, then I'll call the seller and touch bases with her. Just let us know when you want to see it."

"Thanks." Charlie said, taking his card.

"Thank you for your insight." Pastor said. "It will give us a lot to think about."

"As long as I have you all here, could you show us some condominiums?" Sandy asked.

"My son is free all afternoon. He would love to. Right Junior?"

"Absolutely! I have a new listing that just came on the market."

"I was going to show that to your mom." Red Senior said. "You see, I'm thinking of retiring, at least semi-retiring. Don't want to put too much on Junior all at once."

"Yes, I'm taking some time off also, it would be so much easier to travel without a yard to take care of. I could leave anytime I wanted." Sandy said looking at Pastor.

Changing the subject again, Pastor said. "Who do you think will win the game Sunday."

Charlie and Sandy both laughed.

"What's so funny." Junior asked.

"He doesn't even know who's playing. He doesn't follow sports. Ask him." Sandy said.

"The Red Sox and the Yankees are playing. I think the Yankees will win." Pastor said.

"Where did you hear this?" Sandy prodded. "You didn't get it from the sports page."

"I overheard it when we came in. Two guys were talking at the counter."

Red Senior headed back to the office and the four of them got into Jr's Toyota SUV, and he drove them over to the condo.

201

AUGUST 9 THURSDAY 2 PM
FORD DEALERSHIP

An hour later the Police Chief walked into Jen's office, with Leon in tow, shut the door and sat down in front of her desk, pointing to the other chair for Leon to sit in.

"You're going to give Leon a complex, not talking to him. What do you have? And it better be good!"

"Not the least bit intimidated, Chris responded.

"You can decide if the information is good or not. According to Jenny, at Jenny's Beauty solon."

"More gossip from the hair place."

"There are always some facts behind the gossip."

She filled them in on everything she'd heard. When she finished, the Chief got up and, standing at the door, said, "Next time tell Leon, he's the detective." When they reached his car, he told Leon to drive. Once inside he asked Leon,

"Did you have any of that before we went in? Not the details. Some of the clients told me she was not very honest. I want her husband brought in today. I want you to interrogate him. If you don't think he's spilling it all, tell him we will get a court order and pick up all his records. You can drop me off at Pastor Boyd's."

Leon dropped him off, when he tried the door it was locked, so he went over to the parsonage and rang the bell.

After a few minutes Jack rolled his wheelchair up to the door and motioned for him to come in.

"Where's Boyd? I want to talk to him."

202

"He's out looking at houses, to see if he can catch the killer, I think. If you want to stay and wait I'll let you make us a pot of coffee. As you can see, he made me a sandwich for lunch and a salad, but forgot to set the coffee pot up."

Jerry looked around, the remains of Jack's lunch was sitting on the table by an empty coffee cup. And there was a mess by the coffee machine where Jack had been trying to fix his own.

"I might as well. I'll have to have Leon come back and get me. I let him take my car. Always a bad idea to be left on foot."

"Thanks a lot for making the coffee. Pastor normally does a good job. But now he's out with Charlie and his secretary, playing detective."

"That's what I want to talk to him about. Before one of them ends up a victim."

Jerry called Leon to come back and get him. Then went ahead and
made the coffee and sat down.

"How are you and Boyd getting along? It must get awfully boring being inside all the time."

"Yes, I hate being confined in this chair. But I did it to myself. Normally I get out every day, sometimes twice. Pastor takes me out almost every day. Jen and Chris come over several times a week and sit and talk or take me out to eat."

"But it's not like being on your own."

"No, it's not."

"If you don't mind me asking, how do you a...get cleaned up?"

"You've never had the tour? Follow me."

Jack turned his wheel chair around and led the way to his room and bath.

"You are set up. I never would have thought it would be this big and nice. It looks like a spa. Well, like I would imagine a spa would look like."

"I'm surprised you've never seen this before. I thought you and Pastor were buddies, friends."

"We are, just not... go to each other's house and watch the game kind of friends. If you know what I mean." We're both very busy I guess."

Leon drove up to the house and honked the horn.

"That's Leon, I'll get you your coffee.

Jerry pushed Jack back to the table and filled his cup. He opened the door to leave, then turned.

"I know it sounds like a cliché, but I am sorry you lost your dad."

Jerry went out and shut the door.

"Where to now, Chief? Did you find out where Boyd is?" Leon asked, after he got in the car.

"It's Pastor Boyd. And you can take me back to the station. Then take your own car and get Markowitz. We'll interview him together."

As soon as he was in his office, he called Pastor Boyd.

"When do you work? I just left your place. Jack said you're out looking at houses. I told you to stay out of the case. If I want your help, I'll ask for it. Now what did you find out?" Pastor filled him in on the information from the realtor. "That's very interesting. Stay out of this murder case! By the way, if you find out anymore you call me. Don't make me track you down."

AUGUST 9 THURSDAY 3:45 PM
OAK RIVER POLICE STATION

An hour later Leon had run Bud to ground and the three of them were sitting in the back room of the police station. Bud was trying to explain about his wife's affairs.

"Tell me again. You were ok with your wife sleeping with whomever she wanted." Jerry asked."

"How many times are you going to ask me?"

"Until you tell me the truth."

"Ok, it bothered me. But not enough to kill her, I loved her."

"Let's go to a different topic. You and your wife have a one million dollar life insurance policy on each other. Is that correct?"

"Yes. But I didn't kill her for the money. We're doing fine."

"Are you telling me she was worth more alive than dead."

"I guess, if you want to put it that way. I couldn't possibly have killed her, I was with a whole family showing them a house out of town at the time. You know that."

"Do you do mow your own lawn."

"My lawn, what does that have to do with it?"

"Just answer the question."

"No, we hire a lawn service."

"If you needed a new roof would you do that yourself?"

"No, I don't know how to roof a house. I just know how to sell them! I'd hire a professional. Hey, wait a minute. Are you trying to say I hired someone to kill my wife?"

"Did you?"

"No!"

"You are aware your wife sold a large farm not too long ago, let me see, as part of the estate of Ed Hoffman, 2000 acres?

"Yes."

"Do you remember how much it sold for?"

"No not exactly."

"Come on now. If my wife made a sale that big, I would remember."

"Sixteen million."

"Do you remember who bought it?"

"Some corporation back east. Ag-Adverturess or something like that."

"Did you know they sold it the next week to Stanley Granger, for twenty million dollars. That's a pretty good profit, don't you think?"

"Yes. But that's not illegal. What could that possibly have to do with my wife's death?"

"Did you know your wife and another partner were Ag-Adventures."

"No! I did not! That's not true!"

"Are you scheduled to go to a Realtor Conference in two weeks?"

"Yes."

"How long will you be gone?"

"The conference is a week. But I'm staying an extra week to play golf. Look, my wife isn't even buried yet. I haven't thought about the conference. Can I go now?"

Bud was looking very tired. He didn't look like he could hold it together much longer.

"One more thing. Are you aware your wife has sold your house and the real-estate business? The sales are to close the day after you leave for the conference. And I think, but haven't confirmed it yet, she was going to auction off all the household furnishings. So, when you came home the only thing you would have is your suitcase and car."

"The car's leased. It's up at the end of next month.

"Look, I didn't kill her and I didn't hire it done. I just don't have the guts. Even if I would've known about all this, I still wouldn't have hurt her."

"You can go for now, but don't leave town. Not even to show a house."

"Ok. Thanks."

Bud slowly got up and left.

"Do you believe him Chief?"

"Do you Leon?"

"Find out who and where this partner is. Check out his background and bring him in."

"What if he's out of state?"

"He won't be. Just get him."

AUGUST 9 THURSDAY 4PM
OUT FRONT OF THE OAK RIVER CAFÉ

It was just after 4 pm when Red Jr. dropped them back off at the Café. He'd shown them two condos and a town house, with a second trip back to the first condo. When they parted company, Red had made a sale, and Pastor and Charlie had taken a short course in real-estate. The last information they got was the name of the listing agent for the Hoffman farm, and the Kingsley house. Ted Wise originally listed the farm, but when it sold the listing agent was Julie Markowitz.

Sandy went with Red Jr. back to the office to write up her offer for the condo. Pastor and Charlie went inside the Café where they were led to a booth. Both ordered coffee.

"That's very interesting." Charlie said. "Ted listed both properties. That gave him access and knowledge of the Kingsley house. And since there was no lock box on the door, Julie would have had to pick up a key from him to show the house. Which means he would have known Julie would be there."

"As Chief Watson would say, 'That gives him means, motive, and opportunity'." Pastor added. "But how are we going to prove it?"

"If he killed her, that means he also stole Bud's shoes. No one has found them yet, so he must still have them."

"You don't think he's thrown them away?"

"I hope not. Even if his fingerprints are matched to the ones in the house, he could easily explain it. We need some hard evidence before we can tell the Chief."

"Right now, you need to run me home. I have to check on Jack and make dinner."

Charlie dropped Pastor off, then went home to have dinner herself. Since Judge Hartley had ordered her to live with Paula, life had changed in every way, including what she ate. Charlie had grown up on fast food, pizza, and easy-to-fix fried foods, with a lot of hamburgers, hot dogs, pork and beans, frosted flakes, and cheap cuts of meat. Paula's table was filled with vegetables, fresh fish, and high-end meats. Things were not just thrown together. If Paula had a hobby, it was cooking. She planned her week's menu on Wednesday. Thursday evening she went to the store. Friday night and Saturday were for trying new dishes she found on tv cooking shows, like Pati's Mexican Table, Lidia's Italy, and Julia Child. Charlie usually watched and helped on Friday. On Saturday Paula would sleep in and then have coffee, yogurt with fruit or granola and just lounge around. Charlie was up at 6:00, her usual time, and either worked out in Paula's home gym or went for a run. Then it was a big breakfast-eggs with sausage or bacon. Her personal favorite was a pork chop with a muffin and a big glass of milk. Usually for lunch it became Paula's Cooking Class. Charlie really enjoyed it.

Paula was a good teacher. She was patient and forgiving when Charlie made a mistake. Charlie also liked learning about new foods. Some she liked right away, like stuffed flounder, and others would take getting used to. Lots of them used ingredients and spices Charlie had never heard of, let alone eaten. Like saffron, which she learned came from a flower and was very expensive. Sage, rosemary, and thyme, she had heard of them in a song, but had never tasted. Also, cooking with wine was totally new to her. Her uncle Paul cooked the fish he caught with a beer batter. He used a little for the batter-and a lot for Paul. Which usually resulted in the fish being burnt. Tonight was Charlie's debut at cooking supper. She had helped Paula twice make stuffed flounder from a recipe Paula had seen on Chio Italia with Mary Ann Esposito. She got the recipe card from the file, looked it over, then organized all the ingredients and cooking utensils needed. She took a deep breath and started. Something she'd heard one of her aunts say came into her mind. "If at first you don't succeed, fry, fry, the hen."

This was her first time alone.

"Well Father, we don't have any chicken so this better work. You know all about cooking fish, so please help."

From Mary Ann Esposito

Ingredients

1 lb. fresh spinach, well washed

1 medium carrot, scraped and shredded

1 tablespoon grated ginger

5 tablespoons butter, melted

4 flounder fillets, each weighing 5 to 6 ounces

Salt and pepper to taste

Directions
1. Preheat the oven to 400 degrees
    a. Cook the spinach, covered, without any additional water, just until the leaves wilt. Drain and squeeze dry. Coarsely chop and place in a bowl. Cook the carrots with the ginger in 2 tablespoons of the butter until the carrots begin to wilt. Transfer them to the bowl with the spinach. Season with salt and pepper.
    b. Divide and spread the mixture on top of the fish. Starting at the short end, roll each fillet up like a jellyroll.
    c. Brush a casserole dish with 1 tablespoon of the remaining butter. Add the fillets and drizzle the tops with the remaining butter.
    d. Bake for 20 to 25 minutes or until the fish turns white and is easily flaked with a fork. Serve hot.

Dinner had turned out... mostly ok. The fish was fine but the rice was a little sticky. And the steamed broccoli, Glenda said, could have cooked a little longer. But, all in all, not bad she thought.

Right after supper they went to the grocery store. Paula always shopped from a list, right down to what flavor of yogurt she would get. She also shopped with purpose. Being very familiar with the store, her list was laid out in the order she would find it. Occasionally, Charlie would ask if she could get something she saw as she was walking past. Paula never said no, but Charlie could tell it would've been better to mention it while they were making out the list. After they got home and the groceries were put away, they watched a cooking show Paula had taped. When it was over, Paula got her briefcase and began working on some legal case she was involved in. Charlie went upstairs, worked out a little with the weights, took an early shower, and went to the library to read. Just after eight, she went downstairs to get a snack. She was eating the last piece of tonight's fish when she heard Paula's phone ring. She wasn't trying to listen in, but it was easy to overhear what Paula was saying. Right after she hung up, Paula went to the stairs and yelled, "I'm going out for a while. Not sure when I'll be back." And then she heard the back door shut.

Charlie sat there thinking. She was sure Steph was Stephanie, Bud's secretary. And the money had to refer to the farm sale or perhaps a large life insurance policy. And Paula, if not already their lawyer, she would be now. She was even more sure Bud and Stephanie were innocent. It was clear Paula knew her or she would have called her Stephanie, or Ms. So, and So. Charlie wondered what her last name was. Maybe that would help. It was also apparent they'd talked about the murder before. Charlie went to bed at ten, still unable to figure out how to prove Ted killed Julie Markowitz. Her last thought before she fell asleep was what she should say to Paula in the morning.

AUGUST 9 5:30 PM
OAK RIVER POLICE STATION

Leon left and Jerry leaned back in his chair. He was sure Bud had no idea what was going on. He felt sorry for him. He wondered if Julie's partner in all this was as clueless as Bud. No, he would be a lot smarter than that.

AUGUST 9 THURSDAY 6:00 PM
MARKOWITZ REALITY OFFICE

Markowitz Realty was on the corner of Main and third street. It started life as a barbershop built in 1928. It was frame construction with a nearly flat roof. It sat back on a large lot with parking in front, there was a large electric sign with the company's name on top. The sign would flash pictures of homes for sale. Besides the new sign, the building had a new brick veneer all the way around, with new windows and a new roof.

As you entered the building, Bud's office was on the left and Julie's on the right. Directly ahead was a desk for Stephanie, the office receptionist/ secretary.

When Bud returned to the office, Stephanie was hanging up from a phone call.

"That was another one of Julie's clients wanting to know if we were still open. I told him we would be taking office visits starting next Wednesday. He made an appointment for two that afternoon."

"Thanks, I want to talk to you about some of my wife's sales."

She followed him into his office.

"Just take a seat Steph, this could take some time."

"Yes sir."

"What can you tell me about the Hoffman Farm sale a few months ago?"

"Do you want me to get you the file?"

"Yes, and also the file on the sale of our house and the real-estate business. Oh, also everything you have for Ag- Adventures."

"You know about that?"

"Yes. I found out from the Chief of Police. Everyone but me seems to know what is going on in my office."

"She told me I would be fired if I said anything. Most of those files are locked up in her desk. I only saw some of it by mistake. Are you going to fire me?"

"Do you know where the key is to her file drawer?"

"She always kept it on her."

"You get what you can. I'll be right back."

Bud went to his car and came back in with the tire iron.

"Which drawer is it?"

"The big one on the right."

He tried to 'jam' the tire iron into the top of the drawer, but missed. He tried twice more unsuccessfully.

"Would you like me to try?"

Bud stood back and handed her the tool. She got it on the first try.

"Figures"

"Don't put yourself down Mr. Markowitz. I play softball and I've had a lot of practice swinging a bat."

Bud began taking out files and putting them on the desk. There were over twenty. When they were all out, he was surprised to find a hand gun in back. He left it there.

"Did you know about this?" he asked.

"Noo, I've never seen it."

He shut the drawer and picked up some of the files.

"You get the rest and come back to my office."

When he had all the files he said, "Make sure the closed sign is on the front door and lock it. Then turn the phones over. I don't want us to be disturbed."

When she returned, he was arranging the files.

"It looks like my wife was running a separate office of her own."

It took them almost two hours to go through all the files.

"Do you know where the banking is for all of this?"

"It's all on her computer. But it's locked out."

"Do you know how to get in?"

"Yes, but I never did."

They both went back to his wife's desk.

"Show me what's in there." Stephanie sat down, turned on the computer and worked her way in, until she came to Julie's private file. She entered the password. Y78O25U37.

"How did you get this again?"

"I saw her type it in one day. I have a photographic memory. Plus I'm kind of anal I have the numbers on the phone memorized with the letters. I almost laughed out loud when I saw it. The letters spell 'you', and the numbers spell 'sucker'." She put her hand over her mouth. "I'm sure she didn't mean you Sir."

"Yes, she did." The file opened. Most of the money was in a bank in Australia–$4,399,514.74.

"I don't believe it." Bud said."

"That's Australian dollars in, US dollars it's less." She got out her phone and quickly had another number. $2,784,503.00.

"That's still a lot of money. Are there any other accounts?"

"Yes. There's one in a Swiss bank." Stephanie punched another key. "1,088,000. Swiss francs. "It's a little bit higher than the dollar. Do you want me to convert it?"

"No. Is there any more?"

"There's the business account and her personal account here.

"How much is in those?"

"The business account has," she switched files, "$8,533.92. Her personal account has $36,092.56."

"How much is the total?"

Stephanie picked up her phone again and did some quick figuring.

"$3,828,983.00 over seas, $44,626.46 here in town grand total is $3,873,609.46."

Bud was getting more upset with the ever-increasing amount.

"How much is she getting for the house and business again?"

"The house sold for $252,000.00. After the mortgage and other expenses, you will get $182,099.61. The business, including the building, sold for$199,000.00 net proceeds. There's no mortgage so you will get all of it except closing costs which are," she checked the papers. "$1,980.79."

Bud sat back in the chair and looked up at the ceiling.

"What am I going to do?" He said mostly to himself.

"I think you should give the two million she scammed from Stanley Granger back to him and move all the rest into a new account in your name. Let the sale of the house and business go through and move to Australia with mee…"

Stephanie realized she had said way too much.

"I'm sorry I…"

Bud sat there and thought for some time. Finally, Stephanie said.

"I was way out of line. I can go if you like?"

"Where would we go in Australia? Have you ever been there?"

She was suddenly cautious.

"No. I don't want to give the wrong impression. I don't…I didn't mean aaa… I thought we could move there and start a new business. You will have the capital."

"I never understood why you worked here." Bud said. "You are much smarter than Julie or I. You have an MBA, right?"

"I just thought … well … we, you could start all over.

Just then there was a loud knock on the door. Startled they both looked to the front of the office, then at each other. The knock returned, followed by a voice.

"This is Chief Watson. I know you're in there. Your cars are both in the parking lot. I would...."

Just then Bud opened the door.

"Thanks. I just had a couple more questions. Is it Ok if I come in?"

Bud moved to one side and opened the door all the way. The first thing Jerry saw was Stephanie standing in the doorway to an office. She'd quickly closed the file and had gotten up to join Bud.

As Jerry walked in, he said, "I hope I'm not interrupting a meeting. Mind if I have a look around? I've never been here before. This is very nice. Did you do the decorating?

"No, Julie picked it out."

Walking on in he asked Stephanie,

"You must be Bud and Julie's secretary."

"Mostly I answer the phone. More like a receptionist."

"Is this your office?"

"No. My desk is over there." she said, pointing to a desk in the center.

"Whose office is this?" He walked around Stephanie and noticed the tire iron and the pried open drawer. "Have you had a burglary? I hope you didn't touch anything. We will want to get fingerprints."

Bud came over, picked up the tire iron from the floor, and set it on the desk.

218

"This is my wife's office. After what you told me at the police station, I thought it would be wise to check into some of my wife's files. As you can see, she kept it locked and I don't have a key. So I had to break in myself. Stephanie has been helping me sort things out. You were right. Julie was doing a number of things I wasn't aware of. If you want you may take a seat and we will show you what we have found."

Jerry sat in the chair Bud was using while he pulled another one around.

"Who exactly opened the drawer?"

"I did." Stephanie said.

"I see."

Bud went to his office and returned with the files.

For the next twenty minutes, Stephanie gave a run-down on what they'd discovered, except for the bank accounts. When she finished, Jerry pushed his chair back and looked at both of them, sure they were hiding something.

"Could you tell me where you were last Tuesday between one and two pm?" he asked Stephanie.

"I was here in the office."

"Was anyone with you? Or maybe you talked to someone on the office phone during that time?"

"I don't remember. There were a few calls, but I don't know what times they were."

The Chief pulled a notebook from his pocket. "I checked. There was one call at 12:05. It wasn't answered. The same number called back at 2:13. You talked for one minute, forty-six seconds. Could either of you tell me where the money from the sale of the farm is? That's a lot of money and it's not in any of your accounts in town."

Bud answered, "We are trying to find out ourselves. When we do, I'll let you know. I haven't had time to talk to my wife's other partner yet."

"I talked to him. His name is Jerry Gold. He lives at 10344 Rock Circle, Cedar Falls. He told me they split the money right away, fifty-fifty. Leon is on his way now to meet with him and get a copy of his files pertaining to the sale. Is there anything you want to share with me?"

They both shook their heads 'no'.

"Don't either of you leave town for a few days. If you find out anymore let me know."

"We will." Bud said.

"I'll give you some advice. Don't either of you play poker. You'll lose. I'll see myself out." Jerry stood to leave. "It would be best to have the rest for me by noon tomorrow."

He left the office and a moment later they heard the front door close.

Bud started to say something but Stephanie put up her hand.

"Before you say anything, I did not kill her. I was here in the office just like I said." Bud started to speak again. "Let me finish. I didn't like the way Julie treated you, giving you no respect, doing deals behind your back. But I could not, did not, kill her."

"I believe you. I was going to ask you what you think we should do now. He knows we know where the money is. He asked me if I hired it done. Now he is wondering if you and I planned it together. I'm sure if we don't tell him everything, he will arrest us both for murder.

"Tomorrow morning, I think we need to see him and show where the money is. Then he will know we didn't have access to it."

"No, I think it's time to get a lawyer."

"The only lawyer I know is the one who handles things for the office, I don't know a criminal lawyer."

"If you want, I can call Paula Collins."

"Does she handle criminal law?"

"Yes. And she is very well respected. She even speaks at conferences."

Bud thought for a moment. "Yes, call her."

"I'll put her on speaker phone so we can both be in the conversation."

Stephanie took out her phone and dialed

"Steph, how are you doing? Have you found out any-more? Have the police talked to you yet?"

"You're on speaker phone Paula. I'm at the office, Bud Markowitz is here. The Police Chief just left. I'm sure he thinks we planned it together, and is trying to find enough evidence to charge us."

"We would like to meet with you as soon as possible." Bud said. "We are not very good at evading questions. We told him the truth, but left out the financial details. He knows we didn't tell him everything. He gave us until noon tomorrow. Then it sounded like he would bring both of us in for questioning, then arrest us."

"I don't have an alibi for the time of the murder." Stephanie said. "I'm sure he thinks I killed her, and that we are involved with each other, and going to take the money and run."

"How much money are we talking about?"

"Several million."

"I'll be right over."

Paula listened as they explained everything.

"I am going to ask some questions you probably won't like. But I need you to be honest and candid. It will be much better to face them here for the first time, rather than down at the police station."

They both shook their head yes. "Did either of you know about what she was doing and how much money was involved?"

Bud said, "no". Stephanie said, "I didn't know exact amounts but I knew there was a lot of money involved."

"Are you two romantically involved?"

They both said, "no."

"Jerry is going to try very hard to connect you two. If there is even a rumor floating around out there and he finds it, well, I need both of you to think carefully. For example, how often did you eat lunch together without Julie?"

"Once in a while, but we work together. Isn't it normal for coworkers to eat together sometimes?" Bud responded.

"How often Steph?"

"Two or three times a week, usually at the Oak River Café."

"Do you sit in a booth or at a table?"

"A booth."

"Do you have feelings for Bud?"

She did not answer right away.

"You're hesitating. They will assume the answer is yes. We need the truth here."

"Yes, I am very fond of Bud." She looked over at him her eyes getting red. "I have never done or said anything to let him know."

"Bud, did you know? I need the truth. If you lie, he will know."

"Yes, I know he will. And yes, I knew, or suspected."

"How do you feel about her?"

"I am, or I was, a married man. Unlike my wife I took my vows very seriously."

"I'm not asking if you had an affair. But Jerry will, and he will push the point. Your wife was unfaithful. She was dishonest. You were sued twice over her business deals. And this farm sale is fraud, but no way to prove it without a witness or something in writing. Even so, I'm surprised you weren't sued over it. Four million is a lot to cheat someone out of. On the plus side it is also a good motive for murder. If you want, I can have a private detective look into the buyer."

"How much will that cost?"

"Not as much as going to prison will, if you're convicted."

"Neither of us did it."

"Let me ask you another question. What size shoe do you wear?"

"A ten."

"Do you have a pair of wingtips?"

"I did, but not anymore. They disappeared about a week ago. Why?"

"Because shoe prints were found at the murder scene, from a size ten, Florsheim wingtip. Let me see your shoes."

Bud bent over and took them off and handed them to her. She turned them over and looked at the heels. The left one was worn down on the outside."

"That ankle was hurt playing baseball in school. I'm supposed to wear inserts to keep it straight. But I don't."

"Have you looked for the shoes?"

"Yes. They were in the back seat of my car. I was going to take them and have the heel fixed. It's much worse than these. But they were gone."

"It looks to me like someone took your shoes and wore them to kill your wife. They also left a very distinct print in a flower bed, hoping it would be discovered. You were set up. Now, let me tell you how it looks to the police. Your wife cheated on you, not very subtly, and was planning to run out on you. The two of you are having an affair."

"We did not have an affair!" Bud said.

"It will look like it to them. Stephanie has no alibi, while yours is rock solid. There's enough money involved to kill a dozen people.

"As soon as you admit your feelings for each other... and they will get it out of you... There is means, motive and opportunity. I think he will arrest both of you for the murder of your wife."

"You have us convicted." Stephanie said. "How do we prove we are innocent?"

"The best defense we can use is to find out who really killed her."

"Isn't that the police's job?"

"Once they charge you, they're not going to put a lot of effort into finding someone else. I will get a detective on this right away. I would advise you to put all these files and the computer in the safest place you can. Preferably an actual safe off premise."

"I don't have a safe. We don't even have a security system, here or at home."

"I'll take them with me if you want. I have a quality safe at the office and state of the art security. I'll give you a receipt. Steph can make out a list and I'll sign it."

"Do you really think this is necessary?" Bud asked.

"Someone already stole your shoes, and used them to commit murder. They knew where your wife was and had access to the house. Yes. I think it's a good idea. And see if you can find those shoes. They're going to turn up somewhere to incriminate you."

The three of them carried everything out to Paula's car. After she left a silver SUV parked half a block down the street followed her. She drove to her office, parked and began carrying everything in. When she went back for the second load there was a man standing there holding the computer.

"I thought you could use some help."

It was Chief of Police, Jerry Watson.

"That's personal property I'll take that."

Jerry handed it over.

"Yes, it is. It belongs to Bud Markowitz. What are you doing with it?"

She headed back into her office. Jerry picked up the rest of the files, shut the

trunk and followed her in.

"Is all this from a new client?"

"Yes, and everything we talked about is privileged information."

"You don't have to talk. Just listen. I'm sure they told you I was there right before you. They probably called you as soon as I left. I've seen everything you just brought in except where all the money is. Julie was quite a piece of work. She probably has it in some offshore account."

After putting everything in the safe, Paula locked it and sat down at her desk.

"Take a seat, I'm listening."

"They have the means, motive running out their ears, and opportunity. My mother could lie better than the two of them. She's sweet on him and he's too dense to see it. Look, I don't think they did it, but you can see how it looks. I asked them to come into the office by noon tomorrow and give me what they're withholding. As soon as I get them there, they will call you. You'll come over and that will be that. I'll have to charge them. I'll tell the judge about all the money sitting offshore. He will deny bail. They will go to trial and probably be convicted."

"I'm a better lawyer than that. They're innocent and I'll prove it."

"Have you called that PI of yours? What's his name, Mike Gargoyle or something?"

"You know very well his name is Michael Griffin."

"Look, I want to get home, have some supper, watch tv and forget about this mess for a while. If I tell you to tell your clients not to come in tomorrow, I won't have to arrest them, etc, etc."

"And what do you want from us?"

"I want you to grill them like I would. Get them to cough up everything. Get them to tell you things they don't even know they know. And another thing, I want that shoe. It's going to turn up somewhere. I was thinking your detective could get right over and put some cameras around their office, house and even bug their cars. If we're really lucky, we might get a picture of him returning the shoe. Whoever did this has a lot of inside information. They knew where Julie would be, probably had a key to the house, and was familiar with it. I think that footprint was carefully put down in the neighbor's garden so we could get the print. They wanted two for the price of one: kill the wife and let the state take care of the other one. You don't need to compromise your client to turn over to me anything you come across that would point to someone else."

"How long are you willing to give us. It's not unending."

"No, it's not. Let's start with seventy-two hours."

"Seventy- two hours. We'll take it."

Jerry left for home. Paula called Michael Griffin.

"How can I help you?"

Paula laid it all out. "When can we have the cameras?"

"I can have a man there in less than an hour."

"Good I also want tails on both of my clients, round the clock. Can you do that?"

"That's a lot of money. For how long?"

"As soon as possible, plan on three days."

"You suspect your own clients?"

"Let's call it client protection. Someone killed the wife and set the husband up to take the fall. If they see he's not going to be charged, there's a chance they might try to finish the job themselves."

"We're on it."

"Oh, I forgot. Also check on Stanley Granger. He bought the farm, and was cheated out of four million dollars. And Jerry Gold. Apparently he was involved with Julie Markowitz, our victim, in a company called AG-Adventures." Michael added this to his notes.

"I should have all the rundown on these people by noon tomorrow. And I'll have a tail on everyone before midnight."

"That sounds great. Talk to you later."

AUGUST 9 THURSDAY LATE
PAULA'S BEDROOM

Paula almost jumped out of bed! She had been asleep only about an hour when her phone rang.

"This is Michael Griffin."

"Yes. Good morning, or whatever it is."

"You sound wide awake."

"Thanks, what's going on?"

"You can check Jerry Gold off your list. I just got a call. The man I sent over arrived the same time as the police. Jerry was shot walking up to his front door. The neighbors thought it was someone setting off fire crackers. The killer emptied eleven rounds into his back. If nothing else, the killer is passionate about his work."

"Thanks, I'll pass it on to the police here in town. Do you have someone covering Bud and Stephanie?"

"We have Bud covered. He's at home sleeping. Stephanie, we haven't found yet, she hasn't come home. I'll keep my man there."

"Let me know as soon as you find her."

"Under the circumstances, I would like to double up on both of them."

"I agree. Were there any witnesses?"

"No. Some guy out walking his dog found him a couple of minutes after the shots, but he didn't see anything. He was around the corner when the shots were fired."

"I'm going back to sleep now."

"Good night."

CHAPTER NINE
AUGUST 10, FRIDAY 2:30 AM
PARSONAGE JACK'S ROOM

Jack was in his wheelchair in the back of the church. He could feel his anxiety begin to build as the sermon was ending and the piano player took his place playing softly. Swiveling his wheelchair, he headed toward the back door. The usher opened it, and Jack rolled out. As the door closed behind him, he moved on down the foyer. Passing the reception desk, he saw Charlie sitting on a bench.

"I can't do it." he said.

"Do what?"

"Surrender."

"You're being lied to you know."

"You mean Pastor is lying?"

"No. The voice in your head is lying to you. It's telling you, you're better off being in charge of your life rather than letting God be in charge."

"That's surrender."

"But it's not the truth. You are not better off. For one thing you know you are a sinner and you know you will go to Hell if you die the way you are."

The scene faded into smoke when the smoke cleared he was back in Montana watching the man on the motorcycle circle around and come back straight for him. Then he saw Charlie pick up a pistol from the ground. She stood up and walked toward him. stopping in front of him, protecting him. He heard the sound of her pistol, saw the man tumble off the back of the motorcycle, his gun firing as he fell... his last round striking Charlie. She fell back into his lap. He looked down and saw blood starting to stain her shirt. And then their eyes met. Jack sat up in bed, a cold sweat covered his body. He looked at the clock. It was 2:30 Friday morning. The dreams were getting closer together. At first it was only Sunday nights. Now it was almost every night. His father's killers were behind bars and would be in prison for life. He had set up a generous scholarship for Charlie, quit making fun of Bill, and even started calling him Pastor. Why was he still having these nightmares? He decided it was all the stress that was causing his feelings of guilt.

He laid his head back down and thought about where he would go from here. Today he would get both casts off and life would begin returning to normal. Only in his new normal he would have money. His substantial inheritance, plus the payoff for the tavern fire. Yes, life would be very different. Jack shut his eyes and drifted back to sleep.

AUGUST 10 FRIDAY MORNING, PAULA'S BATHROOM

Paula had just stepped out of the shower when her phone rang.

"This is Michael. Stephanie just showed up at home. We put a tracker on her car."

"Any more information on Jerry Gold's murder?"

"Not yet. I'll text when I have something."

Paula finished getting ready and went downstairs for breakfast. She had just sat down with her coffee and yogurt when Charlie came in from her run. Instead of going upstairs to shower, she came in and sat down across from Paula.

"You look like you have something on your mind, want to share?"

Charlie hesitated then spoke.

"Yes, I know who killed Julie."

Paula stopped stirring her yogurt.

"You think you know, or you can prove it."

Charlie hesitated again.

"He has means, motive, and opportunity. I don't think anyone suspects him. He's off everyone's radar."

"So, you don't have proof."

More hesitating. Charlie could tell by the tone of her voice she had made a mistake.

"No."

"This person is very dangerous. You need to leave it to the police. That's what they get paid to do. Don't go getting into trouble. If you have any information you should tell Leon, he's working the case. He can check it out."

"You're right. It's just a hunch, I guess. It's hard not to think about it. I've got to get ready I work 10 till 2 today. Do you want to go to the fair tomorrow? I was scheduled to work but there was a mix-up, so I'm off."

Charlie knew she would say no. She just wanted to change the subject.

"No, I have a case I'm working on. Why don't you call Chris or Jen. They might want to go? I think Jack is getting his cast off today, maybe you could all go."

"Thanks. That's a good idea."

Charlie got up and ran up the stairs, then got in the shower. She let the hot water run over her relieving the tension, and at the same time reminding herself how tired she was. The dream had come back in the night, and she was up for three hours reading the Word and praying before she could go back to sleep. "Well Lord, that didn't go like I thought it would. What should I do now?"

Nothing came to her. She finished showering, dried her hair, and dressed, then went down and made her breakfast. Paula had already left for work. After she finished eating, she got out her notebook and looked through it. There was a list of names, each one with a check in front of it, except Ted Wise.

John and Willie, ridiculous.

Sharrie and Kelly, Just as ridiculous.

Bud Markowitz – husband solid alibi.

Stephanie? no alibi Paula thinks she is innocent. So do I.

Mrs. Kingsley family.

Ed, no children, Seattle.

Tim, 2 children, Lincoln.

Robin, never married, Iowa city.

All no known motive. Highly unlikely.

Stanley Granger bought the farm, paid too much. Motive-Cheated out of 4 mil. Solid alibi. On vacation, Alaska cruise with family.

Jerry Gold. Julie's partner in fraud. Maybe but I don't think so. Check out alibi.

Ted Wise. Motive: (money) cheated out of the Hoffman farm listing. Opportunity: listed house has key, would have known Julie would be there. Means: iron pipe left at scene of crime.

She wrote at the bottom. HOW CAN I GET PROOF? Then she headed over to the parsonage to ask Jack if he would go to the State Fair tomorrow.

AUGUST 10 FRIDAY 7:00 AM
PARSONAGE JACK'S ROOM

It seemed like only a few minutes when Pastor was shaking his shoulder.

"Time to get up, if you want a shower before we go to the doctor and get those casts off."

"Let's get it done. This should be the last time I need your help."

235

At nine o'clock Jack was sitting in Doctor Rubin's office, his casts laying on the floor. The nurse moved a walker in front of him.

"Let's see if you can stand." He said.

Jack grabbed the arms of his chair and stood not expecting any problem. An instant later, to his embarrassment, he slumped back in the chair.

"Let's try again." The nurse said.

This time she held the walker and, with Pastor on one side and Dr. Rubin on the other, Jack stood up again. It went much better. He took a step, then two. His left leg was much weaker than he expected. But he walked five steps then turned around and five steps back, turned and sat back down.

"That's pretty good. Your strength should come back quickly. We can set you up with a therapist at Belknap Care Center if you like."

"No thanks. I'll be fine on my own." Having rested a minute, he stood, this time on his own. He was a little shaky, but he made it. He walked three steps over to his wheelchair, turned again and sat down. It was not a soft landing.

"Let's go Pastor." Jack said.

As the nurse handed Pastor some papers to take to check out, Jack was already

going out the open door.

When they were back in the van Jack said, "I guess it'll be a few days before I can move out."

"Have you decided what you're going to do?"

"I'm going to rent my dad's house from my sister, at least for a while. I appreciate the church pitching in to get it cleaned up after the killers ransacked it.

My sister is looking for a house to buy, now that she can afford one. She doesn't want to live in Dad's house. Neither one of us do, really. It will go on the market soon."

"What about your dad's tavern? I suppose you're going to rebuild it."

"No, I won't be staying in Oak River long, and I am not the business owner type. Don and Gloria already have new jobs at the Dew Drop Inn down town. It will be a boon to their business, most of the customers have already followed them there."

"Chris told me you were offered a job at the Ford dealership. Are you going to take it.?"

"No. Now that I can afford it, I might go to college. Although I'm not sure what I would take. I guess I don't know what I want to be when I grow up. I do know, I am going to take a vacation, somewhere people aren't shooting at me."

"Like in Montana?"

Jack didn't like the reminder about Montana.

"No, like Iraq! I'm thinking, Hawaii and the South Pacific, then maybe Australia. Some place without winter, with lots of sun and sand."

Pastor pulled into the drive and unloaded Jack and they went into the parsonage.

"You going to be alright? Pastor asked. I need to go over to my office for a little bit. Be back in time to make lunch."

"I'll be fine. Time to start my rehab. Do you think Nate would come over and help me with some exercises?"

"I think he would like the chance to get out of the house for a while."

"Could you give me his number? I'll give him a call."

Pastor looked up the number and then headed over to the church office.

Nate was glad to come over, said he could be there Monday morning.

Jack started practicing standing and sitting. Then he took a short walk over to the fridge opened it, got a Coke and headed to the table.

Trying to use the walker and hold the can at the same time was too much. He dropped it. As he was wondering how he was going to pick it up, Charlie pulled in the drive. He waited for her to come in.

"Look at you. You're walking!" Charlie exclaimed.

"If you can call this walking."

Seeing his predicament, she picked up the can.

"I think I'll get you a different one. It's better than having the casts on and being in a wheelchair isn't it?"

"You're right there." Jack finished walking over to the table and sat down.

"How would you like to go to the State Fair tomorrow? The weather's going to be nice, no rain. It'll give both of us a chance to get out of town for the day."

"I don't think I'm quite ready for an all-day walk yet."

"We can take your wheelchair. You can use it as a walker and I can push you when you need a ride. It'll be great therapy. What do you say?"

"I thought you were working at the Dairy Queen."

"I am, but they messed up on the schedule and had too many for tomorrow. They said I could have the day off. Come on. What else are you going to do, sit here alone and play with your walker all day?"

Jack was hesitating with an answer.

"Come on! I've saved my own money and I am dying to spend some of it. You're not afraid of being seen in your wheelchair, are you?"

The wheelchair was still embarrassing, but the real reason was, every time he saw Charlie, his mind went back to the incident in Montana. He had been avoiding her as much as possible since they had got back. "Kill or cure, he thought", maybe I'll get it out of my system, and the nightmares will stop.

"I'll go, when do you want to leave?"

"Seven in the morning."

"Nine."

"Eight."

"It takes me longer to get ready than you. I'll see you at nine."

"Ok nine, I'll be here. I got to go to work. See you in the morning."

AUGUST 10 FRIDAY MORNING
LESTER'S FARM

Lester helped Jacob with his trunk so it would open and close until he could get it properly fixed.

"Don't worry about the trunk. Between them they were carrying just under seven thousand dollars. I guess they weren't big on using credit cards, at least not their own I found three that didn't belong to them."

Afterward they took the fossils back to the lab and worked on them some more.

"As hard as it is to believe," Lester said, "these are the real deal. When we put them together with what's back in Montana, it will rock the paleo world. My men are expert diggers. We can have it all in your lab in Bozeman in less than two weeks. At least one of you needs to be on-site to supervise."

"I used your phone this morning and called the University. I am now on a sabbatical." Dr. Bullock said.

"I haven't called yet, but I will be there also," Glenda added. "One way or another."

They quit in time to load the fossils into Jacob's car and the two of them left, planning to get lunch in town before going to the sheriff's office.

Lester stayed behind making sure all the security was set. It was past time for him to leave when two men drove up and got out of their car. Red went over and gave both a warm greeting.

"How long this time?" they asked.

"I'm not sure but, plan on an extended stay. You'll need to call in some more help."

He explained what had happened. Just before Lester left to go to town, he made one last call, to his team at the site. They were now firmly in control.

Lester was the last one to arrive at the sheriff's office. He was nearly a half hour late. They took him back to a meeting room where Glenda and Jacob were already telling someone their version of what happened last night. The three of them had spent some time last night trying to decide what to tell, minus any mention of the barn or the fossils.

AUGUST 10 FRIDAY
PAULA'S KITCHEN

Paula had just finished breakfast when Chief Watson called.

"We need to talk." He said as soon as she answered the phone.

"Ok." she answered, "Has something happened?"

"You probably already know. Jerry Gold was shot to death last night outside his home. I need some questions answered. Number one. There was a 9 mm hand gun in your client's desk. Is it still there? Two, where were they last night between 10 and 12?"

"I don't know about the handgun. I haven't seen it. Bud was home all night. Stephanie arrived home about twenty-five minutes ago. I have no idea where she was last night."

"I'm getting a lot of pressure to make an arrest."

"We have a deal." Paula said before he could continue.

"I know. I'm going over to Markowitz Reality. I want you to meet me there with both your clients as soon as possible." Jerry hung up before she could say anymore.

Paula grabbed her things and headed out the door.

Jerry was there in less than ten minutes driving his personal car, without his uniform. He checked all the doors and windows. They were all locked, with no signs of a break in. He was standing by the back door when Bud pulled in, followed closely by Paula.

"I would like to wait for Stephanie before we go in."

It was ten more minutes before she arrived, looking every bit like someone who had slept in her car.

Bud unlocked the door and Jerry led the way in.

"You two stand here, Paula and I will take a look around."

The first place he went was to Julie's desk. The drawer was still open but the pistol was gone. Paula followed as he finished taking a survey of the office. Nothing else looked disturbed. He went back to where Bud and Stephanie were standing.

"Ok. Did either of you take the handgun that was in that drawer yesterday?"

They both answered no. Jerry motioned for Paula to follow him, moving far enough away they couldn't be overheard.

"This is getting really tough." Jerry said, looking out the window. "Those two cars parked down the street, do you know who might be in them?"

"I might."

"Darn it, Paula! The mayor is on my butt, and today's morning paper is questioning my competence, and the safety of the community. How tight do you have them covered? Are they covered? No, I don't want to know. I hope she has an alibi, and it needs to be rock-solid, or I am going to have to take her in".

"You promised us 72 hours."

"That was before there was another body. And Stephanie looks like she was out all night, not to mention the possible murder weapon is missing. I'm going out to my car and give you ten minutes to clear her of all possibility she killed Jerry Gold or I'm going to arrest her on suspicion of first-degree murder."

Jerry left, walking past Bud and Stephanie without saying a word.

Eight minutes later Stephanie came out followed by Paula. Bud stayed at the door watching.

Stephanie held out her hands.

"Paula said you want to arrest me on suspicion of murder."

Jerry handcuffed her, read her her rights, and put her in the back seat of his SUV. When he pulled out of the parking lot, one of the cars down the street pulled out and followed him. After he turned the corner and headed down Main St., another car parked on the other side of the street did a U-turn and joined the parade, with Paula bringing up the rear.

As soon as Stephanie was processed, they all met together in the conference room in back. Stephanie and Paula were sitting on one side, the Chief and Leon on the other.

"Just to bring everyone up to speed." the Chief said, "There was another murder last night in Cedar Rapids. Jerry Gold was shot in the back eleven times with a nine mm. He was also involved in the sale and resale of the Hoffman Farm. Can you give me any information on what happened to the pistol, and your whereabouts last night between 10pm and midnight?

Stephanie looked over at Paula who shook her head yes.

"I do not know where the gun is. I did not take it, and I am sure Bud didn't either. We both left together, right after Paula, and locked the door."

"Are you sure the door was locked properly when you left, both front and back?"

"Yes, I checked the front door and Bud locked the back. We each got in our own car and left."

"Did you meet anywhere after you left?"

"No. Paula said it wouldn't be good to be seen together. People talk."

"Where did you go after you left the office?"

"I know now I should have gone home, but I panicked. I left town and drove to Waterloo."

"Where did you stay, and when did you return home?"

244

"I know I drove around awhile. Then I found a park. I drove in and took a parking place and tried to sleep in my car. It was not a good night."

"Did you buy gas or food? Something we can trace to show you were there?"

"I didn't need any gas and I couldn't eat. I bought a cup of coffee this morning at a McDonald's on my way home. But I paid cash."

"Why didn't you get a motel room?"

"I don't know, I just wanted to be alone I guess.

"I would like to search your apartment and your car. Do we have your permission, or do I need to get a search warrant?"

She looked over at Paula again. Then gave her permission.

"I'll leave you here with Paula for a few minutes. Then a lady will come and take you to a cell. Let her know if you're hungry and she will get you something to eat."

Jerry and Leon left the room and went to Leon's office.

"I want you to go over everything again. There's something we are missing. Use your imagination. Find someone else who is connected to the sale of that farm." Jerry said.

Leon started at the beginning. He drove up to the Church Camp and questioned John and Willie, then Kelly and Sherrie. Then he went to the farm and talked to Stan Granger, who'd just returned from vacation. All he got was a rehash of the same answers as before. As a last resort he went back to the crime scene, hoping he would see something new. He was standing in the kitchen looking where Julie's body had been when his phone rang.

AUGUST 10 FRIDAY NOON
PARSONAGE

Chris and Jen drove into the parsonage driveway as Pastor was walking up from the church to make lunch. They all entered the parsonage at the same time.

"Wow, sitting at the table in a regular chair!" Jen said, going over and giving her brother a kiss on the forehead.

"How does it feel to have your casts off?" Chris asked.

"I want to see you walk." Jen chimed in.

Jack needed no more encouragement. Grabbing his walker, he stood up and walked over to Jen.

"How's that, Sis?"

"That looks great! How far can you go?"

"Not as far as I would like, but it sure beats using the wheelchair all the time."

"We thought we would see if you two were up for lunch, our treat." Chris said. "Can you get in a car?"

"I'm up for the challenge." Jack responded. But I'll need to take my wheelchair. A man needs to know his limitations. And mine is about twenty steps."

Pastor got the wheelchair and pushed him out to the car. Jack stood up, grabbed the open door, lifted in his left leg, and swung into place. A big smile was on his face. They decided on the Oak River Cafe. There was no wait, Susan took four menus and led them to a table in the corner.

"Did your friends get ahold of you, Pastor Boyd?" she asked, setting the menus down.

"I don't think so. Who was it?"

"He didn't tell me his name. But he sure drives a big fancy car. Everyone that came in noticed. It was old bright red Cadillac convertible."

She went on to describe them. "He asked about you, called you Billy Boyd. I guess he doesn't know you're a pastor."

"That would be my uncle. He's the only one who still calls me Billy. Did he say where he was staying?

"No, but they were not getting along. She was crying and it looked like they were having an argument."

"Thanks for letting me know. When did he come in?

"Yesterday mid-morning."

"I'll be looking out for him."

After Susan left with their drink orders, Pastor asked,

"What is everyone hungry for today.? I think I'll get the special, fried chicken."

Jen and Chris both wanted shrimp salad. Jack said he was getting a double cheeseburger and fries.

Not one to let a question hang in the air, Jack asked, "So, who's this uncle of yours, long hair, ponytail, and a classic Caddy? Sounds like someone I'd like to meet."

Everyone was all smiles and eager to hear the story.

"The last time I saw Uncle Jacob was at my dad's funeral a little over ten years ago. I've probably only seen him half a dozen times, all at someone's funeral. The car is a red 1959 Cadillac Eldorado convertible that he keeps just like it came off the showroom floor. He also has a red 1966 Jaguar XKE and, I believe, a 1953 Mercedes-Benz convertible, also bright red. He's never been married, except to his cars and his work. He's a Professor of paleontology at the University of Chicago. If he is here, it's either a new fossil discovery or has to do with one of his cars. I could check with Rob at City Auto, they have a reputation far beyond Oak River. Neither of which seem very likely. But he didn't come here just to say hi. He must want something."

"If he hasn't contacted you by now, maybe he just kept going." Jen said.

"I'm surprised, given your relationship, he even knows you're here. He must have either kept tabs through someone, or made the effort to find you." Jack added.

"If that's true. Why hasn't Pastor Boyd heard from him? That was twenty-four hours ago. Oak River is not that big, and most anyone in town could have given him directions to the church. Also he must have a smart phone. He could just look it up. It just seems strange you haven't heard from him. Maybe he had an accident or something." Chris said.

Their waitress brought over the drinks, and took their orders. While they waited for their food everyone kept asking questions about uncle Jacob.

Lunch was served, and the conversation turned to Julie's murder.

After lunch Chris and Jen went back to work, dropping Pastor and Jack at home on the way.

"If you and Charlie are trying to solve the murder of that lady, I don't think it's a good idea after what happened last time." Jack said, once they were inside.

AUGUST 10 FRIDAY 2:00 PM
DAIRY QUEEN

All the time Charlie was working, her mind kept returning to Ted Wise and what she should do, finally she decided to call the police like Paula had told her. As soon as she was off work, she made the call and asked to speak to Leon.

"Leon is not here. Can I take a message?"

"I have some information on the Julie Markowitz murder."

"Hold on, I'll put you through."

"This is Chief Watson. You have some information for us?"

"I know who did it."

Charlie was cut off.

"Charlie, I told you to leave this alone. This guy is dangerous. Jerry Gold was, shot last night. It was probably the same person. He has a real hate on. This is not a case for you and Boyd. Do you understand?"

"Yes sir."

The phone clicked off. That was the second time today someone had told her it was dangerous. She decided to call Pastor Boyd.

"New Life Church. This is Sandy."

"Hi, Sandy. Is Pastor Boyd available?"

"Only for a minute, we're working on the annual report. I don't want him to lose focus."

"Hi, Charlie. What can I do for you?"

"I thought you were going to do the report next Tuesday."

"So did I, but she caught me in a weak moment. What's up?

"I know who did it... Who killed Julie."

"Jerry just called. He told me there was a second murder, and that this guy is very dangerous. Maybe we should just let them handle it. Give him or Leon the name. They can take it from there."

"Thanks, that's good advice."

Charlie hung up. "Two dangerous and one very dangerous. I guess I should be very careful how I prove he did it. Before he kills someone else." she said to herself.

"Did you say someone else was killed?"

Charlie didn't realize she had spoken out loud.

Charlie looked over. She was sitting at one of the outside tables at work and there was a young woman with two children, just sitting down with their lunch next to her.

"It's just terrible." she went on. "I don't feel safe in my own home anymore. Someone should do something, don't you think?"

"You're right. Someone should."

Charlie got up and went to her car. She sat there in the shade with the top down, occasionally sipping her coke, thinking. She got out her notebook and went down the list again. She was sure she was correct. She called Chris... Ted Wise had never bought a car from them and Chris didn't really know him.

Next, she looked up Wise Insurance and Real-estate, on her I-pad. She made a note of his business address and phone numbers, including cell phone and Fax. Next, using her phone book app. she found his name and wrote down his home address and phone number. Frustrated she couldn't think of anything else to do, she decided to go to Jenny's Beauty Salon, see if she could get in. "You never know." she said to herself, "there is always some truth to gossip. Right?"

Jenny's was busy. All the chairs were full and there was one person waiting. They told Charlie it would be about a half hour. She looked over at the waiting area. Charlie guessed the lady was maybe 40. She had short brown hair, eyes to match, and was wearing shorts, a sleeveless top, and flip-flops. She was reading a woman's magazine. Charlie picked up a copy of the Oak River Star. The headlines read.

JULIE MARKOWITZ MURDER BAFFLES POLICE

Three days after prominent real-estate agent found murdered police have yet to make an arrest.

The lady looked at Charlie, who took advantage of the eye contact to start a conversation. Showing her the headline she said.

"This is the second murder this summer. Someone told me today the killer is very dangerous. I don't feel safe anymore."

The lady put her magazine down.

"I know. We just moved here, right when that other guy was found dead in the cemetery. Imagine being killed next to your wife's grave. I told my husband, Bob, he works at the wind generator factory-maybe he should've taken the job in Omaha. We thought it would be safe and peaceful here, you know a good place to raise our kids."

She continued talking non-stop until they called her name. Charlie hadn't been able to say anything. A few minutes later she saw another lady leave.

"Charlene." Hearing her name called she looked up. She followed the beautician to a chair right in the middle.

"This is your first time here, right? I didn't know your name was Charlene. That's real pretty. I should have known your real name wasn't Charlie." As soon as she said 'Charlie', everyone turned to look at her.

"You're the one who found the body, right?" 'Said' The lady next to her.

Charlie walked out twenty-five minutes later with a shampoo and a trim. Eighteen dollars poorer but a lot wiser. She had learned nothing about Ted Wise, but a lot about gossip, now that she would be the main topic for the next four weeks.

Back in her car, she decided to drive past where Ted lived. It was a newer home on the west side, a nice ranch with a weed free-yard, nicely mowed. There was a flag sticking up next to the sidewalk announcing, Raymond's Lawn Care-Your Complete Lawn Service. There was no landscaping, no children's toys and all the curtains were closed. 'Lifeless' was the word that came to mind. Charlie drove down an extra block turned around and slowly drove back. All of the other houses had some land-scaping and obvious signs of life. Kids out playing or toys left in the driveway. A lot of them had fenced-in yards with a dog lying in the shade. Ted's place stuck out.

AUGUST 10 FRIDAY
SHERIFF'S OFFICE, GROVER IOWA

Finally, they were all finished at the Sheriff's office and allowed to leave. It was almost four o'clock.

"I don't think they believed our stories. Glenda said, "They're not stupid. They know there are missing pieces."

"Just the mass murder in Montana, and the reason we were at Lester's in the first place." Jacob said.

"I've known Jim since he was born." Lester said. "I'm related to his mother. My wife and I used to babysit. I told him I would give him the rest of the story in a week... that it was very sensitive and would only put our lives more at risk. The barn is older than he is. He used to play all over the farm. He knows about the barn, but not what's inside. He's been dying to see the inside since he could walk. I told him I would give him a complete tour and explain why those two broke in, a week from today. Otherwise we'd still be in there, until we told the whole story. He hinted

253

he could get a search warrant. That would not be so easy. I am well acquainted with all the judges, Lodge buddies."

"Is there anyone you don't know?" Glenda asked."

"I am either related to, or know, everyone in the county. My family homesteaded this farm in 1855. I'm the sixth generation to live here. And I'll be the last. My wife and I were never able to have children. Let's go down to the Water Hole. It's just down the street. They have a back room and we need to make a plan."

As they headed down the street Glenda looked around. What she saw was a clean town, made up mostly of brick buildings surrounding a court house.

"If your family has lived here so long how come the town isn't named after you?" she asked.

"It is. Grover is the first name of my third great-grand-father's brother. He donated an acre of ground for the court house to start the town. Don't think he was being generous. He owned the land on all four sides. He started and owned most of the original businesses in town. He was elected mayor, and held the office until he died. His son was sheriff, followed eventually by a great-grandson, Jim's father. Now Jim holds the job. The town is only just over 2000, and the county about 8000. Here's the Watering Hole."

Lester held the door open, then led the way to a back room. It was a bar/ restaurant. The floor looked like they were the original floor boards. The outside walls revealed the original brick. It seemed to Glenda that all the workers had brought in their tools when their trade died out and hung them on the walls. There were old blacksmith tools, old carpenter saws, wooden block planes and hand-held farm equipment. Some looked like they came from the colonial period.

They all ordered coffee, Glenda added a piece of pie. When the waitress left she had orders for three coffees and three slices of apple pie.

Glenda began the conversation. "I need a new cell-phone and we must find out more about the explosion. I have parents to call, and a University to answer to, assuming I still have a job."

"Do both of you agree the fossils are legitimate?" Jacob asked. "And are you willing to risk your reputation on it?"

"They're real, Jake". Lester said. "We all know it. The skull is a modern human skull. The Edmontosaurus rib has a Clovis point imbedded in it. We all looked at it under a microscope. It has been there since death. When taken with your pictures, which the men I sent over have veri-fied, it is without a doubt an Edmontosaurus. And there are two more Clovis points in situ, one with part of the shaft still attached. There's more than enough evidence to prove a human, or humans, killed an Edmontosaurus with spears. It will be called a fraud. There will be contro-versy and debates. You will have to let others examine it. In the end it may never be settled in our lifetime, without finding other sites, other proof of human and dinosaur co-existence.

THE PAST COMES ALIVE

"If we're all agreed it's real, we need to call a press conference right away. Once it's public, they will stop trying to kill us." Glenda said.

"Where do you want to do that?" Jake asked. "Here in Grover?" he said sarcastically."

"Of course not!" Glenda said, "We need to go back to Montana, to the University and have a press conference there. Then we can take them out to the site and show them everything. Lester already has security in place. We can put a building over it for protection, not just from the weather, but it will be much easier to guard, until we move it all back to Boseman."

"As important a find as this is..." Lester continued, "Perhaps it would be best to leave it right where it is, and build a museum over it. It could be a focal point for further research. It could be called the Bullock, Crenshaw, Pearce Museum of Modern Paleontology."

"No!" Bullock said emphatically. "No press conference! There are too many questions that need answering. I've been giving this some thought. We need to look at the bigger picture. It's unlikely he was hunting alone. So why was his body left there?

If word gets out there will be a stampede of people out there. Not just the press and other paleontologists, but everyone with a pick and shovel will be all over the place, hoping to make the next great discovery. They will unwittingly destroy all the evidence we need to prove this is not a fluke."

"But how are we going to work on this when people keep trying to kill us? We need to get lucky every time. They only need to get it right once. They're hiring people, Jake. These are professional killers." Glenda said.

"It seems to me one of your students sold you out. You said only six of you knew about the discovery. If you two are not responsible, it must be one of the students. Who do you think it might be?" Lester asked.

"They're all ambitious in their own way. But I can't believe any of them would commit murder. Not mass murder." Glenda said.

"Ok, they didn't think anyone would be hurt. What could be gained from the information they had?"

"That's just it." Jake said. "The agreement is with both Universities. It was for twenty years. There are still eight years left."

"What happens if all of you are killed? But no one knows what you found, except the killers?" Lester asked.

"Normally we would've stayed at the motel also, and died when it was destroyed. But I wanted to leave immediately. If we'd stayed and died with everyone else at the Motel, and there was no evidence or knowledge of the find, one of the other professors would take over. Without any evidence of our new find, and with a tragedy of that magnitude, the site might have been abandoned all together. If that were the case someone else could come in, work out a deal with the Striker ranch, and then... rediscover it."

"Who would most likely take your places?" Lester continued.

"You mean, would any of them be willing to commit mass murder?" Jake asked. "I don't know. That's just it. This isn't just another great fossil discovery. This will change everything. The stakes are infinite. Dangle enough fame and fortune in front of someone, you don't know who will crack. There would be just as many wanting to cover up the whole thing as those who would want to be credited with the find. Probably more.

The students all knew their futures would be made by having their names connected to this find. I can't imagine one of them doing anything to throw that away."

"Unless…unless 'they' didn't want it to be made public." Glenda said. "Unless someone convinced them it needed to be kept secret for the greater good. The only one I know who has any family connections, who might have a stake in this, is Ruth Biskup. Her father is a geologist. He may have strong feelings about the discovery."

"But would he kill his own daughter?" Lester asked.

"I don't know. The family does have money, they could have hired it done. I've only met her father once. He seemed very controlling."

"So, where does this leave us?" Lester asked. "Since we've decided not to have a press conference. I recommend the two of you go back to the site and continue working, including looking for more evidence. We can set up a more permanent campsite. Right now, that looks like the safest place. You will have my men to protect you and the fossils. What do you think?"

"Glenda and I could pick up my car and leave immediately. I want you to check into Ruth Biskup's family, especially her father. We can stop in Des Moines and get new cell phones."

With the fossils back in Jacob's car, they left Lester's farm a little before six and headed for I 80. Their first stop, a Verizon store.

AUGUST 10 FRIDAY 4 PM
106 SPRINGDALE

Leon's phone rang. It was dispatch.

"Where have you been? I've been trying to get a hold of you. Charlie called a while ago and wanted to talk to you."

"I was out of town. The cell service is not the best."

After he hung up, he went through his notes, found Charlie's number and called.

Charlie was parked two businesses down from Tim Wise Insurance, partially hidden by a delivery van for the flower shop, when her phone rang. She didn't recognize the number but answered it anyway.

"This is Charlie. Who is this?"

"This is Detective Summer. You wanted to talk to me?"

"I think I know who killed Julie. I think it's Ted Wise. He had the listing for the farm and somehow lost it to Julie. He also has the listing for 106 Springdale. The door didn't have a lock box, so the only way Julie could get the key

259

to show it was to get it from Ted. So, I figure he went to the house and came in the back door with a second key. They had an argument, which the girls overheard. Wait a minute! He just came out the back door. He's carrying a gun! It looks like a shotgun! And a bag... big enough to hold the shoes. He put them in the front seat. He's going to leave!

"I'm going to follow him!"

AUGUST 10 FRIDAY, 5:00 PM
INTERSTATE 80 HEADING WEST

"We need to stop for the night in Des Moines, Jacob, I'm beat. We haven't slept a whole night since we left the dig. I also think we need to rent a car there. Your car is really nice but if anyone is still looking for us, we stick out like a sore thumb."

"You're right, I'm worn out too. And I don't want any more damage done to my car."

Jacob pulled onto I 80 and headed west. At the next entrance a black suburban entered the Freeway and stayed about a hundred yards back. Jake didn't notice the Suburban moving into the other lane, picking up speed and beginning to pass. As soon as it was alongside, the driver swerved and hit the Cadillac forcing Jacob onto the shoulder. Jacob was outraged.

"He did that on purpose!" Jake yelled.

To get ahead of him and back onto the highway, Jacob pushed the gas pedal all the way to the floor. His car surged forward. He was almost all the way back on the road, when the SUV caught up again. This time Jacob hit him first. They hit hard, and the two of them stuck together. Jacob kept his wheel turned into the other car. The weight and power of the Cadillac was too much for the smaller SUV. Jacob was gaining ground. He pulled back into his lane just as they came to a bridge. Jacob kept the pressure on, pushing the smaller car until it hit the other side of the bridge knocking the rear view mirror off and smashing in the side. Jake kept him there, the two cars speeding down the bridge. The SUV scraping his way across. When they came to the end there was a bump and the two cars were free again. Jacob turned to the right and then hard back to the left, knocking the other car off the road. Desperate to get away, the SUV drove across the median and into the oncoming lane, where they collided head on with a semi. Jacob stopped on the side of the road.

"They destroyed my car! My door won't open! I think I have a broken leg!"

Glenda had sat there silently holding onto the armrest. Now that it was over, she began to cry. She was shaken but otherwise ok. When she regained her composure, she screamed.

"They were trying to kill us Jacob! I thought we were going to hit the end of that bridge!"

She looked around to see what had happened to their would-be assailants. Traffic was stopped. She saw a semi turned sideways blocking both lanes. She could not see the other car.

Jacob reached over and squeezed Glenda's shoulder. She looked at him. He was obviously in a lot of pain.

"Stay with the car and have it towed into town! Then rent a different one, get the fossils and go to Montana."

"I can't leave you like this."

"Yes, you can. I'll call my nephew and get him to take me to the site. Lester's men will be there. You'll be safe."

"Are you alright?"

Glenda turned. There was a man and a woman beside the car. They opened the door and Glenda got out. Her legs felt weak so she held onto the door for a minute.

"I'm fine, but my friend has a broken leg." She said.

"Help is on the way. We saw the whole thing. That black car deliberately rammed into you! You're lucky to be alive! It's a good thing you have a big car!"

Glenda had her strength back. She walked around and looked at the driver's side.

"It's not good, Jacob. I don't think even all the king's horses and all the king's men can put it back together again. I hear sirens. They will have you out soon."

"Do what I said. I'll only be a few days behind you."

"When will this end, Jacob?"

"Just do what I said. We will get through this. We'll figure out something."

The ambulance pulled up. In no time they had Jacob out and were loading him into the back of their ambulance.

The last thing he saw was Glenda holding her hand over her face, crying again. He gave her a thumbs up.

AUGUST 10 FRIDAY
106 SPRINGDALE

Leon took off running out of the house, talking into his cell phone as he went.

"Charlie let me take care of it! What kind of car is he driving?"

"He has a dark blue Honda Accord. It looks new. He turned on to Main street and is heading south. He just turned at Markowitz Reality."

Charlie punched the gas and quickly caught up. She slowed as she came to the corner, and as soon she turned she saw Bud walking out the back door of his office, carrying a sign. Ted was getting out of his car holding the shotgun. As he pointed it at Bud, Charlie floored the gas pedal, her tires screamed. Ted turned to see what was happening. All he saw was a bright yellow car heading straight at him. He backed up against his car as far as he could. At the last second Charlie swerved just enough to miss Ted, but her car caught the barrel of the shotgun and sent it flying. She continued down the street did a J-turn and headed back. Ted ran over, picked up his gun, and was crossing the street. Bud froze next to his car, holding the for-sale sign in front of himself for protection. This time Charlie caught Ted right in the middle of the street. She headed straight at him. He turned and faced her, pointing the gun at her. But as she barreled down on him, instead of firing, he dropped the gun and put up his hands. Charlie hit the brakes, stopping inches from running him over. Ted collapsed, just as Leon turned the corner. Shutting off his siren, he blocked the street and left his lights on. Charlie backed up a little and got out of her car.

Leon called for an ambulance as he walked to where Ted was. Charlie joined him and helped a shaking Ted to his feet.

"I told you to let me take care of it!"

"You can. There's the shotgun he was going to kill Bud with. I think you'll find all the evidence you need in the front seat of his car."

Bud put down his for-sale sign and came over. Ted was standing on his own now while Leon put handcuffs on him.

"Why did you kill my wife?" Bud asked.

"She and that Jerry Gold stole my farm listing. I didn't care if they sold it, but she stole the listing, cutting me out of any commission at all. I needed that money. My wife had a stroke and has been in a care facility for five years. I'm losing everything we have just to keep her there. That commission would have been enough for several more years."

The Police Chief drove up right behind the ambulance. When he got out an old man who'd been walking his dog crossed the street and came up to him.

"I saw the whole thing Chief! It was just like in the movies! That guy over there got out of his car with a shotgun just as that young girl turned the corner!" He continued with a vivid account of everything.

"Thank you very much." Jerry said, jotting down his name and phone number. "We may need you as a witness. Are you sure you can recognize that girl again?"

"Charlie? I'm surprised you don't know Charlie! Everyone knows Charlie! She just stopped a murder all by herself. I nearly peed my pants when she did that quick turn, just like on tv, and came bearing down on that guy with him pointing that gun at her all the time. Wait till I tell my Mable. They will have something to talk about at that beauty shop of hers that's actually true."

Ted made a complete confession of both murders. Bud's shoes and his wife's pistol were both in the front seat of Ted's car. His prints were all over it, and ballistics would prove it was the gun used to kill Jerry Gold.

When everyone had left, Bud put the sign in his trunk and drove down to the police station. A half hour later he drove Stephanie back to the office.

"Did you mean it when you said you would go to Australia with me and start a new business?"

"Yes."

"I need to return the two million to Stanley Granger. And I want to take care of Ted's wife. There won't be nearly as much left."

"You also owe Paula and the detective agency."

"Right."

"It's not about the money. We just saw what greed can lead to. I just want to be with you." Stephanie said.

265

CHAPTER TEN
AUGUST 11 SATURDAY
CHARLIE'S BEDROOM

Charlie woke up at twenty to six, twenty minutes before her alarm. She shut off the alarm, got out of bed, changed her nightshirt for running clothes, and went down the hall. Looking into the spare bedroom Paula had converted into a fitness room, she remembered the first time she'd seen it. She had just moved in. Paula was her lawyer and Judge Hartley had put her in Paula's custody until he held a hearing on Monday morning on charges of theft and assault and battery. At the end of the hearing she found herself temporally in Pastor Boyd's and Paula's custody for a month, continuing to live with Paula. She can still hear the judge slam his gavel down and call her by name 'Charlene Ruth Ann Bolton'. A lot had happened in that month. She had accepted Jesus as her Savior, helped track down T.J.'s killers, and been shot in the process of protecting Jack, who was in his wheelchair about to be shot. Falling back onto Jack's lap, before losing consciousness, their eyes had met and she knew, Jack knew... he was unsaved and if he had died, he would have gone to hell... and Jack knew she knew. That was the problem, she knew too much.

She'd expected Jack to give his heart to Christ but he had just clammed up. When they came back, he'd avoided the topic... and her. He had been more than generous, setting up a scholarship to any university she could get in, complete with a monthly stipend to cover her living costs.

"Wow, Lord! You sure have changed my life and future", she said as she continued down the hall, down the stairs and out the front door.

"Yes." she said out loud. "Getting arrested, was the best thing that ever happened to me. I found You. What will it take for Jack?"

She walked quickly down the side walk. Just before the street she stopped, did a few stretches then headed down the street at a fast walk, then picked up her pace. By the time she reached the corner she was jogging. She often talked to God as she ran and today was no different.

"Father, today Jack and I are going to the State Fair. I need Your help to talk to him. To somehow let him know how wonderful You are."

She finished her run and went upstairs to get ready for her day. Paula was out of town meeting with a client, and wouldn't be back until tomorrow night. She liked being on her own. One more year of high school and then off to college, she couldn't wait.

She pulled into the parsonage drive at eight thirty. She figured she would have a few minutes with Pastor Boyd before Jack was ready. She found him at the kitchen table and he waved her in.

"Good morning Charlie. You and Jack going on a date." He teased. "Won't Chris be jealous."

"You know better. But I do want to talk to you about today. I feel like Jack has been avoiding me, and God. What can I do to help?"

"You're right. He is avoiding both of you. And he's guarded about what we talk about also. Jack is running from God. You should know about that. I recall you had to finally be arrested on serious charges before you stopped running."

"You're right. But I know Jack knows he is lost. He knows hell is real, that he will go there if he dies. Why won't he just surrender?"

"You used the right word, 'surrender'. Jack knows the cost of coming to Christ and right now he thinks he can avoid paying. Some people give their hearts to God but when some conflict comes with their faith, they fall away. They never intended to surrender to His Lordship. They think they can have salvation without the cost. Like a 'get out of hell free' card they can keep in their pocket for an emergency. Jack is actually, ahead of that game. He has seen the change in you and others and knows he will have to go all the way. It's a good thing."

"But what can I do? What can I tell him that will cause him to give his life to Jesus?"

"Pray."

Charlie waited a minute for Pastor to finish, but when he didn't add anymore, she continued.

"I do pray for him every day, more than once a day."

"Then trust God to answer."

She heard Jack coming down the hall with his walker.

"Good morning you two. See! I'm getting stronger already. I think I'll be ready to be on my own in a week. Then I can get out of your hair, Pastor."

"You're not in my hair. In fact, it's been a blessing having you here. I never did like living alone. You will be welcome back anytime you like. Well I've got to go to the office, and you are headed off to the fair." As he went out the door he said, "Remember! Controlled power."

Charlie went to the door and held it as he left.

"Can I show Jack a J-turn?"

Pastor held up one finger as he walked toward the church.

"What happened to the van?" Jack asked.

"I thought we could put your wheelchair in the back seat. But if you want to, I can get it."

"No, this is much better."

Charlie helped Jack with the door and then followed with his wheel chair. When they were in the car and headed out the drive Jack asked,

"What did he mean by controlled power?"

Charlie, feeling a little feisty and dying to show off, said, "I'll show you if you want."

"You're not going to do something stupid are you?"

270

Charlie turned the car back into the church parking lot, stopped, put it in first, revved it up, and popped the clutch. The car roared to life with the tires smoking, trying to find traction, pushing Jack back in the seat, racing across the parking lot. Soon they were running out of space headed to the empty lot next door. Jack was about to tell her to stop when she hit the brakes turned the wheel and spun in a perfect 180 and started back where she had come from. She came to a gentle stop back at the entrance, ready to pull back out onto the street.

"I've watched you practicing with Pastor's car. It's a lot different being in the car instead of watching from the kitchen window." Jack said, relieved he wouldn't be going back to the hospital. "Where did you get this car?" he asked.

"Pastor won't tell me where it came from. Just said it was a gift from an anonymous benefactor. Who does that? right."

"What have they done to it? What about the motor? That's not stock."

"No, none of this car is stock. They rebuilt the whole thing... brakes, suspension, even the driver's seat. You may have noticed it adjusts to me perfectly. And you're right, they put in a custom engine and transmission. Pretty cool, hua!

"I'm glad you've had a lot of practice."

"I have, but that's the best one I've ever done. Sometimes it doesn't work out that great." she said with a smile. "Let's go to the fair."

An hour later they were in line to enter the fair, without ever going over the speed limit. When she reached the head of the line, she handed the lady her ten dollars and followed the line to her parking spot. While Charlie retrieved the wheelchair, Jack got out and stretched, taking in the sights, sounds, and smells of the Iowa State Fair. He walked around to the back of the car on his own, while Charlie opened his chair.

"Wow! All on your own. You didn't even hold on to the car."

Looking how far they had to go to get to the entrance Jack said, "Well, I'll let you push me until we get inside. This ground is pretty rough. I think I'll save myself for the pavement."

Charlie took it easy through the grass, but when she got to the smoother driveway, she took off running.

"Is this too fast for you?"

"Not as long as you don't do another 180!"

She slowed down at the ticket booth, walked past, took two tickets out of her back pocket, and handed them in at the gate. Once they were through, she stopped the wheelchair so Jack could get out.

He stood up, and reached for his wallet to pay her for his ticket.

"Please don't." Charlie said. "I know it's a guy thing to pay your own way but, please don't pay today. Let me do it." Her eyes were on the verge of tears. "I want to give you a gift. I saved this up from my paychecks. You are doing so much for me. I can never pay you back. I wanted to say thank you. Ok?"

"Ok." Jack said, putting away his wallet. "Just remember I eat a lot, and fair food is expensive."

"What's your favorite fair food? I'm starved."

"Let's start with a Monkey Tail and take it from there."

"Ok, what is it, and where do we get it?"

"You've never had a Monkey Tail? Follow me."

"I've never been here before. But I'll try anything you do."

"Well," Jack said. "Let me be your guide. We came here every year when I was a kid, sometimes twice a year."

Jack did well, using his wheelchair as a walker.

They'd entered in the far east gate and worked their way downhill, through the barn full of exotic chickens. Next, into the Mountain Man camp, where they took turns throwing hatchets. Jack didn't do so good. The first one didn't even get to the target.

"I can't believe how weak I am. I think I'll let you push me for a while."

Charlie was fascinated by everything. By midafternoon they had: worked their way through the Cultural Center; watched a performance on the MidAmerican stage; seen the butter cow; gone through the Isle of Breeds, where they were both awed by the bull elk; and had thought the winning boar was gross; and they'd each chosen their favorite horse. In addition to the Monkey Tail they'd consumed three lemonades each, corn dogs, deep fat fried snickers, a funnel cake, a large nachos which they shared, and Sloppers, which they didn't, and were sitting on the porch of the administration building, each eating a pig leg Jack was wishing he'd said 'no' to, but didn't want to let Charlie eat more than he did.

"Where do you put it all? I don't think I want anything to eat for a week. How big are you? Do you even weigh a hundred pounds?"

"I'm five feet tall and weigh one hundred and three pounds. And apparently that's big enough to eat you under the table. By the way, if you're not going to finish your pig leg, I'll take it for later."

The day was sunny with a high in the eighties, so the shade was nice. Jack had alternated walking and riding in his wheelchair and for a short while, Charlie sat while he pushed. An hour went by fast, talking and listening to the music coming from the Bill Riley stage. When they got up to leave Jack had trouble getting up.

"I think you're going to need to push me the rest of the way. My legs are done for the day."

"No problem. I can push. It'll help build my appetite. This place is huge. We've only seen about half of it. This is only the second day of the fair. Would you consider coming back next week? Maybe we could get Chris, Jen, and Pastor to come?"

"I'll think about it. How's that."

"Sure. I need to check my work schedule for next week to see which days I'm off."

"If we're going to come back next week, how about seeing one more thing and then going home?" Jack asked.

Charlie checked out her map of the Fairgrounds. She'd been checking off everything they had seen.

"That's fine. We can check out the Varied Industries Building. That sounds interesting. What's in there anyway?"

"Well, you can figure it out. What have we seen the most of so far?"

"Lots of people."

"And?"

"Farm stuff, animals, and food venders."

"Ok. So now we are going to see?"

"Industries. Thing's people make?"

"You got it. But first we need to make a stop. I need to use the rest room."

After their pit stop, they went on down the walk, turned and went to the northeast door and went in.

"I thought there was a lot of people outside! It's packed in here."

They went up and down a couple of rows accumulating a bag here, or a pen there.

"You need to have a house to use most of this stuff." Charlie said, her enthusiasm waning.

"Yah, I hated to come in here when I was a kid, but my dad made us go up and down every isle. The only bright spot was the bucket of cookies you can get down on the end."

"Even I'm not interested in cookies. If you don't like it either, let's go down one more row and head home." Charlie said.

"Works for me."

Charlie finished the row made the turn and headed back toward the end where they had come in. About halfway down the aisle they came to a large double booth. Charlie stopped to look, and a young man handed her a flyer.

"What's this?" she asked.

"Have you ever heard of Noah's Ark?"

Charlie looked at him a little closer. He was only a few years older than her and only about three inches taller, with red hair, green eyes and a nice smile.

"My name's Charlie." she said.

"My name is Rocky Schulz. "Charlie gave him a funny look. "I know, I'm too small to be a boxer. I used to get into a lot of fights in school, because of my name. Not so much anymore. What about the Ark? Have you ever heard of it?"

"Sure, in Sunday school."

"Have you ever seen it?"

"Of course not. No one has."

"This is all about Noah's Ark. Not the one Noah built, but a replica of the original one. It's in Williamstown, Kentucky, about 40 miles south of Cincinnati, Ohio. It shows just how Noah could've built it, with technology available at the time, and how all the animals would fit in it, along with Noah and his family."

Jack was uncomfortable with what he saw. He didn't believe in Creation, at least not the way his sister described it. And for some reason, he just didn't like being here.

276

Jack interrupted, "I hate to break this up, but could we go on home Charlie? My legs starting to hurt. Too much walking for one day I guess."

"Yes. I'm sorry Jack. Sure. Isn't this great! Look at all the stuff.

Did you know there was a full-sized ark, just like Noah built?"

Jack started to rub his leg.

"I've got to go Rocky. Nice to meet you.

Charlie turned to leave. While she was making her way back out to the isle Rocky gathered some literature and put it in a bag for her.

"Here take this. You can look at it at home. Maybe you can come back later?"

"Thanks." Charlie said. "I hope so. It looks really cool."

Charlie made her way down the aisle as quickly as she could, considering the crowd of people there.

"I'm sorry. We probably should have left sooner." she said to Jack, "I hope your leg will be alright."

"I'll be fine. Just time to quit is all."

Charlie left the building and headed for the gate they had come in.

"Let's go the other way. It'll be much quicker. We can pick up a ride in a golf cart. The Shriners do it to raise money for their hospitals."

Charlie turned around and headed back the other way. The crowd was getting bigger and it seemed to Charlie that everyone was coming in, while she was trying to get out. She followed Jack's directions down to the corner and turned right. Not too far down on the left, she saw a golf cart stop and let some people out. She picked up the pace and started running toward the cart. The driver saw her coming and waited. Jack got in the front seat while Charlie held the wheelchair and sat in the back seat. When they reached the gate, she heard the driver ask Jack where their car was. While they were riding back Charlie pulled out one of the pamphlets from her bag and tried to read it but the ride was too bumpy. All she could do was look at the pictures.

By the time they reached the car Charlie was glad she had a ride instead of pushing Jack all the way.

"Are you ok putting the top down?" Charlie asked, as she loaded the wheelchair and got in.

"Yah, that's fine." Jack answered. "It'll feel good to cool off on the way home. I had a great time today. Thank you. I didn't realize just how bad I needed to get out. It's like I'm back to normal. Well almost, anyway." he said, looking back at the wheelchair.

"You won't need that long. You'll have all your strength back in no time."

"It doesn't take much to lose it. I don't think I will take it quite for granted anymore. Can we talk for a minute?" Jack asked.

"Sure."

They were almost to the highway entrance.

"Then go on through, and pull into that motel parking lot."

Charlie did as he asked, not sure what he wanted, but she felt it must be something serious. Breathing a quick prayer, she parked under the shade of a tree and shut off her car.

"This is hard for me." he said. "But I need to get it out. I've been avoiding you, because every time I see you, my mind goes back to Montana, and you standing in front of me, shooting Billy, and saving my life. I even dream about it. I thought if we were together today, just having fun, I could shake it off. It was working great until you stopped at that Creation booth. See, that's one of the things I just can't believe in. The earth is way older than six thousand years. It wasn't created in only six days. I just can't believe like you do."

"You know you are being lied to. That voice in your head is telling you, you're better being in charge of your life than letting God do it. But it's not true. You know…"

Jack interrupted. "I know I'm a sinner and that I will go to hell if I die the way I am. That's what you say to me every time in my dream."

Jack turned his face away.

Charlie waited a minute then said. "What would it take for you to believe the Bible is true, the whole thing from beginning to end?"

Jack turned back, but didn't answer.

"You said, Genesis is not true. If God shows you that it is, will you surrender? Will you ask Jesus to forgive all your sins and to be the Lord of your life, let Him be Boss?"

"He can't do that. It's not true."

"You're hedging. Yes or no."

"If God proves to me that dinosaurs and humans lived together, I will believe."

"And...."

"And surrender and make Him my Boss."

Charlie just smiled and said a silent prayer. "God, you heard him. Please answer his challenge."

CHAPTER ELEVEN
AUGUST 12 SUNDAY
MORNING AT THE PARSONAGE

Jack went to bed at nine the night before worn out from his day at the fair. He woke up a little after two, hurting all over. He got up on his own and took three ibuprofen and went back to bed. At 7am he woke up again stiff and hurting. He got up and used his walker to go to the shower. This time he took four pills. The shower felt good he sat down on the stool and let the hot water run over him. His muscles began to loosen up and the pain pills started to kick in. He sat there for a half hour before he showered and shaved. He was grateful the house had continuous hot water. To say Jack was sorry he ever said he would go to church this Sunday would be a huge understatement. And after yesterday he decided he would leave town as soon as possible... permanently. But right now his sister and Chris were waiting for him to finish dressing and walk with him over to the church. When he was ready he walked out to the kitchen using his walker. Jen was gone and Chris was sitting at the table. She stood up as he came in.

281

"We're already almost ten minutes late." she said.

Jack made his way over to the table without responding and sat down.

I'm sorry. I can't go. I went to the fair yesterday with Charlie. It wasn't a good idea. I hurt all over, not just my leg which is killing me, but my arm and every muscle I have. I'm not going to be able to go today. Maybe next week."

Chris sat down. "Jen is saving us seats. I can push you in your wheelchair. Charlie is singing a solo today. I know she is anxious for you to hear her sing. She is really very good."

I'm just hurting right now. I over did it. I'll be ok. But you know how it is when you really over do a workout well this is much worse."

"Ok, I get it. Would you like me to fix you some coffee and maybe breakfast. You look like you had a rough night."

"Thanks for understanding, Coffee sounds great. I think I'll pass on the breakfast for now."

Chris put on the coffee, got out two cups and sat down. "I've been wanting to talk to you alone for some time. I hear you're going to take a vacation soon. Are you coming back?"

Caught off guard, Jack hesitated.

"Or are you just leaving… again. You know I love you Jack. But I can't, I won't wait anymore. I will continue to pray for your soul but if you leave again, I will not pray for us… anymore."

"Then come with me. I have enough money we can go anywhere we want."

"Is that a proposal of marriage? I was hoping for something more romantic. You know I won't just move in with you."

"Are you going to let that church come between us again. You know I love you too. I always have."

"It's not the church, not Pastor Boyd. You might as well get it right. It's Jesus Christ. God Himself. No matter how much you try to deny Him. You know He is real. You know there is a heaven and a hell and you know where you are going if you die without Him. Charlie told me... You know... Why won't you surrender to life instead of walking in death?" I have prayed and waited for so long. I thought after Montana you would..."

"Would what. The whole thing is not real. It's all only in your head. You're brainwashed... that's all. There is no God!" Jack found himself standing and shouting.

Chris got up, poured him a cup of coffee, and left without saying a word.

Jack sat down and took a drink, burning his mouth. Then he threw the cup on the floor, breaking it on the tile.

CHAPTER TWELVE
AUGUST 13 MONDAY
A HOSPITAL IN DES MOINES IOWA

Oak River was in the beginning of a heat wave, expected to last at least through the next week. The last time it had rained was July 31. Charlie parked the van under an awning in front of the main door of the Hospital, lowered the lift, and got out the wheelchair. Entering the building, she was immediately hit by a rush of cold air. Her first stop was the reception desk.

"I'm looking for Dr. Bullock. Could you tell me what room he's in please?" she asked.

The receptionist looked up from her job of stuffing and sealing envelopes and typed his name into her computer.

"He is in room 327." She pointed down the hall. "You'll find the elevators over there."

Charlie went up to the third floor and followed the sign toward his room. She could hear him long before reaching his room. Then she saw an aide run out his door, followed by a coffee cup that bounced off the wall, just missing her head. When she saw Charlie with the empty wheelchair she stopped.

"Are you here for Bullock? I hope so! Is someone else with you?"

"There's only me."

"You should have someone else to help."

"I'm only small on the outside. I'll be fine."

The aide quickly went on down the hall.

Charlie picked up the coffee cup on her way in. "Hi. I'm Charlie. Pastor Boyd sent me to pick you up. That was a pretty good throw, by the way. You almost got her right in the back of the head."

"I wasn't aiming for her head or I would have hit it!"

Pastor had just asked her to take the van and pick-up a Dr. Bullock at the hospital and bring him to the parsonage, without saying anymore.

Charlie discovered he wasn't a medical doctor, but held PhDs in Geology and Paleontology. He was sixty-eight but didn't look it, six-foot tall, thin, long gray hair tied in back with a leather strip, brown eyes, with deeply tanned skin.

"Where's Billy? They said he was going to pick me up, not a sniveling kid."

"I am a young woman and I don't snivel."

I don't care who you are, just so we can get out of here."

Dr. Bullock was not going anywhere on his own. His left leg was severely broken, from his auto accident three days earlier. An external fixator now held it in place. His welcome here was wore out by noon of the first day, when the drugs started to wear off. Unable to leave on his own, he'd been trying to hire one of the staff to take him to

Montana. No takers. Finally, when they were going to release him to a care facility, he told them to call Billy Boyd in Oak River to come and get him.

"Let me call for the nurse and we can get you in the wheelchair."

"We don't need a nurse. They're useless anyway. You just bring that thing over here and keep it from moving."

Charlie pushed the wheelchair to where he had pointed and locked the wheels. Dr. Bullock stood up on his right leg, pivoted himself around and sat down.

"Well, let's go! I don't have all day."

Charlie released the brakes and headed for the entrance. Just then the nurse came in along with an aide pushing a wheelchair.

"I have my own transportation." Jacob said.

The nurse started to protest but Jacob cut her off.

"Let's go, Charlie. Billy still has that special van and can take me where I need to go, right?"

"It's Pastor Boyd. And yes. He has a 'handicap van'. It's parked right out front. As for taking you where you want to go, that would be up to him."

The nurse and aide moved to the side and let them leave.

"I need to be in Montana as soon as I can get there."

"Like I said, you will need to take that up with Pastor Boyd."

Charlie reached the front door and pushed the button for it to open. They went through the first set and when the outer doors opened, she pushed Dr. Bullock out into the hot Iowa summer.

Two men, just getting out of a black Cadillac SUV, stopped and watched as Charlie loaded him into the van. Then they got back in their car and waited, following them out.

Red Cleave, the driver, said, "I'll follow them until they turn off I 80. Then when we find a nice spot, I'll pull up beside them. You shoot the driver. They'll have a wreck, then like good citizens we'll stop to help, and make sure they're both dead."

"It's a girl. She doesn't even look like she's old enough to drive."

"Look! Ed and Lou botched this job already and got themselves killed. You take out that girl and then we'll make sure the old man is dead this time."

"What about the woman?"

"One thing at a time."

"Why can't we just run them off the road?

"This running people off the road didn't work out so good for Ed and Lou. They're both dead. Not to mention Tom and that other guy. They both got caught breaking in to some house. Look. They were all stupid. Are we stupid? No. We're not going to get caught or killed."

Red stayed back, just keeping them in sight. He knew where they were going and didn't want them getting suspicious. After turning off the Interstate he closed the gap. About seven miles later they came out of a curve to a long straightaway.

"How did you have that accident anyway?" Charlie asked."

"Why?"

"Because there's a large black SUV behind us. I noticed them after we left the hospital. When I slow down, so do they, and when I speed up, they keep pace. When we turned off the inter-state they followed. There's nothing up here but Oak River and it is not a tourist destination."

"I'm sure it's just a coincidence."

Charlie didn't really hear what he said. She was focusing on the car, which was now rapidly catching up to her. In response, she increased her speed, soon going well over the speed limit.

"What are you doing?" Bullock said. "You'll get us killed. Just let them pass."

Charlie checked her speed. The needle was just past 75. She held it there. Red pulled out and came alongside. Tony stuck his arm out and pointed his gun at Charlie's head. Just then she looked at him and their eyes met. He hesitated just a few seconds, but it was long enough for Charlie to register what was going to happen. She slammed on the brakes just as he fired. The first shot hit the doorframe. The second one hit the side of the wind-shield. As she braked, she turned hard to the left hitting the Cadillac in the rear bumper. The unexpecting Red lost control. His car spun to the right, flipped over twice, then slid down the center of the highway on its top.

"Now look what you've done! I told you, you would cause an accident."

Charlie stopped, got out, and looked at the front of the van. The only damage was some black paint on the bumper. She called 911 and told them what had happened and where they were. Ignoring Dr. Bullock's complaining, who she was sure was all right, she walked down to the car to see if she could help. The driver was hanging out the window, the side of his head split open. Charlie walked around to the other side got down on her hands and knees and looked in, the man who was going to shoot her was lying on his back in the middle of the car, his head bent at an unnatural angle. Charlie reached in took hold of his wrist and felt for a pulse. She could not find one. Slowly she walked back to the van.

"You could have got me killed!" Bullock screamed. "Driving like that!"

"I think I just saved your life. Both of our lives."

Charlie walked on past to the back of the van, sat down, and began to pray. Cars began lining up from both directions. She ignored them. Someone came up and asked her if she needed any help. She continued to pray without answering, first in English and then in the Spirit. The sirens came closer and then stopped. The words were flowing uninhibited now, and a peace came over her at last.

She opened her eyes and smiled at the paramedic touching her shoulder, asking if she was ok.

"Yes, I'm fine. The two men in the car are both dead. There's a gun somewhere. The police will want it for evidence. They shot the van."

The paramedic left, hurrying down to tell the others about the gun.

Charlie went to the side of the van and opened the door to get Dr. Bullock out.

"What did you mean about saving our lives? You're the one who hit them."

"Only after they shot at us."

Charlie unlocked Bullock's wheelchair, pushed him to the lift and then lowered him down to the highway. He didn't say a word.

"You have some explaining to do, Dr. Bullock. And here comes the man who will want the answers." she said.

Charlie was looking at Pastor Boyd running up to the van. Although in his fifties, the former Navy SEAL kept in shape.

"Are you alright? I heard you were shot at."

"They missed me. But hit the doorpost and the front window." Charlie said.

They walked around to the other side of the van and Charlie showed him the hole in the door, the bullet still lodged inside.

Just then a lady walked up from the back of the van holding a 22. Caliber pistol with a silencer. She had one finger through the trigger guard. "I found this next to my car when I stopped. I didn't touch it." The Chief of Police for Oak River, Jerry Watson, who had joined them, held out a plastic bag.

"You can put that right in here ma'am." he said. "Show me where you found it."

The two of them started walking back toward the lady's car.

Hearing a noise, Charlie and Pastor turned around. It was Dr. Bullock coming around in his wheelchair. He locked the brakes and stood up on his one good leg and put his finger over the bullet hole.

"I thought it was over when the two men were killed running me off the road." He said.

"I think we deserve an explanation Jacob." Pastor responded.

"It's a long story. And I don't want to get you involved."

"We are already involved. Don't you think?"

"It's something I'm not ready to confide to anyone at the moment."

"Oh, that's alright. We don't feel ready to take you home with us."

"You know him Pastor?" Charlie asked.

"Yes. He's my uncle on my father's side. I haven't seen him in, what's it been Jacob, ten years? At my father's funeral?"

"Things were awkward. It seemed better to just slip away."

While they were talking, a deputy sheriff told them the highway was open. They could leave. "We will be in touch. You and Dr. Bullock will need to make a written statement. Where can I find you, Dr. Bullock?"

Pastor looked over at him. He nodded his head. Pastor took out a card and handed it to the officer.

"You can find all of us here the rest of the day." Looking over at Charlie he continued. "I got a ride here with Jerry. I'll ride back with you."

"I'll get in back." Charlie said.

"No, you drive. It looks like you've done alright so far. Where did you learn that maneuver? I didn't teach you that yet."

"I saw it on YouTube."

Back at the parsonage the three of them sat at the kitchen table.

"Well let's hear it." Pastor said.

"Like I said, it's a long story." But convinced they would call a care center to come and pick him up, he began.

"I would ask you to keep this to yourselves. A number of people have already died, and this is the second attempt on my life. The first one was August 10. We were headed west on I-80 about seven in the evening. Traffic was light."

"How big is the number?"

Jacob hesitated.

"Probably 6 or 7." I don't know for sure.

"Pastor interrupted, "You said 'we'. Who is the other person?"

"A colleague of mine. I saw a car coming up fast behind me."

Pastor interrupted again, "Look Jacob. It's going to be all or nothing."

"Ok. But I'm telling you, whoever's behind this is ruthless. They have already blown up a motel, killing everyone in it. Her name is Glenda Pearce. She's a professor of

Paleontology at Montana State University in Bozeman. We've been working together on a ranch in north central Montana for about twelve years."

Pastor gave him a look.

"Ok. The Striker ranch north of Jordan, Montana."

Jacob brought them up to date, including every detail.

"I thought that would be the end of it, that whoever was after us was now dead themselves. I don't know how they tracked me to the hospital and then followed your van. I thought it was finally all over."

"Where is Glenda now?"

"Glenda should be back at our dig in Montana by now. It's very important that I get back to our site as soon as possible. There's no way to get a hold of them except to go there. After what happened today, they could be in grave danger."

"Can't you just phone them?" Pastor asked.

"There's no cell service. I need to get there right away."

"What about Lester? Have you tried to get in touch with him?"

"Yes. I called him from the hospital phone five or six times. There's no answer."

"What about the Sheriff? We can get in touch with him and he can send someone out."

"I would have to explain everything to him. We are not ready for this to go public yet."

"Are you concerned about her or your fossils?" Pastor asked.

294

"Both. Surely you understand how important this find is. Not just for Glenda and me, but also for how everything is viewed. The skull is clearly that of a modern human. We need to do a lot more research. If it goes public now, the place will be overrun with idiots, digging up everything and destroying vital evidence. The academic community will apply unbelievable pressure. They will call it a fraud. We must have collaborating evidence. I have to get there right away. If you won't help me, I'll find someone else or I'll drive myself. I can drive without using my left leg."

"Why did you really call me, Jacob? You could have hired a driver, or like you said, you can drive with a broken leg."

"Lester. I don't completely trust him. The only one he's concerned about, is Lester. And you're a Navy Seal. I want you to cover me. I want you to do whatever you do, to sneak into a spot where you can observe, until I'm sure it's ok.

"Look, I'm desperate! Lester has armed men at the site. Maybe he's good as gold. But I need to be sure.

"I wasn't there for your mom when your father died, I know. But I don't fit in. I'm the black sheep, the only one who doesn't believe. I knew they would take care of her. But it wasn't that way when you were born. Your mother was only 15 when you were conceived. Your biological father was 22. Their noble Christian character didn't show itself right away. Your grandfather threw her out of the house and ran off your biological father with threats he would have him thrown in jail for statutory rape if he didn't leave. I was at college on a basketball scholarship. She lived with me until you were almost one, when she married the father you know. He was one of the three roommates I had. We shared a house together."

"So, you think I owe you because you were kind to my mother, your sister, before I was born."

"No, you don't owe me anything. Glenda is like my daughter. She's all I have. No one else would put up with me. I made a terrible mistake after we left Montana. I really hurt her feelings. I don't want anything to happen to her. I met her 18 years ago at the University of Chicago, first as a student. After she earned her PhD, we worked together until she got her professorship in Bozeman. We still work together. You don't owe me, but I am asking for your help."

Charlie sat quietly, listening. "I should be going home. You can let me know if I can help. I have a new car and I'm supposed to give people a ride who need it." Charlie said as she started for the door.

"You wait here. I may need you to help drive."

Jack, coming in from his bedroom, overheard the end of the conversation, and said, "If you all are taking a trip I want to come too. Look I can walk." He let go of the door frame he was holding on to and walked over to the kitchen table and sat down. "See."

Seeing Jacob in his wheelchair and looking down at his broken leg he said.

"My name's Jack. I just got out of one of those. They take care of strays here. Who are you?"

"This is my Uncle Jacob. You heard about him at the Cafe the other day." Pastor said.

"See. He did have an accident. What did I tell you?"

"Does this mean you are going to take me?" Jacob asked.

"Yes, we are going to take you." Pastor said.

"I'm ready to go. If we leave now, we can be there by," Jacob looked at his watch, "4am. That will be perfect. You can be in place by sunrise."

"It's not that easy." Pastor said. "I have some arrangements to make first. I do have a job here."

"We need to leave immediately."

"There are enough bodies already. I don't want to add ours to the list. We will leave in the morning."

"I think I missed something." Jack said. "What's this about bodies? I thought we were going to take Jacob home, 'or something'."

"It's more the or something. Pastor said. Then to Jacob he said, "I need to know as close as you can tell me, exactly where the location is."

Jacob gave him the GPS coordinates. "Is that good enough for you?"

"Yes." Pastor said as he left, heading to the church. He let Sandy know he would be on vacation, but would be back for Sunday service. He called Jonathan Wilson, a close friend from the Service who agreed to meet them in Montana. Then he called his friend at the old go-cart track.

"I know I haven't done any work yet, but I could use some intel and equipment."

In an hour he was sitting at her desk explaining exactly what he needed.

"What did you say you needed all this for?"

"I'll fill you in as soon as it goes public."

"Ok. I'll remember that."

After he loaded everything he needed, he gave her a hug.

"I owe you one."

"I'll put it on the books. Are you sure you want to take Charlie? That's a lot to expect from a seventeen-year-old."

"Like I told you, she's special. And I've seen her when the chips were down."

"Just the same, you be careful. I don't want to lose you before you even start work."

CHAPTER THIRTEEN
AUGUST 14 TUESDAY 6 AM
STRIKER RANCH MONTANA

They pulled out of the driveway as the sun was coming up. Pastor and Jacob were in the van. Charlie and Jack followed in her car. After the first two hundred miles Jacob finally quit trying to get Pastor to speed up and resigned himself to going the speed limit.

A little after ten pm Pastor turned off the road and followed a dirt drive a quarter of a mile to two metal sheds. He parked the van in one of the open spaces and Charlie parked beside him. She got out of the car and just as she turned around, a large man wearing camo, including face paint stepped, out of the shadows. Charlie screamed a warning to the others, even as she brought her foot up to kick him in the groin. Ready for her, he grabbed her foot and held on.

The rendezvous with Jonathan at the Striker ranch was on time. He kept hold of her foot as she swung her fists, unable to make contact. Pastor came over. "This is my friend Jonathan Wilson, and this is Charlene Bolton."

"Charlie!" she said, looking up to Jonathan's face a foot above hers.

"You can call me Bugs and I'll call you Charlie. Deal?" he said, letting go of her foot and holding out his hand. She took it and gave it a shake.

"I'm glad you warned me about her kick or she would've caught me off guard." Bugs said.

While Pastor was introducing everyone, Charlie checked out the large open shed. There were two small camper trailers, a kitchen on wheels, plus an old jeep, a 4-wheeler, several tents and awnings, and other camp gear stored on shelves. Pulled in crossways was a Humvee, on top of which was an armored gun turret with a machine gun. There was a trailer behind, carrying two motorcycles like she had never seen before.

"They're electric." Bugs said. "You don't want to miss my briefing do you."

"No, Sir."

"Just Bugs, ok?"

Charlie looked up smiling. "Yes sir, just Bugs."

He grabbed her head and turned her around.

"Isn't that a little overkill?" Charlie asked.

"I always like overkill."

"Our position is here." Bugs said, pointing it out on a detailed topographic map.

He was interrupted immediately by Jacob. "This is all way overboard. This is not Afghanistan or some other Middle East war zone."

"Tell me again, how many dead at the motel? And how many attempts on your life? If you will let me finish, I'll take complaints and questions at the end. As I was saying... This is our position. They're camped here. Aerial photos and ground recon show they are maintaining sentries here and here, guarding their front door. They're dug in and camouflaged and appear to have fully automatic rifles. I left microphones at both locations so we can pick up their chatter. There are six more men under a tarp here. And one standing guard here under another tarp."

Bugs put another mark on the map. "What's interesting are these two tents, here and here. The big tent is where they're holding Dr. Pearce, Lester, and his four men. They have their legs chained together."

"Are you saying they have kidnapped them?" Jacob asked.

"That's exactly what I'm saying, Dr. Bullock."

"How do you know all this Maybe they're just in there sleeping."

"I also bugged both tents and the large tarp. From what I've picked up they're expecting some big shot tomorrow morning, early. It sounds like, if Jacob has not shown up by then, they will destroy the fossil site and kill all their hostages. Then leave some men behind in case you do show up. They would've done it as soon as Glenda arrived, but she didn't have the fossils with her. They're not very good at interrogation. They slapped her around a little, but she kept insisting you have them with you,

Dr. Bullock. She said you would never let them out of your sight."

"I don't have them. She was supposed to get them from my car and take them with her."

"My guess-she was smart enough to stash them some place."

"How are you expecting to get them out alive?"

"Good question. It would be easy to subdue all of them tonight when most of them are asleep, except... they respond with a random code word each time they talk to whoever's in charge. I'm sure he will call before he drives in, and if he doesn't get the correct response, he won't show up. So timing is very critical. We need to wait until he calls and gets the all-clear and then take them while they are awake."

"What are you planning? Jacob asked. "You can't just kill all of them!"

"No. We are non-violent commandos. No one dies." Pastor said.

"How long do you think we have from the time the call is made until they arrive? Charlie asked.

"That's a good question." Bugs said. "Dr. Bullock, you have a lot of experience. How long would it take you to get there after you turned off the road?"

"I wouldn't drive there in my car. Glenda and I leave our cars here and take the jeep over. We only travel in four-wheel vehicles after that. You can go thirty with no problem, forty or fifty if you're in a hurry. I'm usually in a hurry. But from our base camp to here is a different story.

It's quite rough even in the jeep. If you don't want to jar your teeth, ten would be too fast. If you're not familiar it could take you an hour or more."

"How long in a helicopter?" Charlie asked. "I wouldn't drive out here. If I had the resources they seem to have, I'd fly in, especially if I was so concerned, I set up a code word. I could check it all out from the air. You're talking kidnaping and mass murder. He wouldn't come here at all except he wants to see the fossils for himself before he destroys them."

They all looked at her. It was the first time anyone had thought of that.

"She's right! He's gone too far just to let everyone go. He may even kill his own men to make sure there are no loose ends." Pastor added.

"If I could say something else." Charlie said. "It seems to me the priority is to free all the hostages. Then worry about catching him. And I'm sorry, but the whole thing needs to be made public. Let the chips fall where they may. Invite other professionals and the press. Then you and the fossils will be safe."

Once they had a plan figured out, they all went to work.

Dr. Bullock used some materials that were stored there to create realistic plaster casts, resembling the real fossils. Jack checked out the Humvee, while Pastor and Bugs unhooked the trailer and unloaded the motorcycles.

CHAPTER FOURTEEN
AUGUST 15 WEDNESDAY BEFORE DAWN
STRIKER RANCH

When everyone was ready, Charlie loaded Dr. Bullock into the van, then backed out of the shed and headed down the drive, followed by Jack. Taking a different route Bugs and Pastor disappeared into the night on the motorcycles with scarcely a sound.

Charlie had no problem all the way to their base camp. After that, it was very slow-going in the van. She was grateful Jacob was with her. He knew every rock, dip, and bump. There was no need to worry about being announced... Before she left, Pastor had poked several holes in the muffler, so you could hear it coming a mile away, then he'd loosened two brackets.

"We're getting close." Dr. Bullock said. "There is a hole..." Before he finished, the van hit it dead center. The already loose muffler began dragging on the ground.

"You hit it on purpose." he said.

Charlie just smiled.

A minute later lights came on, revealing a large canopy. She headed for it. By the time she pulled up next to the other vehicles, two guys were waiting for them. One came to her window, the other to Dr. Bullock's side. Charlie looked out. He was standing right next to her window.

"Shut it off! Shut it off!" he said. Then he put his hand up, turning his wrist to indicate what he wanted.

With all the racket Charlie was making no one noticed the jeep. Jack, parked in a low spot, just deep enough to hide in, about fifty yards back and off to the right.

She shut off the motor and rolled down her window.

"Hi, I'm Charlie. I'm sure glad to see you. I didn't know if I was going to make it or not. I've been driving nonstop to get here. Someone is going to have to pay for fixing this van. I can't drive it home like this. I rented it. Well, actually Dr. Bullock did. But I have to return it, just like I got it. He can't drive you know. He has a broken leg. I'd appreciate some help getting him out. He's in a wheel-chair." Charlie kept talking as she turned around in her seat and got out in back to help unlock the wheelchair. "He wouldn't let me wait until morning when I could see. I think something fell off."

Charlie looked over. Another man was already opening the side door. She backed the wheelchair up and put it on the lift, grabbed the remote and lowered Dr. Bullock to the ground.

"We've been very worried about you, Dr. Bullock." the other man said. "When Glenda showed up without you, we didn't know what to think. Did you bring the fossils with you? She said you had them."

306

"They're in the back of the van. Just leave them there for now. Where are Lester and Glenda?

"I'll take you to them right away Doctor. Everyone's been asleep."

"I have a truck coming sometime early this morning with lab equipment. It must be handled very carefully. Glenda and I will take care of it ourselves."

"Thanks for telling us."

Charlie stepped out of the van, raised the lift, and shut the door.

Dr. Bullock was already being taken toward the canopy. She could see a group of men standing there. They all looked armed.

"How do you know Dr. Bullock?" the man walking with her asked."

"My name is Charlie, what's yours?"

"You can call me Will."

"Ok, Will it is. I just met him a few days ago. My sister is a nurse where they fixed Jacob's leg. That's his first name, Jacob. He wanted a ride out here and no one would take him. He's not a very nice guy. He told my sister he would pay $1000 plus expenses to whoever would drive him out. She told me and here I am. I can really use the money... School you know."

Will took her to a large tent, unzipped the flap and held it open for her.

"Go on in. Everyone is waiting for you."

"What about Dr. Bullock? He said he would pay me as soon as we got here."

"We'll bring him right over. We just have a few questions to ask him first."

Charlie went in, quickly followed by Will.

"I don't understand. Why are they all chained up?"

When Charlie turned around, Will was pointing a gun at her.

"You just sit down on the end there."

Charlie did what she was told. Will took out a pair of handcuffs, but instead of putting them on her wrists he used them to hook one of her ankles to the chain.

Charlie began to cry.

"I don't understand. What are you doing? Please let me go. I won't tell anyone. You can keep the money."

Will didn't say anything. He just left. About ten minutes later they brought in Dr. Bullock, took him out of his wheelchair and locked up his right leg next to Glenda, who was on the other end of the chain.

"Please let me go." Charlie said, tears running down her face. "I don't belong here. I don't even know any of these people."

"Now you'll have time to get acquainted, but don't take too long."

He laughed as he left, zipping up the tent door.

"Are you all right?" Glenda asked Jacob.

She started to cry and hugged him.

"I think they're going to kill us and destroy the site." she said.

"I don't think so." Charlie said, dropping her act.

She took off her shoe and removed some keys, then put her shoe back on. She tried two of them. The third key worked. She unlocked herself and went quickly down the line unlocking all of them.

The only one who wasn't awestruck was Dr. Bullock.

"Who is she, some teenage secret agent or something?" Glenda asked.

"Something like that." Jacob answered.

Charlie put her finger to her mouth. "Don't be scared and don't make a lot of noise. We're all going to leave out the back." She coughed twice. and immediately a knife cut through the back of the tent.

Charlie pointed to the two biggest guys and then to Dr. Bullock. They shook their heads in understanding, picked him up, and went out the back. The others followed. Pastor was waiting right outside the tent. Charlie came out last, and Pastor handed her a pistol. She tucked it into her belt. Then he handed her a walkie-talkie and a small flashlight. She took the lead and headed away from the camp. Pastor handed a second flashlight to the fourth one in line. Charlie followed the dry river bed for about a hundred yards. Where it made a sharp turn to the right, she had everyone sit down behind a large pile of debris. When everyone was seated she spoke.

"Go ahead, turn off your flashlight." She did the same.

"My name's Charlie. Don't worry. We'll be safe here until they've taken care of your kidnappers."

"Who's they? The police?" one of them asked.

"We have one more to catch, then the sheriff will be called."

The sentries hadn't gone back to their post. All nine of the kidnapers were under the canopy looking at the fake fossils laying on a table. One of them pulled out his knife and was going to cut the plaster off. Brad grabbed his arm and told him to stop.

"Not yet! The boss wants to do it himself."

Just as Pastor and Bugs hoped. Brad took his sat phone and made a call.

Glancing down at his notebook he said, "B is for bacon." Then he continued. "We have Dr. Bullock and the fossils. He has a broken leg. Yes sir. Yes, the charges are all set. I'll expect you then." He hung up the phone, took a pen and crossed off the code word and put the notebook back in his shirt pocket.

"The boss will be here at sunrise to finish the job. Then we all get paid, and can take a nice vacation... out of the States for a while.

Pastor gave the signal and Jack started the Humvee. He turned on his lights and drove out of his hiding place.

Everyone went outside. Jack stopped about thirty feet away and quickly took his place in the turret. He turned on the extra lights, blinding everyone. Pastor and Bugs quickly came out from hiding and stood behind them.

"I want all of you to kneel on the ground and put your hands behind your head."

Jack pulled the bolt back on the machine gun and sprayed the ground with a burst right in front of them.

310

"Do as he says, or the next burst will be right on target.
"Now!" Bugs shouted.

They all got on their knees and put their hands behind their heads. The one who had made the phone call reached into his pocket and pushed a button on a small remote. Immediately there was a large explosion. He sprang up and started to run. Before he got two steps, Bugs shot him in the knee, and down he went.

"Anyone else want to try?" Bugs asked.

No one moved. Pastor and Bugs zip-tied their hands behind their backs. Then using their own chain and cuffs, hooked them all together, and had them move back under the canopy, sitting back to back in a circle. Next, they duck taped their mouths and put hoods over their heads.

"Charlie, you can come in now." Pastor said over his walkie-talkie. "They're all trussed up."

While they were walking back, Bugs took out a medical kit and bandaged Brad's knee. He gave him a shot of anti-biotics, and another one for pain, which also contained a sedative. Pastor walked over and took the notebook from his pocket. He opened it and flipped the pages. Each one had a list of words that were scratched out. Four pages in, he found the last one, B is for bacon, with a line through it. The next code word was L is for lettuce, followed by T is for tomato. They carried him over and chained him up with the rest.

When Dr. Bullock arrived back at the site, he was furious.

"What was that explosion? It better not be my fossil bed! Get some lights and take me over there."

They followed the Humvee. It's lights revealed a large hole where the fossils had been. Charlie grabbed the wheelchair and opened it so Dr. Bullock could sit down. Glenda and Lester were standing next to him.

"That solves the threat against our lives." Glenda said, turning away and heading back, tears running down her face.

"You still have the fossils you took, right Doctor?" Charlie asked as the crowd disappeared.

"Without the site they're worthless. Glenda and I are the only ones alive who can verify them. With the site destroyed, all we have is a human skull and a bone with a Clovis point in it. There's no longer anything to connect the two. If we try to publish, we'll only be laughed at. Take me back."

Charlie turned the wheelchair around and worked her way over the rough terrain.

Jack drove the Humvee back where he had been hiding, and covered it with camouflaged netting. Then he joined the others, leaving Lester standing there alone as the sun began to rise.

Pastor stayed under the canopy. As the group gathered just outside, the radio came to life.

"This is Vulture. Over."

"This is Brad. L is for Lettuce. Over."

"Is it safe to come in? Over."

"Roger that. Over."

Minutes later they heard a helicopter. Pastor quickly herded everyone under the canopy.

"I want all of you to stay in here." Then he looked over Lester's men and told them to pick up a rifle and follow him outside. He quickly sent two out to the sentry points and told the other two to take up places where they could be seen when the helicopter flew over. Then he went over to Charlie and whispered in her ear. She shook her head 'yes'.

As it became eaiser to see, Lester had walked over to a large rock he saw about twenty feet away. Looking down, a big grin crossed his face. At the sound of the helicopter he hurried over to where the tarp had come down after the explosion. He grabbed it and took it back. Spreading it out where it had been before, he crawled under and sat down, his mind racing with the possibilities.

He had just settled down when he heard the helicopter fly over. It made a wide turn and flew back again. This time it landed.

It sat there for a moment, then the engine shut down and the door opened. A man stepped out. He was wearing a dark business suit, dark blue shirt, and a red tie. He was medium height, thin, with short brown hair thin on top. His name was Henry Staten. He looked around before moving. Then he saw Pastor standing in a hole to hide his six-foot four height, waving. Satisfied things were ok, Henry reached up and took the hand of a young woman. She stepped out beside him. They had only taken a few steps when it looked like he stumbled. Ruth looked down and reached out her hand to help him up. Then she saw a dart sticking out of the back of his neck. She knelt and pulled the dart out, then looked around. She couldn't see anything except the helicopter with the pilot still sitting in his seat. Charlie came out of the canopy and began running toward her, waving.

"Hi! I'm Charlie. Is everything ok? It looked like he fell." Unsure now what to do, Ruth froze, and just stood there. As Charlie came closer, the pilot made up his mind. He was leaving. He unhooked his seat belt and crawled over the passenger seat to shut the open door. Reaching out to grab the handle, he stopped. He was looking down the barrel of Bugs' Desert Eagle .50 caliber pistol.

"You can just keep coming out." Bugs said.

Ruth turned at the sound, and seeing Bugs, she held the dart up high to stab him. Before she could take a step, Charlie, almost there, jumped, and tackled her. She grabbed her arm and twisting it around behind her. She removed the dart, pulled out a zip tie and put it around both wrists.

"Ok, let's see how your uncle is doing." she said.

Bugs stepped back as the pilot came out and, without being told, turned around and put his hands behind his back. Bugs put on the zip tie and led him toward the tents.

Pastor sent two of Lester's men out to help. They secured Henry and carried him back to camp, while Charlie escorted Ruth.

Pastor radioed the sheriff's office and explained the situation. While they were waiting, Bugs loaded the two motorcycles on the Humvee and left. A short while later a semi pulling a stock trailer drove out of the Striker Ranch. A few miles down the road it passed the sheriff's car heading in. Bug's waved and kept going.

Sixty minutes later the sheriff bounced into camp and stopped in front of the tents. Jacob and Glenda were waiting in front, with Lester and his men a couple of steps behind. The sheriff looked to be in his early forties, about five foot ten, and twenty pounds overweight. His deputy was the same height but thin, and looked about half his age.

"Who's in charge here?" the sheriff asked.

"We are." Jacob said, "I'm Professor Bullock and this is Professor Pearce. We were both kidnapped and held at gun point, along with our colleague Mr. Crenshaw and his men. You'll find the kidnappers in the tent. They've all been subdued and are waiting for you... including their leader Henry Staten, and his niece Ruth Biskup, who turned out to be a spy. The other one is their pilot. I'm sure Henry Staten is responsible for the attempts to murder of Dr. Pearce and myself, along with the murder of three other students in the explosion of the motel in Jordan."

"That's a lot of accusations. Can you prove any of it?"

"They are certainly guilty of kidnapping and destroying University property. We are all witness to that."

The sheriff and his deputy walked past Jacob and into the tent.

"And who are you three?"

"I'm Dr. Bullock's nephew, William Boyd. And this is Charlie Bolton and Jack Donavan. Their friends."

"How do you fit into all this?"

"We freed my uncle and captured the kidnappers."

The sheriff looked down. Henry, Ruth, and the pilot were sitting on the ground.

"You are Mr. Staten, is it, and Ruth, and who are you?" he asked, looking at the pilot.

"I'm Mr. Staten's pilot."

"You have a name I presume."

"Yes, Able, Able Miller."

Henry was still groggy from the drug. Ruth spoke up.

"I don't know what's going on here. They shot my uncle in the neck with a dart and tied us up. I want to press..." She stopped mid-sentence when Jacob and Glenda walked in.

"Before you listen to her complaint you should ask her why her uncle blew up the Elks Rest Motel, killing Linde Phillips, Steve Bell, Tim Blocker, and five others who were there." Jacob said.

"It's not true." Ruth protested." My uncle never hurt anyone."

She looked at Glenda. Tears were running down her face, and she was shaking her head up and down.

"Yes, Ruth. They are all dead." Glenda said, wiping away her tears with her sleeve.

"Near as we can figure, your three friends, the Motel manager and his wife, a truck driver, and another couple were all killed in the explosion." the Sheriff said.

"Ask her how she got out before it blew up. Ask her who picked her up. She's responsible for all of this." Jacob said.

"Is it true? Did someone pick you up at the motel?"

Ruth hung her head down. She couldn't face them anymore.

"My uncle and two other men picked me up. He said no one would be hurt. He just wanted to see the fossils."

Henry was coming to, and understood what Ruth was saying.

"Don't say anymore Ruth. I'll have my lawyer here before we get back to town."

"Why do we need a lawyer?" she asked, looking at him. "You did it, didn't you? You killed them all! How many others have you killed?" She head-butted him, giving him a bloody nose, and started to cry.

An ambulance pulled up along with two other sheriff's cars and a large SUV.

Brad was loaded into the ambulance, and the kidnappers in the SUV. Ruth, Henry and Able were split up, each in the back of one of the cars.

Charlie had watched Lester come out of his hiding place. He took the tarp and covered up a large rock. After the sheriff and everyone left, she walked over and pulled off the tarp. It was roughly a two-foot by three-foot section of the fossil bed intact, and showing the other two Clovis points including a section of the Edmontosaurus. Hearing someone walk up behind her, she turning around. There was Lester.

"I'm sure you were going to tell Jacob and Glenda right?" she said.

"Isn't it magnificent!" Lester remarked, his face grinning from ear to ear.

While they were standing there, Pastor and Jack came over.

"There's your proof, Jack." Charlie said.

Jack stood there staring, not sure what he was looking at. Gradually the rest of them came over. One of the guys was pushing Jacob, with Glenda walking beside him.

"I don't believe it!" Jacob said, looking down at the fossil.

"That's because you don't believe in miracles." Pastor said. "What are you going to do with it?"

Glenda answered quickly. "We are going to load it on a truck, add the two I have at home under my bed, and take them to Lester's. Right Jacob?"

"Yes. I think that would be a good place for them. If that's all right with you, Lester?"

Lester stood there with his huge grin still in place. My place is a little crowded." He said. If I could find a place for my T-Rex, I think I could find room for them."

"Are you offering to give it to us?" Glenda asked.

"More like on loan, to any museum the two of you agree on. I think it's time the rest of the world met him. Just remember his name is 'Lester'. I already have the bronze plaque."

CHAPTER FIFTEEN
AUGUST 20 MONDAY 8 AM
STRIKER RANCH MONTANA

Dan Luther got out of his truck and cut the barb wire, opening a way onto the Striker ranch. Then he stepped back and watched as his drilling rig and support equipment went through. When the last of them were in he got back in his truck.

"This is a big day for me." He said to Archie, who was sitting next to him. "Today Luther Petroleum turns the corner to the big time."

Dan had put everything he had into this. Close to bankruptcy, he was only able to convince one investor to put money into the project. He borrowed everything he could, including mortgaging his personal property.

All the equipment was staged close to the road, while a bulldozer was unloaded, and began putting in a road over the rough prairie, to the spot indicated on his grandfather's map. It was about a mile to where they would set up the drilling rig. Dan, too excited to wait for the bulldozer, headed off with Archie in his truck. When they arrived, Dan parked and they both got out to look the site over. To Archie it all looked the same, empty prairie. Dan, on the other hand, was very excited.

"This is a perfect place to drill! I can almost see the oil down there waiting for us to bring it up! The bulldozer had an easy time of it, and by 10:00 he made a final pass, clearing off enough ground to set up all their equipment. Unseen to him, he was uncovering a set of tracks that had been there since the earth was new and wolves could talk.

Luther stood there in anticipation. He heard the engines on the big trucks start. Looking down toward the road, he was surprised to see that the first vehicles he saw coming were two sheriff's cars followed by a pick-up driven by Carl Striker. Seated next to him was Justus Craves, Attorney at law.

The Sheriff got out first and slowly walked up to Dan and Archie.

"We've been waiting for you since April. Which one of you is Dan Luther?" Archie took a half step backwards. "I am." Dan said. "You are under arrest for trespassing, destruction of government property, breaking and entering, and, oh yea, theft."

Dan began loudly protesting, while pulling out papers from his jacket pocket. He handed them to the sheriff.

"There's some mistake. I have an oil lease to all the Striker ranch."

"That may well be. The courts can decide if it's valid. But you are not on his ranch. You are on Federal property. His property ended about a hundred yards east of here. You should have checked your GPS more closely. We are also confiscating all the equipment until this is settled in court." One of the deputies handcuffed Dan, read him his rights, and escorted him to the back seat of his car.

"Who are you?" the Sheriff asked Archie.

"His name is Archie Deerman." Justus answered for him. "How is your ankle doing?" he asked, looking at him.

"He can speak for himself." the Sheriff said.

"I'm his lawyer. Right Archie?"

Archie was a little stunned, but not stupid. "Yes, that's correct."

"I think his testimony will be very helpful to the prosecution." Justus added.

"I think we will take him in just the same."

THE END

EPILOGUE

That same August morning Henry Staten, all his men and Ruth Biskup, were indicted for murder, kidnapping, the attempted murder of Charlene Bolton, and Professors Bullock and Pearce, destruction of government property, arms violations, in regards to their fully automatic weapons, plus possessing and using explosives without a license. They all faced life in prison without parole, or possible execution.

AUGUST 20 MONDAY 10AM LESTER'S FARM

They all arrived back at Lester's farm. After showing everyone his T-Rex and private museum. They left for Oak River, leaving Lester alone.

When he watched them turn onto the highway, Lester wheeled the stainless-steel cart holding his newest prizes, over to his walk-in safe, opened it and went in. He carefully transferred them onto an empty shelf. Standing back he got a huge grin on his face, pulled the clean white sheets off four other prized specimens, and began to laugh.

Before leaving Montana, Lester had provided false IDs to his four men, identifying them as coming from the Paleontology department at the university of Chicago, and gave them directions to return to the encampment and follow the riverbed east, carefully looking for more fossils. They started work right away. In a few miles they came to a fork, the larger one went to the right, they turned that way and kept going. On the morning of their third day, August 20, they were only a short distance away and had watched as Luther petroleum drove in, only to be escorted back out again a short time later by the sheriff. When they were all out of sight the four of them went over to check it out. They soon discovered the Edmontosaurus prints overlaid with several sets of human prints the bull-dozer had uncovered. Excitedly, they called Lester on their sat phone. At 11:50, Lester was heading back to Montana in his pick-up truck.

AUGUST 20 MONDAY NOON OAK RIVER CAFÉ

Everyone gathered at the Oak River Café for lunch. Normally prime-rib was only offered on Saturday night, but Glenda had called when they left Montana for home, and reserved the private dining room and ordered a buffet, including prime-rib, roasted chicken and a large deluxe pizza, which they brought in from Soldati's Pizza down the street. And all the extras including dessert, as a thank-you. She used Jacob's credit card to pay for it.

Later that week Charlie started her senior year of High School. Pastor added three of last year's graduates to his driving classes. Professors Bullock and Pearce left to go back to their respective Universities. On Saturday morning, Jen bought the house at 106 Springdale. That same day she drove out of the Ford dealership in her new Ford Escape. Chris went back to work, still hoping and praying Jack would come back to her. Without telling anyone he was leaving, Jack had Don drive him to Des Moines, where he bought a ticket for a flight to Hawaii. After saying goodbye, he gave Don his new phone number told him not to share it. Then he turned and headed for security.

"I think you should go into law enforcement. The bad guys wouldn't stand a chance." Chief Watson said, to Charlie.

"It would be very interesting, but that's not my calling."

CPSIA information can be obtained
at www.ICGtesting.com
Printed in the USA
LVHW050813110621
689977LV00007B/1038